W9-AGJ-560

Praise for *Jaguar Hunt*

"This ferocious feline novel is a passionate love story gently woven into an action-packed plot that will steal readers' breath away."

—*RT Book Reviews*, 4.5 Stars

"Terry Spear brings her jaguar world to life with a lot of humor, plenty of sizzling sex, and of course the spectacular touches of good guy versus bad guy action."

—*Fresh Fiction*

"A stunning package of romance, danger, and some twists and turns to curl your toes."

—*Addicted to Romance*

"Terry Spear's smooth writing style and vivid descriptions are simply breathtaking."

—*CK2S Kwips and Kritiques*

"Filled with action and intrigue... The romance was great, with plenty of steam and witty, charming scenes."

—*The Romance Reviews*

"An adrenaline-pumping, action-packed paranormal romance that will keep you glued to the pages."

—*Romance Junkies*

"A great balance of mystery, romance, excitement, and danger. It'll take you on an awesome wild ride!"

—*Buffy's Ramblings*

Praise for *Jaguar Fever*

"Exciting, funny, and sexy...*Jaguar Fever* has a multi-layered, sizzling plot that will have readers unable to put it down."

—Fresh Fiction

"An action-driven story with twists along the way. The suspense is captivating and the romance is steamy."

—Thoughts in Progress

"Rife with sensuality, heat, danger, adventure, passion, and romance, *Jaguar Fever* will keep the reader up until the wee hours of morning."

—The Royal Reviews

"Spear is arguably one of the best paranormal romance writers out there. Fans will embrace this series and new readers will be fascinated by Spear's laser-sharp focus on these big cats."

—Debbie's Book Bag

"Scorching hot...an action-packed, sensual contemporary romance."

—Romance Junkies

"Ms. Spear's jaguars are highly sensual creatures."

—That's What I'm Talking About

"Sleek, sensual, and spellbinding."

—Booked Solid with Virginia C

Praise for *Savage Hunger*

"Has moments of humor, of tenderness and pure hot loving… Leaves a reader hungering for more of this awesome and exciting new world."

—*Long and Short Reviews*, 5 Stars

"Dark, sultry, and primal romance… The chemistry is blazing hot and will leave readers breathless."

—*Fresh Fiction*

"Well-written paranormal romance featuring a couple that sizzles right off the page."

—*RT Book Reviews*, 4 Stars

"The strength of Spear's writing lies in her ability to keep the reader emotionally in tune with the characters… Spear's lush descriptions of the Amazon…will leave readers hungry for more time in paradise."

—*Booklist*

"A sizzling page-turner. Terry Spear is wickedly talented."

—*Night Owl Reviews Reviewer Top Pick*, 5 Stars

"Terry Spear has created another engaging world that is rich in detail and has fascinating characters."

—*Anna's Book Blog*

"Spear makes the impossible seem real and natural while keeping you in suspense."

—*Thoughts in Progress*

JAGUAR PRIDE

TERRY SPEAR

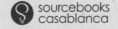

sourcebooks
casablanca

To those who serve to protect the exotic animals in the rainforest. Thanks for making it possible for so many of them to remain in their natural habitat and for stopping those who are destroying the animals or transporting them from their homes in the wild.

Chapter 1

AT DUSK IN THE CORCOVADO NATIONAL PARK IN COSTA Rica, Melissa Overton barely heard the constant sound of crickets chirping all around them. Prowling through the dense, tropical rainforest as a jaguar, she listened for the human voices that would clue her in that her prey was nearby.

Waves crashed onto the sandy beaches in the distance as she made her way quietly, like a phantom predator, through the tangle of vines and broad, leafy foliage, searching for any sign of the poachers. Humans wouldn't have a clue as to what she and her kind were when they saw her—apparently nothing other than an ordinary jaguar. And she and her fellow jaguar shifters planned to keep it that way.

Her partner on this mission, JAG agent Huntley Anderson, was nearby, just as wary and observant. The JAG Special Forces Branch, also known as the Golden Claws, was only open to jaguar shifters and served to protect both their shifter kind and their jaguar cousins. For this mission, JAG Director Martin Sullivan had ordered Melissa and Huntley to capture a group of poachers. The JAG agents were to let the Costa Rican authorities take it from there, which didn't sit well with Melissa. She understood Martin's reasoning, but she'd rather end the poaching in a more...*permanent* way.

Otherwise, the bad guys would be back to poaching

once they'd served their time. And she and others like her would be trying to apprehend the poachers again, before they killed or injured the exotic cats—or took them out of their native habitat and sold them to the highest bidder.

An ocelot caught her eye, but as soon as he saw her, he quickly vanished. It was May and the rainy season had just begun—a time when many tourists avoided the area because flooding made hiking more dangerous. She and Huntley made their way through a tiny section of the park's more than 103,000 acres of tropical rainforest, searching for Timothy Jackson, the leader of the poachers, and his men. Intelligence at JAG headquarters indicated that this was the group's favorite area to poach from.

Jackson was an enigma. He'd fought bravely in the desert on two combat tours and left the service with an honorable discharge. But when his wife took their baby daughter and ran off with another man, the shame and anger seemed to have consumed Jackson. He'd finally quit his job as a Veterans Administration clerk and had turned into something dark and twisted.

Melissa's paws didn't make a sound as she moved through snarled roots and wet and muddy leaf litter at the base of the towering tropical trees, her ears perked, listening for human voices.

Wearing his black jaguar coat, Huntley was sniffing the air nearby and pausing to listen. Darkness had claimed the area, the trees and rapidly approaching rain clouds blocking any hint of light at dusk. Though Melissa's golden coat, covered in black rosettes, was difficult to see at night if anyone should shine a flashlight on her, Huntley was even harder to see, making him hauntingly ghostlike. In broad daylight, his rosettes could be seen, but in a darkly elegant way. She'd never tell him. As hot as he looked, he probably knew it well, and she didn't want him to think she was interested or anything. Not when they were each currently seeing someone else.

She loved working with him, though.

Some would incorrectly call Huntley a panther, but he was a black jaguar. Black jaguars, a melanistic form, accounted for about six percent of the regular jaguar population. The jaguar shifters weren't sure about the ratio within their own kind. Huntley's mother was a beautiful black jaguar, and his dad, golden. Both his brother, Everett, and sister, Tammy, were also golden. For whatever reason, Huntley's coat appealed to Melissa, especially on missions like this. He seemed like a ninja warrior in jaguar form—sleek, agile, and deadly. And she liked that he was wild like she was, making them both able to live in their native environments without a hitch. Unless they had trouble with poachers.

She realized more and more that she should have hooked up with a cat like Huntley—and not a city cat like Oliver Strickland, who didn't ever shift or want to experience his wild side. How boring was that? She had believed that if she showed Oliver how much fun it could be, he might change his mind. She should have known that altering someone's personality wasn't going to happen unless the person wanted it to. Oliver was strictly a human who kept his jaguar persona hidden from everyone. Including her. Not that he wasn't a

gorgeous specimen of a man to savor. He was. She
sighed, wishing he was more…wild, in a jaguar way.

Switching her attention from thinking about her tame
boyfriend and her hot JAG partner, she listened again for
any human sounds. Nocturnal animals were out hunting,
which included all the wild cats that lived there—the
pumas (also known as cougars, mountain lions, and a
variety of other names), margays, ocelots, oncillas (a
small wild cat, also known as the little spotted cat), and
the jaguar. All wild cats were territorial, but the jaguar
was king.

She'd spotted what looked like domestic cat prints in
the mud underneath some of the ferns. In reality, they
were an oncilla's paw prints. She and Huntley were
leaving their own jaguar pug marks in the mud, though
they were not using any of the human-made trails so no
human was likely to encounter them.

They used the coastal track to search for the poachers, which meant having to ford several rivers, the Rio
Sirena being the most dangerous at high tide. All of the
rivers could be treacherous if the currents were strong
enough, especially for inexperienced hikers. The Rio
Sirena also had its fair share of American crocodiles,
bull sharks, and spectacled caiman.

Melissa and Huntley had traveled nearly two miles,
staying hidden in the rainforest near the track, which
hikers could use to make a two- or three-day trek through
the park and camp at five different ranger stations. She
and Huntley would consider anyone they came across as
suspect. Hikers carrying backpacks and camera equipment were probably there for just a visit. Anyone toting
a rifle or gun would be their number one suspect.

Before dusk, she and Huntley had stashed their own camping equipment—single tent and two sleeping bags, clothes, hiking shoes, and insect repellent—high in a tree. They didn't want to tempt anyone who might think to steal their "abandoned" equipment by leaving it lying about.

They searched for the poachers at night because that's when the men were most likely to be hunting. This was the second day of trying to locate the poachers, and she wanted to find them *now*.

Mosquitoes buzzed around her, making her glad to have her jaguar fur coat. She suddenly spied several tapirs as they poked around, looking for vegetation worth eating. She and Huntley made a wide sweep around them, not wanting the animals to believe two jaguars were hunting them. The sound of insects roared in the thick, humid air. An owl hooted. A vampire bat flew overhead. That surprised her because the bats often stayed near herds of cattle. She glanced up at the cloudy sky. Vampire bats didn't like hunting during the full moon when they were visible.

Only the stout of heart would come to the rainforest during the rainy season. That meant more of a chance for her and Huntley to catch those who weren't there just to sightsee. Anyone visiting the area would have to watch the tides. The virgin rainforest, deserted beaches, and jungle-edged rivers were a visitor's paradise. But the park also had vast swamps that were inaccessible to humans. As cats, they could go there, but if the poachers couldn't navigate the swamps, it wouldn't do Melissa and Huntley any good to search for them there.

Martin said that the poachers had been seen hunting

their prey in this area. They were suspected to be hunting here at night, sometimes when the jaguars went to the beach to eat sea turtles. It was indeed the perfect hunting ground for the poachers, who could use the beach to escape with their bounty. She loved it there in the South Pacific region. This was a favorite vacation spot for her, so she hated to think that poachers would be there hunting any of the beautiful cats. Or any of the animals, for that matter.

Melissa was startled to see two spotted cubs sniffing around the ground, and she immediately stood still. A mother would be nearby. And dangerous. Melissa couldn't tell from this distance and without being able to smell the cubs' scents whether they were jaguar cubs or pumas. The two species were so similar before they were six months old that they were hard to tell apart. In the tropics, jaguars and pumas were known to overlap territories to some degree, unlike in other locations. Though if the puma came across a jaguar, he'd give way to the bigger cat.

Her heart pounding, Melissa caught sight of the mother—a tan-colored puma. She nudged one of the cubs, who looked to be about four months old. And then the mother and her cubs disappeared into the rainforest. Melissa glanced back at Huntley. He looked wary, ears pricked, his blue-green eyes focused on where the puma had disappeared. Normally, the puma wouldn't have chanced a confrontation with a male and female jaguar, but any mother with a cub could be unpredictable.

Her heart settling a bit, Melissa continued to explore, finally coming across a human trail. With only a hundred feet of visibility because of the thick vegetation, getting lost in the rainforest was a real concern for a visitor who didn't stick to a trail. But she and Huntley could smell and hear things that humans couldn't—like how far they were from a swamp or a river or the ocean. All rivers lead to the ocean, right?

There the rivers could end up in crocodile-infested swamps before they continued on their way to the sea, so hiker beware.

Men's voices deeper in the rainforest caught Melissa's attention. She couldn't make out what they were actually saying. Huntley was beside her in an instant. Were the men camping in the rainforest? She'd heard at least three different voices. She could smell whiffs of smoke from their campfire. She and Huntley headed in that direction, drawing closer until they could hear the three men talking—about rugby, girlfriends, and sex. *Australians*. Most likely they were not who she and Huntley were looking for.

"Hey, mate, look at this. Hold the light closer."

One of the men was holding a flashlight as they looked at a tiny, neon-orange poison dart frog sitting on a broad green leaf.

They thought that was exciting?

To give the men an experience of a lifetime, and before Huntley could dissuade her—if he thought to, or before he did it first—she ran near the camp and past it. She caught one of the men's attention before she disappeared into the rainforest.

"Holy shit!" the man said, scrambling to his feet.

"Was that a—" another man said.

She heard Huntley chasing after her.

"Two of them?"

"A black jaguar?"

"Did anyone get a shot of them?"

The men were so excited that they continued to talk about their experience, wishing someone had gotten a picture of the two jaguars.

Both Melissa and Huntley were well out of sight, having disappeared into the foliage seconds after their appearance in camp.

Huntley was close enough that he brushed his shoulder against her hip in a playful way—amused at what she'd pulled and playing along. She grinned back at him, showing a mouthful of wicked teeth.

He grinned in response.

He *could* have gone on a path parallel to hers, staying hidden, but *no*, he had to follow her, probably giving the tourists a near heart attack when they saw not one but two jaguars. Or…it might have given them more of a thrill.

She smiled, never knowing what to expect from her partner, whom she'd been with on two missions before. He could say the same for her—never knowing what she might pull. Sure, he would have an inkling of what she was about to do from the way she would shift her footing and tense her body, preparing to lunge or run. But he wouldn't have enough time to react.

Wouldn't the tourists just love to tell the park rangers that they had spied two jaguars running together? Jaguars rarely made an appearance for them. A black jaguar was even rarer. But a female and male running together? In the jaguar world—as opposed to the jaguar shifter world—the big cats only did that when they were courting.

She smelled the salty ocean and headed that way, intending to see if maybe someone had ditched a boat in one of the isolated coves. She and Huntley finally reached one of the beaches, where the warm ocean waters lapping at the sandy shore teemed with marine life, brightly colored coral, and rock formations. She sniffed the ground and the air, trying to smell any sign of insect repellent or suntan lotion. *Neither*. She glanced at Huntley. He shook his head, indicating he hadn't smelled anything either.

Then they spied a jaguar at one end of the beach searching for sea turtles. She'd read that the park used to have more than a hundred jaguars, and now it was down to between thirty and forty. This jaguar was one of the lucky ones.

She and Huntley avoided it and took off in the opposite direction. She ran along the sandy beach, her paws leaving imprints in the sand, and then she and Huntley reached the mouth of the river—and saw fins. Bull sharks, one of only a few kinds of sharks that could survive in both fresh and salt water. She was surprised to see so many because illegal poaching of shark fins was decimating the numbers.

Melissa and Huntley needed to cross the river to get to the other beach and continue their search for a boat tied off on the shore. She was certain this wasn't an ideal spot to traverse. Not that the jaguars couldn't defend themselves against something that had the notion of biting into them while they were swimming. But they didn't want to be injured. Sure, jaguar shifters healed fast, depending on the injury. But then their boss would want to know what had happened, they might miss taking down the bad guys, and Martin would use them as an example of what *not* to do on a mission when lecturing his other agents. No one wanted to have their aborted missions showcased as an illustration of what happened when an agent made a mistake on an assignment.

On the other hand, Melissa found crossing the river there awfully tempting. She attributed having such a reckless nature to her father, who had always encouraged her and her twin sister, Bonnie, to take risks, while their mother would have had a stroke if she'd known.

Melissa studied the water again, wanting to take the quickest path to the beach on the other side. The bull sharks were definitely feeding, their fins showing, then disappearing and reappearing. She thought she counted about eight. The problem was that the farther away from the mouth of the river she and Huntley got, the more trouble they could have with crocodiles and caiman added to the mix.

Huntley nudged her, urging her to move farther through the rainforest. She grunted at him. What did he think? She was a daredevil? Well, she was, to an extent.

Lightning briefly lit up the gray clouds and then thunder clapped overhead, making her jump a little. Then the rain started pouring down. As deep as the river was, they would have to swim, not walk across it like they could in the dry season. Jaguars *were* powerful swimmers, so at one point where the river narrowed a little, they finally made the decision to go for it, side by side, protecting each other's flanks.

Her heart thundering, she crossed the warm river. A small croc was resting on the shore, eyeing them. Another slipped into the water, and a bull shark passed them by. When she and Huntley finally reached the other side, they bolted out of the water and away from the riverbank. They headed through the rainforest again until they reached the beach along the coast.

For a moment, they just stood there, the rain pelting them as they listened for the sound of a boat engine or men talking. She smelled gasoline down the beach. Her heart began to beat faster. The gasoline smell had to have come from a boat. There was no sign of one beached anywhere, and she hoped that if the smell was from the poachers' boat, they hadn't already grabbed what they had come for and gone. She and Huntley loped toward the cove hidden by trees.

When they reached the edge of the beach and looked right, they saw a boat sitting in the protected cove. She felt a hint of relief and the thrill of the chase. If the boat was the poachers' transportation, they could escape with their "catch" without having to leave via any of the park entrances. She had to remind herself that others used boats to reach the shores for tours, so this might not be a poacher's boat.

No one was around. What if the boat was operated by a legitimate company taking a bunch of tourists on a guided tour? But she didn't see any markings on the boat indicating it belonged to a tour group or resort in the area.

She and Huntley drew closer under the cover of the rainforest, though it was pouring and dark. Still, if someone had a high-powered-enough flashlight, they could see Huntley and her. Well, Huntley's eyes mostly—they gave off a fluorescent color if a light was shined on them.

Then they heard something moving through the brush. She and Huntley stopped.

"Hurry up," a man said, heading in the direction of the beach.

His words sounded promising as she and Huntley hid in the ferns, watching and waiting.

A light wavered through the dense foliage. The men had to be human, not shifters, or they wouldn't have needed the man-made light.

Suddenly, someone came out of the rainforest from a different direction. A man yanked up his trousers' zipper while he watched for his comrades. Dressed in a white shirt and pants, he stood out in the black rain that soaked him and everything around him.

"Any trouble?" he asked the four men as they broke through the vegetation and reached the beach.

"Carlton got careless, and the cat scratched him bad," one of the men said. Two of them were carrying a burlap sack between them with what was likely their live bounty inside.

Cat. Which kind?

A second man was carrying another burlap sack, while the last man was holding on to his shoulder as if his injuries were severe, his shirt and fingers bloodied. He groaned in pain.

All of them had rifles slung over their shoulders and sheathed machetes hanging from their belts.

"Whaddya get?" the lookout asked.

"Puma and two cubs."

Melissa ground her teeth, thinking at once of the puma and her cubs that she and Huntley had spied earlier.

"Hot damn."

"Help Carlton into the boat, will ya? Where's Jackson?"

Jackson. The man—and his cohorts—that they'd come for. And he wasn't here? *Great*.

"Taking a dump. Something didn't agree with him, and he's about an eighth of a mile back there."

"And you left him alone?"

"Hell, he told us to get going. If you want to watch him doing his thing, *you* go back and do so."

Melissa had no intention of letting these men remove the pumas from the park. But both she and Huntley hesitated to make a move. If they attacked now, Jackson could all of a sudden show up and shoot them both.

Then, figuring they had to chance it before the men got the cats in the boat, Huntley growled low, Melissa's cue to attack.

They had one attempt to get this right—while the men still had their hands full with carrying the sacks and the lookout was trying to help the injured man into the boat. The men had so many rifles and machetes between them that it was a dangerous move on the jaguars' part.

Huntley went after the two men holding the bigger cat. Melissa lunged after the lone man holding on to the sack with the cubs. The JAG agents wouldn't kill the poachers if they didn't have to. But the agents had to use an economy of movements and quick action to do this right.

Swiping his paw with his claws extended, Huntley struck the first man that he could reach in the head, knocking him out cold. Melissa used a similar tactic with the other man. Thankfully, by sweeping its paw, a jaguar could stun its prey, knock it out, or kill it. She and Huntley were trying hard not to kill the men, as much as she regretted her orders.

She immediately went after the lookout, who was panicking and struggling to get his rifle off his shoulder. The injured man looked dazed and didn't react. She coldcocked the lookout, then went after the injured man. Even if he couldn't fight well, she didn't want to chance it. Once she'd slugged him hard, and he'd joined the lookout lying unconscious on the beach, she turned to take care of anyone else.

Huntley was checking on all of the men to ensure they were really out and not playing dead.

She tore open the first of the burlap sacks with her teeth. Two sleeping spotted cubs. One of them she recognized as the same cub she had seen earlier. Melissa tore the other sack open and found the mother, tranquilized like her babies. She felt bad for them for having experienced this, but glad they would have a good outcome *this time*.

Huntley had shifted into his attractive human form—that she was trying hard not to look at too much—and was examining each of the men's IDs, verifying the poachers' names before he called the park ranger. The agents had to move quickly before Jackson arrived on the scene.

"Wish we'd gotten Jackson, but we might still be able to. At least we got the rest of his men, for now," Huntley said, pulling a cell phone out of one of the men's pockets. Huntley's dark blond hair was dripping wet, and his blue-green eyes were studying her as he called the authorities. He was as tall as her father, six feet in height, muscled, and well…just plain good-looking.

She grunted her approval, then dragged the momma cat in her burlap sack into the rainforest to hide her. By the time she had returned to seize the sack containing the cubs, Huntley was speaking on a cell phone in Spanish, relaying to the ranger station that some very bad hombres had been caught attempting to poach a puma and her two cubs. He read the men's names off their IDs, then tucked the IDs back into their pockets.

"The puma and her cubs are sleeping in burlap sacks in the vegetation nearby to keep them safe, but you can find the men and their boat at the following coordinates." He proceeded to tell the ranger the location of the cove. "One other man, the leader in charge of the poachers, is named Timothy Jackson. According to his men, he's still in the rainforest."

Huntley ended the call and disabled the boat by pulling the control box apart, removing a few things, and tossed them into the ocean, just in case.

Melissa was supposed to watch his back, and that meant any other delectable part he showed off. All his parts were remarkable, as toned as his muscles were, and though she didn't want to admit looking, he was very well endowed. She felt a little bit guilty, especially since he had a girlfriend and she had a boyfriend. Still, she was only human—well, and jaguar—so she blamed the interest on both. Besides, looking but not touching was acceptable, right?

She swore he was fighting a smile, probably flattered just a little that she *was* interested.

"I'd prefer to sink the boat with them on it," Huntley said gruffly as he joined her.

She roared in agreement. A sunken boat would make a great coral-reef structure for fish in the future.

"It will take hours before anyone can arrive, unless they send a boat, and even that will take some time," he said. "Maybe we can still get Jackson."

Huntley shifted back into his jaguar form and quickly joined her. She led him to the mother and cubs and stayed there, watching over them and protecting them. The mother and the cubs would probably sleep through the night, long enough for the park rangers and police to reach this location. Melissa and Huntley climbed high into a tree, not wanting to face a very hostile mother puma that would be protecting her young and danger-ous once she woke.

They listened for any sign of Jackson approaching. They couldn't see the boat or his men from there, which was why it was a safe place to leave the drugged cats. Either Huntley or Melissa could have gone searching in the rainforest for the bastard, but their training had taught them to stick together as much as possible while they conducted a mission in the wild.

They would stay hidden unless they heard Jackson reach his men. Then they'd pay him a visit and knock him out too. Otherwise, they'd wait until the rangers and police arrived to ensure the mother and her cubs remained safe, just in case any other poachers happened onto them. Not likely, but she and Huntley couldn't leave the cats' safety to chance.

A short while later, they heard movement near the cove. Melissa hated leaving the mother and the cubs alone. Huntley indicated with his head that she should stay with the pumas, but she couldn't let him risk his life in case Jackson saw him and fired a shot to kill.

She and Huntley leaped down from the tree, then stealthily made their way to the cove. A couple of tapirs were rooting around. No sign of Jackson. Disappointed, she and Huntley returned to the pumas and jumped back into the tree to wait.

The problem with the rainforest and all the creatures that lived within was that everything made a noise, and because of their enhanced cat's hearing, the JAG agents heard *everything*. So they investigated the cove five more times before they figured that Jackson had to have discovered what happened to his men, found he couldn't start the boat, and taken off on foot. According to the mission briefing, he had lived in jungles for much of his life, so she could see him being nearly as stealthy as them.

Three hours later, they heard men speaking in Spanish—police and two rangers—and surveying the area for any sign of the cats. When they searched the rainforest and found the sleeping cats, they took pictures and checked them over, never looking up to see the jaguars in the tree above them. In the dark, they wouldn't see the cats anyway unless they flashed their lights in that direction, but who would ever believe a couple of jaguars were watching them?

Ensuring that the three pumas were well, the men returned to the beach.

In the boat, they found cages, weapons, and tranquilizers—enough evidence to put the five men in jail. "The caller said there were six men," one of the police officers said. He read the names of the poachers that she and Huntley had taken down. "But the ringleader? Jackson? He's not here."

Letting her breath out in annoyance, Melissa hated that they hadn't caught Jackson too—and in the middle of a poaching job, the perfect scenario. She glanced at Huntley, who had narrowed his eyes and looked just as pissed as she felt.

Chapter 2

HUNTLEY HATED THAT ONE OF THE MEN HAD GOTTEN away. He wished Jackson had shown up. Huntley would have bitten the bastard in the leg and given him a nice bloody wound to deal with, which in the jungle could have nasty repercussions, at the very least. And it would have hobbled the poacher enough to prevent his escape.

He and Melissa would have to track Jackson down, and he would be armed and dangerous.

"The cat sure scratched them good," the one police officer said, sounding glad the puma had paid the men back.

Except that not all the scratches were from the puma. Some were from two pissed-off jaguar shifters. The men were now marked. Maybe they'd see it as a badge of honor—they came out alive after facing the wrath of a couple of jaguars. The scars would also make the men easier for the police to identify in the future if they were caught poaching again. They couldn't easily hide the scratches from their families either—if they'd had no idea what the men were illegally dealing in.

Once the puma mother stirred and had checked out her cubs, she and the two of them headed away from the sound of the men talking.

Melissa and Huntley waited until the police had retrieved the burlap sacks, glancing around warily and probably worried that the puma and her cubs would still be in the vicinity.

As soon as the police left, Huntley grunted at Melissa, telling her he thought it was time to move on. She jumped down from the tree and he joined her. They tried tracking Jackson by smell, but he had to be wearing hunter spray to hide his human identity from his prey. Only this time, he was the prey, hiding his identity from a couple of angry predators.

After searching the area for a couple of hours, Melissa nudged at Huntley, indicating she wanted to take a break. They really needed some sleep if they were going to track the bastard down.

They headed to the location where they'd hidden their gear. Huntley jumped into the tree, grabbed their tent, and tossed it to the ground. Then he seized each of their field packs and did the same. Before he'd even jumped to the ground, Melissa had already shifted into her naked human form.

He admired her for getting started on the tent right away instead of waiting for his help. Well, he admired that and a hell of a lot more: her reddish brown hair curled about her shoulders and her sparkling green eyes that caught him watching her as he helped her to put up the tent. He *was* helping. Just a little distracted. But she always checked him out when they shifted, so it was only fair that he did the same. He couldn't help but be pleased when she revealed how much he appealed to her—mainly because Genista, his current girlfriend, had acted cold and distant the past few weeks, as if she was looking right through him instead of at him.

But Melissa had a guy. Oliver was totally lame, as far as Huntley was concerned. Something about the insurance salesman must appeal to Melissa or she wouldn't be dating the city cat, even though Huntley had wondered— just a time or two—what exactly she saw in him.

Inside the tent, Huntley slipped into a pair of boxers. Melissa pulled on a tank top, and again, he couldn't help but watch as the formfitting, stretchy top took on the shape of her pert breasts. She tugged on a pair of shorts, and then they curled up in their sleeping bags.

"Do you want to call Martin, or do you want me to?" Melissa asked.

"Be my guest."

Melissa was good at her job, and she and Huntley worked well together. He couldn't help enjoying her spurts of being a daredevil. Like he was.

She pulled out her phone and called the boss, putting the conversation on speakerphone. She explained how they'd taken the men down, identified them, and then called the police. "It's mostly done. One of the men escaped before the police arrived."

"Everyone's alive, right?" Martin asked.

"Yes, sir."

As much as Huntley had wished for a kill order, he knew the JAG director wanted to allow the police to handle this in Costa Rica. Hopefully, between them and the park rangers, someone would catch Jackson before he escaped the peninsula.

"He's armed?" Martin asked.

"The rest of his men were, so I assume he is. We'll go after him once we've rested. He won't be able to sleep much in the rainforest without some gear. None of the men were wearing backpacks when we took them down, so he would have had to sneak in and grab some stuff from the boat, if they had anything tucked away there. He probably knows the park fairly well, but the tides are unpredictable and many of the trails and some of the roads are underwater. Do you still want this one alive?"

"Your call. If he sees any jaguars coming after him, he may shoot to kill. Just stop him any way that you safely can. I don't want either of you injured in the process, and I want this to look like an accident, and well, survival of the fittest, if you can't take him down any other way."

"You mean, let the bull sharks and crocodiles finish him off?" Melissa asked.

"You got it. If you can't just take him down and get the police to take care of it, then that should be the plan. Call me when you learn anything."

"Will do, sir," Melissa said and ended the call.

Melissa turned over on her side to face Huntley. "If not for Jackson escaping, that would have been one of the easiest jobs I think I've ever been on."

"Yeah, but it sure could have been a nightmare if any of those men had gotten hold of their machetes or turned their rifles on us."

"I agree." She sighed. "Do you think this will stop them from doing it again?"

He snorted. "As long as someone's willing to pay for stolen cats, no." He let out his breath. "At least with these poachers, the one guy probably won't be doing any more of this. The puma got one of his eyes. Too difficult to move through the rainforest at night as it is, but with limited sight? Really bad news. He'd be a handicap for his partners. So one down. How many more to go?"

"It's sad, really. I heard that some American foundation and other organizations are sending money to help add more security to the park."

"Good thing too. But when people are paying for the souvenirs or the animals themselves, sellers will take the minimal risk involved in poaching the animals."

For a while they were quiet, and he thought about how years earlier these places were a real paradise for the wildlife. Even without poachers, the environment could be ruined by too many tourists visiting the reserve to see the wild creatures.

"You…weren't thinking of crossing the mouth of the river and swimming with all those sharks, were you?" he asked, not believing she'd even have considered such a thing.

She smiled.

"Good thing you weren't planning to." He put his hands behind his head and looked up at the tent ceiling. "Like running past the college kids at their campsite."

She chuckled. "You didn't have to run past them too."

"Sure I did. You couldn't be the only one to give them a thrill." He smiled. "We work well together as a team."

"I agree. We do. I guess it's back to home base and see what the boss needs us to do next after we clear up this last problem. You're due for a break though, aren't you?" she asked.

"Yeah, long overdue. I was supposed to get one two missions ago, but it's been so hectic that Martin wanted me to go with you on this one, since I've been here recently."

Melissa closed her eyes. "Well, it's been fun working with you."

"This isn't over yet. And it might not be for a while. The guy's a hunter, been living in the tropics forever. His American parents were biologists working in the Amazon. He was born in Venezuela, and he knows the jungle life."

With the flooding, some roads were underwater, the swamps had spread, and the rivers had expanded. Trails were also underwater in some areas, and everything was muddy. So, it wouldn't be an easy trek out. They could have managed it as jaguars, but they had to hike their gear out.

For four days, they followed Jackson's trails—where he'd crossed the swamps, where he'd pitched a tent— which meant he'd had the presence of mind to grab gear from the boat before he had run off. They finally located his scent trail where he'd exited the park. They'd been too late.

Irritated, muddy, wet, and tired, they arrived at the cabin resort bordering the park where they'd been staying. The place was mostly empty because of the rainy season. Of the ten units, only three were occupied.

Melissa cleaned up first while Huntley took care of their gear. It was just something they'd started to do. He'd let her shower first, and he'd clean their equipment. Then he'd shower, and she'd cook a meal. She was a hell of a lot better cook than he was.

While Melissa was making final preparations on the meal, Huntley called Martin. "No luck finding

Jackson. He left the park, and we have no idea where he's gone now."

"All right. Pack it up and return home," Martin said. "The other men shouldn't be a problem for a while. Maybe some jail time will cure their need to poach. As for Jackson, I'll have some other agents try to track down where he might end up next. Your mission is done."

Vastly disappointed, Huntley didn't feel like the mission was over. He had never let one slip away like this, not that they could help it.

"All right. We'll report in when we arrive home."

"And you're due for a vacation."

Huntley wondered if Martin was trying to tell him something. That he'd slipped up because he'd needed a break. He didn't want one now. He wanted to catch Jackson. On the other hand, a break *was* much needed. And sometimes taking one really helped him to think more clearly.

"Do you want to talk to Melissa, boss?"

"Yeah, put her on, will you?"

Huntley handed Melissa the phone, wishing he could work with her on another assignment. They were completely compatible, and it was nice working with a woman for a change. But he couldn't come out and say that to the boss. Not when Martin would begin speculating that something more was going on between them. Oh, hell, yeah, she was appealing as a partner—and nice to look at and smart and fun to be with when they could let down their hair a bit. But beyond that, neither of them was interested in dating the other, not when they both were seeing someone. And Huntley didn't want to come off as some Casanova when he was dating someone else.

"Hey, boss. Have something new for me to check out?" She glanced at Huntley and mouthed, "Food's ready."

"I'll serve it."

He headed into the kitchen and heard Melissa say, "A week? Sure, okay. Anything else? All right. Talk later."

She rejoined Huntley and sat down to eat a meal of rice and beans, pork, and fried plantains—typical Costa Rican fare.

"Delicious," he said, forking up another piece of pork. "You could be a master chef if you ever decided this life wasn't for you." On their last assignment a month ago in Belize, she'd also made the most delightful native dishes.

She smiled. "Thanks. I don't think I'll ever want to give up the life of protecting our kind and cousins and taking down the nasties."

"What about when you have kids?"

"Oliver's not interested in having any. Not that I am either. Makes it difficult for someone like me who's away so often. I'd…want to be home with them, raising them, if I had any."

Huntley had wondered during their last mission how her boyfriend had felt about her teaming up with single, male jaguar shifters on some of these missions where they shared such close quarters.

He'd met Oliver once during a Golden Claws office Christmas party, and the man had looked way out of place. Couldn't be helped, really. Oliver sold life insurance, so not exactly a dangerous way of life. Most everyone serving with the JAG was a field agent with lots of training, all wild cats who could live comfortably in jungle habitats during operations and were used to the adrenaline rush in dangerous situations. He'd never heard of Melissa vacationing with Oliver in a rainforest or jungle environment either. Huntley suspected Oliver wouldn't want kids because he'd be the one stuck taking care of them when Melissa was away on missions.

"What about Genista? Is she looking to settle down and have some cubs?" Melissa asked.

The last time Huntley and Melissa had worked together, they had talked about their education, places they'd lived, that sort of thing. Nothing really this personal. It was different when he was with the guys. They talked about hunting and fishing, past missions, and the like. They often compared notes on who had the most dangerous missions. If they didn't heal completely with their enhanced healing, they'd most likely compare battle scars.

"She's like you, not wanting to give up her Golden Claws assignments. Not just yet."

"I can understand that. We took years to train for a worthwhile cause. It's quite a challenge to think about staying home with a cooing baby or two—or more because of our jaguar genetics." She shook her head and took another bite of her rice.

Melissa had checked out the tranquilized cubs to make sure they were all right, both while waiting for the police and after they had arrived. Earlier, when she had spied the mother puma and cubs, he had seen the way she had looked at the cubs—worried that they had lost their mother. Which had worried him too.

He wasn't sure Melissa was being totally honest with herself or with him. She seemed to have the mothering instinct and would have taken care of the cubs in a heartbeat if their mother had been killed.

Now with Huntley? That was totally a different story. He wasn't ready for fatherhood and had much preferred having Melissa take over with the cubs on this mission. He'd take down the bad guys. It wasn't a case of male chauvinism. Just that she had the natural instincts on how to care for the cubs, unlike him.

"So, I take it you've got a break in assignment. Planning on doing anything fun?" Huntley asked her.

"If I can get Oliver to take off from work. He tends to be a workaholic. What about you?"

"Genista's on assignment in Panama at the moment. I had no idea how long this case would take, and she has no idea about hers either."

"I thought Martin would have the two of you working together from time to time," Melissa said.

"I was working with my brother on a case down here, and she didn't want to have to wait for me to return." He hated how that sounded. The truth was that Genista had been like that ever since they'd started dating six months ago, jumping at the chance to go on a mission that wouldn't include him, being gone when he returned, or vice versa. In this business, it couldn't be helped sometimes. Unless they worked together. But every time he had brought it up, she'd gotten all negative on him.

"Oh," Melissa said, as if she didn't know what else to say.

Huntley knew he and his girlfriend's relationship didn't sound like it was going anywhere. He'd known that for a long time, but he'd still been hopeful they could work things out.

He shrugged. "I'm going to miss your cooking."

Melissa gave him a bright smile. "I'm glad you like all of this traditional fare. Oliver is strictly a meat-and-potatoes guy and doesn't like to try anything new."

"Not me. I think that's part of the enjoyment of visiting other countries. Not eating at a hamburger joint or a fast-food fried-chicken place, but tasting the real local cuisine."

"I agree." She took a deep breath and let out a heavy sigh. "I sure wish we could have nabbed Jackson before he fled the scene of the crime."

"Yeah, I hated losing the bastard. He might not end up back in the park, but I suspect he'll be back to poaching before we know it." Huntley helped Melissa clean up the dishes. He would have done it all, but she always wanted to help.

Then they packed, went to bed and, early the next morning, took the bus ride to the airport. They were quiet, half dozing on the trip home, the knowledge that this was the start of their downtime kicking in. Since he had driven Melissa to the airport for the trip to Costa Rica, Huntley had to drop her off at her place, a neat little condo with a no-kids policy. Maybe she wasn't really interested in kids.

Before they arrived at the condo, he wondered how Oliver would act this time. When Huntley had brought Melissa home from the first mission they'd worked on, Oliver had been a real prick, acting irritated with both of them for some perceived slight. Last time Huntley was on a mission with her, the guy had been working late, and Melissa was visibly relieved. This time? Who knew.

After half an hour, they reached the two-story,

redbrick condo in the Dallas suburbs. Oliver was watching out the window, dressed in jeans and a button-down shirt. No smile. No coming out to greet Melissa. Sour-faced and looking pissed, he had his arms folded across his chest. Maybe Melissa's relationship wasn't going anywhere either.

Huntley warned himself off thinking in such a way. Maybe Oliver was afraid of him. Huntley smiled a little at the notion and waved at the man anyway. Oliver didn't acknowledge the greeting.

That didn't bother Huntley, but what did was the icy reception Oliver was giving Melissa. She'd risked her life in the jungle, was tired, and needed a man in her life who would welcome her home with open arms, a loving embrace, and one hell of a scorching kiss. At least, if Huntley had been her boyfriend, that's how he would have handled the situation. He'd have shown her partner that he had what it took to be Melissa's boyfriend—and no other jaguar shifter need apply.

"Sorry, he must have had a rough day," Melissa said, but she didn't sound like she really thought that was the problem. She sounded like she was curbing the urge to growl, ready to take Oliver to task for being so rude.

Huntley hoped so, and he hoped that would straighten the guy out. She certainly deserved better treatment.

After saying good-bye, Huntley drove home to his place in the Dallas suburbs ten miles away. He was ready to relax, watch a movie, kick back, and just become a mushroom for a couple of days. He called Martin to let him know that both he and Melissa had arrived safely as he unpacked his bag, dumping half his clothes in the washer.

"Good. Glad to hear you're both home all right."

"Have you learned anything more about where Jackson went?"

"Nothing. I'll keep you posted."

Martin was good about stuff like that. Even if Huntley never had a chance to take Jackson down, Martin would keep him informed about who did.

"Anything really hot going on?" Huntley asked, already feeling out of the loop.

"Nothing for you to do. Take it easy. Enjoy your break. You'll be at it again soon enough."

"Thanks, Martin. I'm chilling." At least Huntley was trying to. If Genista was here, it would be a different story. Then again, maybe not.

"Good. Talk to you later. Have an incoming call from your partner."

Huntley smiled. He had beaten Melissa by a few seconds. "Talk later."

He started his laundry and made up a batch of popcorn, already missing Melissa's cooking. He cooked, but somehow the way she fixed meals seemed so effortless, and they tasted a whole lot better than his attempts.

He plunked himself down on the couch to watch TV, but then gave Genista a call. "Hey, got home and wanted to check in with you."

Silence.

He frowned. "Are you still there?"

"Yeah."

"So, how are things going on your mission?"

"They're going, all right?"

He paused, considering her situation. "Can't talk right now?" He understood all too well how difficult it could be on a mission, but he'd just wanted to make a connection with her. Let her know he was fine and ensure she was also. "Are you okay?"

"I've got a job to do. All right?"

Okay, this wasn't what he had expected. "Yeah, I got it. Do you want me to ask Martin if he could cancel my leave and I can join you to help with your assignment?"

"No! Huntley, what you see in 'us' is totally one-sided. I don't want anything more than…"

He waited, wondering why the hell he hadn't seen the signs that their relationship was this much in the toilet. Or maybe he had. He'd been working so hard, and she had also, that he'd thought the problem was just that. Hot under the collar now, he said, "Is there someone else?"

"No," she said, her tone softening. "It's not like that. I just…I just don't want what you want. I don't want you to believe there's really any future in *us*."

"*Oh…kay*. Well, where do we go from here?"

"I already moved out. I put in a change of address for my mail. I'll see you around the office. We can still work missions together, but that's it. Okay?"

He couldn't believe it without seeing it for himself. He immediately rose from the couch and headed for the closet and looked inside. Sure enough, all her clothes were gone.

"Sure." But it wasn't okay. He'd met her on a mission, fell head over heels for her, and thought that what they had was something special. Except ever since she'd moved in with him three months ago, she'd been pulling back, finding excuses to be absent or on a mission. God, how could he have been so clueless? "All right. Well, I'll let you get back to your mission then."

"I'm sorry that it didn't work out," she said.

"Yeah, me too. But better that we learn about it sooner rather than carrying this too far. It just would have been nice if you'd let me know before you moved out on me."

Silence.

"Okay, well, have a safe mission." And he meant it with all his heart.

"Yeah, have a nice vacation." And then she ended the call.

He felt numb. He called his triplet brother, Everett, but he was in Venezuela on a mission, and Huntley couldn't get hold of him. He might have been running as a jaguar. He tried calling his sister, Tammy, but all he got was her voice mail. She was probably working with her new mate, David, on training some shifter teens as future JAG agents.

Huntley decided he should just watch TV to get his mind off Genista and the last mission, and just, well, chill. He turned the TV on and flipped from one channel to another. Nothing appealed, not sports, or mystery, sci-fi, fantasy, police procedurals, nothing. He couldn't quit thinking about all the signs Genista had given him that she was interested in calling it quits…signs he hadn't paid any attention to.

It was seven o'clock. Screw this. He turned off the TV, left the partly eaten bowl of popcorn—now cold—on the table, and headed for the jaguar shifter club. Maybe he'd see one of the agents there, have a drink, and at least express his frustration about losing Jackson. Genista? He didn't want anyone to know he'd lost her this week as well.

Chapter 3

Oliver' totally fried her biscuits. Melissa was tired from the Costa Rican mission. Frustrated that Jackson had slipped out of their grasp. And she didn't need Oliver's attitude about now. Yet she realized she'd been bracing for this because as soon as she had returned from each of her last three missions, he'd been sullen, sulky, and then angry with her over absolutely nothing. Itching for a fight. Provoking one. She was sick of it. When she returned from a mission, she wanted romance, togetherness, peace, quiet, and recuperation.

"You could have been civil to Huntley Anderson. He was my partner on the mission, and he was trying to be friendly. You could have had the courtesy to come outside and greet us and at least say 'hi' back to him," she said, slamming the door after her as she hauled her bags inside without Oliver's help.

She had really never given it much thought before, because she always dragged her own bags into the condo after a mission and was perfectly capable of doing so. But she wondered now if it was his way of passively aggressively telling her he wouldn't aid her because the bags represented her time away from him. So fine. Act like he wanted her home and they'd work on things!

Ignoring her comment, Oliver began talking to her about all the sales he'd made while she was gone. She dropped her bags on the floor and headed for the kitchen for a glass of water, not interested in anything he had to say if it was all about his work.

Oliver followed her into the kitchen. His blue eyes were narrowed, and he was scowling at her. She knew that look. He was ready to create a scene. For not being a wild cat, he could sure get all growly with her.

"You don't care anything about what I do, do you?"

"I'm exhausted," she said. "It was a long trip. Huntley and I had a rough time of it."

Oliver looked even more pissed that she would mention Huntley in the conversation again.

"We lost one of the bad guys, and I need time to decompress," she continued.

"Hell, Melissa. I see the way the two of you are all chummy."

She scowled back at him. "Don't you start on me again about working with the men in the agency. They're professionals." Though she'd known a couple who hadn't been, but Martin had fired their butts. "We work together to bring down the bad guys and rescue the cats. That's it. We've been through all this before."

She knew then that it wouldn't work out with Oliver. The longer they'd been together, the more jealous he'd become of her partners. If she had a mission with another woman, he was fine with it. But as soon as she had an assignment with a male partner, Oliver was hell to live with for a week or more before and after the mission.

She realized she'd been avoiding having to deal with this. She just seemed to always be on a mission or trying to recuperate from the last one.

The condo was his, and she didn't have anywhere

to crash while she looked for a place. She would start searching for an apartment first thing in the morning.

"You sleep with them! You can't tell me you're not interested in what they have to offer. They're wild cats like you, for one," Oliver said.

"We sleep in separate bedrooms when we're in a jungle cabin or hut." She didn't know why she was explaining this to him all over again. "Or as cats in a tree. And in a tent? Get real. It's damned hot and muggy down there, and sex is the furthest thing from our minds."

"You're only human," Oliver said, pacing. "You get naked in front of him when you shift."

Wild cats did when they worked together like this. It was hard not to. Oliver never shifted, but that was his deal, not hers. They didn't lust after other cats' bodies. Well, maybe she did a little over Huntley's, but she was totally hands off with him. Eyeing him a little was okay, as long as she didn't touch the goods. Right? And that had her thinking about his goods all over again.

"When you stay in the cabins, *they* are air-conditioned," Oliver said, angry.

Okay, now she was totally ticked off. "We *do* have some scruples," she said, annoyed to the max. He acted as though she slept around with every male agent in the branch.

She sipped her water and studied Oliver, his black hair slicked back, wet from recently showering, his posture rigid. Even when he was angry, he was beautiful in a movie star, heartthrob way—his body sculpted from workouts in the gym and his skin golden from swimming in the condo's pool. But he looked like he wanted to hit something. Maybe even her. He'd better not try it. Despite his workouts, he'd be flat on his back in a nanosecond.

Oliver turned to look out the kitchen window onto the backyard, then eyed her. "Okay, here's the deal."

As soon as he spoke the words, she was ready to tell him where he could shove his deal—no matter what it entailed. She was through having these "discussions" when she returned from a mission.

"I looked into how hard it would be for you to get a license to sell insurance. You should be able to do it," he said. "My insurance company will sponsor you. You'll have to take an exam and be fingerprinted, and that's it."

"What?"

"Then you could work with me at the insurance agency. We have a new opening. We could take off at the same time and be together nights, and we could drive in the HOV lane, and…"

"Wait, *what*? The HOV lane?" She couldn't believe what he'd conjured up while she was away. How long had he been thinking of this?

"The high-occupancy vehicle lane—you know, for cars with more than one person riding in them during rush hour."

She was still staring at him like he'd gone insane. "You want me to quit my job so I can work at yours?" So they could drive to work in a faster lane on the highway? She was usually quick on her feet, but she hadn't expected this.

"Yeah. It's the only way it's going to work between us."

"It doesn't matter that I love my job?" she asked, not

that she meant for him to answer her. She didn't give a damn what he thought. She *wasn't* quitting her job. And certainly not to work at his agency. Selling stuff? She wasn't a salesperson at heart. Sure, he was always telling her about the Texas codes concerning insurance, which she halfheartedly listened to, and that meant she didn't know enough to pass any test. *If* she'd even wanted to do that, which she *didn't*.

She was a fighter, a rescuer—that's how she lived. If she and her sister, Bonnie, hadn't been rescued when they were young and that hadn't made such an impression on her, maybe she wouldn't be doing this today. She was a survivor. When he was just a JAG agent ten years earlier, Martin had led the team that had rescued her and her sister. From then on, both had wanted to be just like Martin. He finally had become the director of the branch, and when they were old enough, she and her sister had proudly applied to work there. She wasn't ever quitting her work.

"I don't know why you're so hung up on that job. It's an addiction for you. That's all you think about. All you want to talk about. After the mission. Before the mission. What went wrong, and what you have to do differently next time. I just don't give a damn."

She could say the same about him and his insurance work.

"They're looking to fill that insurance position by the end of the week. I'll work with you to get you up to speed to take the test. I made an appointment for you to take it on Thursday, hoping you would be back before then so I could prep you. You're perfect for the job."

She stared at him, not believing he thought he could

just rearrange her life like this and she'd be happy with it.

"That's my ultimatum," he said, folding his arms. "It's not going to work between us if we don't do this. I don't want you to go on one more mission away from home."

She smiled, albeit a little evilly. "Okay, how about we do this instead. Since you want me working by your side, you can join the JAG agency."

Not that Martin would take him into the agency as a field operative when Oliver was a city cat.

"I love what I do. And if I worked for your agency, Martin Sullivan wouldn't put me out in the field with you."

Right, because Oliver would be a handicap and get them both killed.

"Not that I have any intention of changing jobs," Oliver added.

"Ditto for me."

"We wouldn't be together any more than we are now if I took a job like that," Oliver said, frowning at her.

She sighed. "All right. True. I get your point. Really I do. You want more 'us' time, and I understand. It's just not going to work out. I don't want to quit what I love doing."

"Fine. Then pack up your stuff and leave."

She couldn't believe he wanted this over between them so soon. "Okay. Glad we could work this out so well."

He walked into the living room, sat down on the couch, turned on the TV, and acted as though she had already vacated his life for good.

"I'll have to come back for the rest of my things as soon as I have some boxes and a place I can stay."

Oliver raised his brows. "Stay with what's his face."

She ground her teeth. Oliver really believed she was going to move right in with Huntley? "He's got a girl-friend. I told you that already." She just barely stifled the urge to add, "you jerk."

"Boxes are out in the garage."

Her jaw dropped a little. He had known all this time that she wouldn't go along with his ultimatum and had planned for her to leave? Even prepared for it.

"Huh? Thanks, I guess. But I still don't have a place." And it was too late to do anything about that. "Unless you already thought of that and have one lined up for me. Just in case."

He shook his head.

"Guess not, then. I'll be back tomorrow when you're at work and will pack up my stuff."

Crap. Well, at least Martin had given her a week off, so she had time to look for a place. But she wasn't leaving until she had a shower and changed clothes.

After that, she grabbed her still-packed bags and was about to leave the condo when someone opened the door to the guest bedroom. She nearly had a heart attack, realizing someone else had been in the condo all this time while Oliver and she were talking. She was certain Oliver had a girlfriend now, and that all his talk had been—well, just that. Talk.

But when she saw their next-door neighbor, hot and sexy Chadwick Stephano, wearing only a pair of black boxers on his buff body, she just stared at him, openmouthed.

He smiled a little, then frowned at Oliver. "Why don't you just tell her the truth about us?"

"It just happened," Oliver said, standing and looking sheepish. "Just today. We…we were talking about his organic garden, and…one thing led to another."

Melissa was so stunned that she just stared at Oliver. Then finding her tongue, she said, "What about you wanting me to work with you?" Talk about doing a 360-degree turnaround. She was still unable to grasp all that had just been said and, well, all of this.

"Oliver thought that might make a difference between the two of you. If you were working together and you weren't off on wilderness trips all the time." Chad walked over and squeezed Oliver's shoulder. "But he's known for a long time that this isn't working for him any longer."

She chewed on her bottom lip. "Okay." She thought of herself as truly enlightened and mostly aware of what was going on around her. She'd seen Oliver talking with Chad before and knew they'd become great friends. But she hadn't expected *this*. "All right. Well, is it still okay if I come and get my things as soon as I get a place of my own?"

She asked Chad, because he seemed to be the one in charge.

He smiled sweetly at her, as if he appreciated that she'd asked him. Or maybe he was just amused.

"Yeah, sure, I said so," Oliver said, giving Chad an annoyed look back.

"I'm all right with it," she said to Oliver. "I just wish you'd told me sooner."

"He wasn't ready to admit it…before," Chad said. He shrugged. "It just sort of happened."

"Okay, um… Well, let me get out of your hair," she said. "I'll call you before I return for my stuff." She hadn't thought she'd need to, if he hadn't been seeing anyone. She sure didn't want to walk into the place and find they were…busy.

"Yeah, sure," Oliver said.

Still reeling with the news as she left the condo and tossed her bags into the car, she tried to tell herself she understood now why Oliver had been acting so strangely. She only wished she'd known before she moved in with him. Now she had to find a place of her own on such short notice.

Before she left Oliver's driveway, she called several people who might put her up for the night—but all of them were out of country on missions. Damn it. She knew one who wasn't. Huntley. And his girlfriend was away on a mission, but she wouldn't go there. Genista would smell Melissa's scent in their apartment, and then there'd be trouble between the two of them. And she certainly didn't want that to happen.

She'd even tried to get hold of Huntley's sister, Tammy, now married to another JAG agent. But Tammy and David were training four teens in night-time operations and couldn't take any calls. She left a text message that she was looking for a place to crash for the night and decided to go to the jaguar club where she might run into some other agent who would be willing to allow her to stay the night. Otherwise, she was stuck getting a hotel, and she really didn't want to be alone tonight.

When she arrived at the club, the first vehicle that caught her eye was Huntley's. She shook her head. If nothing else, she could share a drink with him and see if he knew anyone else who was still in town that she could stay with for the night.

———※———

When Huntley arrived, the Clawed and Dangerous Kitty Cat Club was not all that busy, since it was a Monday night. As the jungle rock music played inside and the scantily dressed dancers in leopard skin danced on platforms around poles, he took a seat at one of the empty tables. He glanced around the half-filled establishment at the mix of humans and jaguar shifters there. Telling the two apart was impossible unless he got close enough and could smell the scent of jaguar on the person, or saw the individual shift.

"Hell, brother, you got back!" Everett said, heading for Huntley's table and instantly brightening his brother's mood.

Huntley rose from his chair and gave Everett a brotherly hug. "Hell, I didn't think you'd be back this soon, either. I tried calling you."

"Phone charger went out on me." Everett took a seat across from Huntley.

"How was your mission?"

"Not good. Can't give you all the details here, but suffice it to say, two of the bad guys got away. Killed one, though. How about you?" Everett asked.

"Took down five, but one got away. Police are holding the five men."

"Better result than we had. How's Melissa?"

"She's good."

"Better than working with me?" Everett teased.

Huntley smiled. He liked working with his brother. They knew each other so well that he never had to second-guess Everett. Like many twins or triplets, they had that secret communication down pat. Melissa was an unknown commodity at times. He found working with her refreshing. More…complicated.

"I have to admit she's a damn good cook."

Everett laughed. "I figured between you and Genista, you'd both starve to death. I never before knew a woman who hadn't ever used a microwave. Thought she'd burn down the house when she cooked with aluminum foil lining the glass pan, and fire and smoke started pouring out of the microwave that one time I went to your place for dinner. Your place smelled like smoke for weeks, not to mention the smoke alarm going off and nearly deafening us."

Huntley chuckled. "Yeah. I'd nearly forgotten about that. And then the baked potato burst all over the floor when she poked the fork into it to take it out of the microwave."

"Hell, yeah."

Huntley smiled at the memory. "I think that was about the last time she cooked."

Smiling, Everett nodded. "So I take it you're on break now?"

"Yeah, you?"

"Nah. Got another assignment. I'm off for the night. Tomorrow night I'm checking into a missing jaguar-shifter case. The man disappeared last year and no one could figure out what happened to him, so the case went cold. Martin wants me to look into it and see if I can get any new leads."

"Good. I don't know what he has planned for me next. But I'm not going to worry about it."

"What about joining Genista in Panama?" Everett asked.

Huntley snorted. "She called it quits with us. Walked out on me while I was gone."

Everett stared at him in disbelief.

"Yeah, believe it. I wasn't sure there was anything there for us to build on, the way she'd been acting so distant the last few weeks, so it wasn't a complete surprise. Though I thought our work might be interfering too much, and I hoped we could get on track."

"Well, crap on that. So sorry to hear it. But if it wasn't meant to be, I'm glad you got out of it this early in the game. What about Melissa?"

"Melissa? She's got a guy. Remember?"

"Ha! The life insurance salesman? Are you kidding? So how's that going for her?"

Not good, Huntley didn't think. But then what did he know? "How would I—"

"Speak of the devil." Everett grinned, stood, and waved for someone to join them.

Chapter 4

HUNTLEY TURNED TO SEE WHAT "DEVIL" HIS brother was referring to while a few more patrons walked into the club. Along with *Melissa*. No longer wearing khaki shorts and a cool shirt like she had for the jungle heat and humidity and the trip home, she was dressed to kill in a strapless dress, short on the leg, with high heels that would make great weapons and showed off her shapely tan legs, and she had a sweater slung over her arm. She glanced in Everett's direction and smiled. Then she saw Huntley, and her smile broadened.

That cheered him up a little.

"Maybe the guy she's with isn't working out for her either," Everett said to Huntley.

"Or she's meeting him here after a while." He really didn't believe it. Not the way Oliver had acted toward them when Huntley had dropped her off at their place. More likely, she was here to cool her heels after a fight with her boyfriend.

As soon as Melissa joined them, Everett got her a chair and pushed it in for her once she was seated. "Well, how's my favorite agent doing these days?"

"Get me a Singapore sling and I'll let you know."

Everett raised his brows a little, smiling. He motioned to a server, then ordered the drink for her. "I'll have a beer," Huntley said to the server.

Everett didn't order anything for himself.

"I didn't think you'd be home so early," she said to Everett before Huntley could make a comment about Everett *forgetting* to order a drink. "I thought you were still on a mission," she added.

"Nah, just got home a little while ago. Thought I'd pop in for a moment and see if anyone I knew was here, when I saw Huntley's car parked outside and wanted to ask him how the mission went. I didn't think I'd be back so soon either. Partial bust. Huntley was telling me that one of the guys you were after also got away from the two of you. Sorry to hear it," Everett said.

"Yeah, so were we," she said.

"Don't I know it. Well, I've got to go. Enjoy your drinks. Got to get packed. Leaving on another mission tomorrow," Everett said, standing.

"You just got here." Huntley had never seen his brother go to the club and not have a drink before he left.

"Yeah, but you know how it is. If I rush tomorrow, I'm more likely to forget something really important. Besides, I need to take care of some stuff. Call you before I leave. Take care. And *enjoy* your leave." Then Everett smiled and hurried off.

Huntley stared after him. His brother always did things at the last minute. He *never* packed a day ahead of time. Everett swore he forgot more things when he started early than when he packed right before rushing to the airport.

The server brought their drinks, and Huntley paid for them.

"Now I know why he was in such a rush to get out of

here," Melissa said, laughing. "He orders the drinks, and you pay for them."

Huntley smiled, suspecting Everett had other reasons for leaving the two of them alone. "I'm kind of surprised to see you here. Is Oliver joining you later?" He sure as hell hoped not. He could really use this. Some nice downtime with a fun partner.

"No." She let her breath out on a heavy sigh. "We called it quits tonight."

That sort of shocked him. And pleased him. He felt relief—for her, because from what she'd told him, Huntley didn't feel the guy was perfect mate material for her. He'd figured they'd break up eventually, but not this quickly.

He bet it had something to do with Oliver's downright ugly attitude when she arrived home. He just couldn't imagine acting that way with a woman like Melissa.

"What happened?" He tried not to sound growly when he was ready to pummel the guy if he'd been violent with her. Though he reminded himself that Melissa could take care of herself and would most likely have knocked the guy out cold if he'd threatened her physically.

Lifting the cherry by the stem from her Singapore sling, Melissa slipped the red fruit between her teeth, still holding onto the stem with her fingers, and gave a little tug.

He swore he'd never seen anyone eat a piece of fruit like that. She made it look so…erotic. She finished the cherry and licked her lips, which had him staring at that sweet, kissable mouth of hers and wishing he'd been the one she'd come home to. They wouldn't be here. That was for certain.

She gave a little one-shoulder shrug. "His next-door neighbor walked down the hall wearing only a pair of boxers and wanted Oliver to tell me the truth about their relationship."

Huntley frowned a little. "You have two neighbors, the little old lady on the left of his place and the"—his eyes widened—"the chef at the Italian restaurant downtown who grows his own organic vegetables?"

"Uh, yeah."

Huntley's smile broadened. "Want to dance?"

Melissa looked a little startled that he'd ask. "I…don't think so. I wouldn't want Genista to get the wrong idea."

Hell, he was so glad Melissa and Oliver were no longer together that he'd forgotten to mention his girlfriend calling it quits with him. "It's over between us. She moved out while I was in Costa Rica. I didn't even know until I called and she gave me the news from Panama."

First, Melissa looked surprised. "You're kidding." Then she shared that sunshiny smile with him that he loved so much: part minx, part sexy woman, and a whole lot fun. "What are we waiting for? Let's dance."

She took his hand and pulled him toward the dance floor, and before he knew it, he was holding her close. He thought it was important to keep some distance at first, since they'd just lost their "roommates," but then he didn't want to. He wanted this. And she seemed to need it too, as she swayed in his arms to the music. It didn't matter that the music was rock and better suited to dancing apart. Being close was the only way he wanted to be. And she seemed to want that too.

"I thought he believed you were actually *sleeping* with me, and that's why he was so annoyed-looking when I dropped you off at your place," Huntley said, thinking of her naked and setting up the tent in the rain-forest, and then putting on her tank top inside the tent. Just imagining her like that—and how she studied him when he was checking out the poachers' IDs naked, and her moving against him now to the steady jungle-rock beat—was turning him on.

"I told him we were. You know. In a tent. Not in the same sleeping bag. Can you imagine how hot and sweaty we would have been in that case? We would need to find a colder location to do that kind of work."

He was ready. To do a mission in a colder climate. But he thought that it wouldn't matter. That if they'd had the time and the inclination—and he was certain he'd have had that—they would have made love in the tropics and been two satisfied cats.

"But then I learned what was really bothering him, which had nothing to do with me or you or anyone else," Melissa said. "If he's happy with Chad, I'm happy for him, though I still was shocked to see Chad there."

He should give her a chance to get over the ex, Huntley told himself, but then he pulled her closer. "So, you've got some time off and I've got some time off. Do you want to do something together?"

"What do you have in mind?" She had settled her body right against his as if she felt comfortable there, like they'd always been this close, her arms encircling his neck, her green eyes bright with interest, her scent a combination of aroused she-cat, peaches and cream, and…intrigued.

The way she was rubbing up against him was making it difficult to think with his thoughtful head and not the other.

"A movie? Dinner out? Something completely out of the ordinary for us. No climbing trees, forging crocodile- or shark-infested waters, no dodging venomous snakes. Just something nice and relaxing and fun." Or something a little hotter. Though he didn't want to pressure her into taking this too far, too fast and then have the whole thing blow up in their faces. He did enjoy working with her, and he didn't want to ruin a good thing.

With Genista, it was different. She was totally businesslike on missions, and he realized now that sex had been that way too. Just a way to satisfy an urge. But with Melissa, he felt…different. Maybe it was the way she was so playful with him and…well, interested. But he didn't want to hurt their work relationship.

"Hmm. Sounds a little quiet, but quiet can be a nice change of pace," she said, her hands sliding down his shoulders.

"We can watch a wild action thriller."

She chuckled.

"Is Oliver moving out of the condo, or are you?" Huntley asked, already taking this in a direction he shouldn't be thinking of. Her place or his, her choice.

She sighed. "Considering he paid for it, I'm moving."

"Got a place to stay?" Huntley asked, his hopes instantly shooting to the moon that she might stay with him for a few days until she could find a place. And he could get to know her better in a strictly friends-with-*no*-benefits way. Though he wanted the benefits, even as he told himself to slow down. She was making it awfully hard to think of slowing down though, given the way her body was stroking his big-cat urges.

"I figured someone might put me up. I was going to ask my cousin, but he's out of the country for another couple of weeks. And my sister lives too far away."

Trying not to sound like a much-too-eager cat and knowing he shouldn't be glad that she had no one else to stay with, he said, "If you want to stay at my place, you can crash there for as long as you need."

"Hmm, I wouldn't want to impose."

He quickly said, "No imposition at all. Now that Genista is gone, it feels kind of empty. I only need to mention one thing before you make a decision." A really *big* thing to mention, and it might ruin the whole *she-cat staying with him* scenario.

She arched a brow.

"It's a studio apartment." He was still hoping she'd say yes. On the other hand, he understood if she didn't, and it was really better if she *didn't*. For the both of them.

"As in…?"

"The sofa makes into a bed. No bedroom. One bath." *Simple, honest, direct.* He almost wished he had a bedroom now, so he could have offered, at the very least, to let her sleep in his bed while he took the couch. Then again, he could say that she could use the bed and he'd sleep on the floor as a jaguar, but he really didn't want to. Not when he could be sleeping with her on the sofa bed.

Feeling as though he had to explain his reasoning for why he had such limited accommodations, he said, "I have it because I'm gone so much. I didn't have any need to get a bigger place."

She pondered that for a few minutes. He realized how much he wanted her to stay, yet he understood how she might want to keep more distance. And sleeping in a bed together wouldn't allow them the distance they probably needed.

"We…would be sleeping in the same…bed," she finally said.

"With the air conditioner on," he quickly said.

She smiled.

"You can crash there. You can come and go as you please."

She wasn't saying yes or no. The anticipation was killing him.

She finally sighed against his chest and he thought it could be a yes. Or…maybe not.

She nodded. "Okay, as long as you don't mind. I'll stay a couple of days until I find a place of my own."

Hot damn, *yeah*! Hell, he hadn't been this excited when Genista moved in with him. That had to tell him something, didn't it?

Trying to sound perfectly businesslike and not like he wanted to pump his fist in victory, he said, "You're welcome to stay as long as you need. I'll enjoy the company until the next assignment." And he would, if he could keep his body under control. He was losing the battle at the moment.

And she could tell. Her face was turned up to his, and she smiled a little. But it wasn't a sweet, innocent smile. Rather one that said she just might like some kitty-cat loving. Not that he thought they should go there…but if they did, he wouldn't object too strenuously.

"Have you eaten anything? I was too upset to eat anything earlier, but now I'm getting hungry," she said, not making a move to pry herself loose from him and leave.

He wanted to continue dancing with her. Then again, the way she was getting him worked up, he wanted to take her home to bed.

"Are you cooking?" he asked. What he wouldn't give for another one of her home-cooked meals. "All I had was some popcorn." He hadn't thought beyond having a couple of drinks at the club.

She laughed.

He didn't want her to believe that all he cared about was her cooking for him. "Or we can eat out. Your choice."

"How about baked chicken and a homemade German potato salad, the recipe handed down by my family? I've been dying to have some ever since we got home. But it's no fun making it just for myself."

"Sounds great to me. I can be a good kitchen assistant. We'll make a trip to the grocery store first. Want to dance some more?"

She sighed. "No, really, I'm just starving."

"All right. Let's go." In truth, Huntley hoped they could come back here and dance some more. Genista was a good dancer, but she liked to dance the faster dances, not holding him close like Melissa seemed to enjoy. Genista always said the slow dances made her too hot. But now he was thinking she didn't want the intimacy. Maybe tomorrow night he and Melissa could come back.

He liked getting close to her and smelling her sweet, intoxicating she-cat scent. He kept telling himself that he was just offering her a place to stay for now and that he shouldn't see this as anything more. But he realized just how much he'd missed having any real intimacy with a she-cat, and he needed some loving. Then again, Melissa needed his friendship. And he sure as hell didn't want to mess up a good thing with a fellow agent that he enjoyed working with on missions.

After shopping, they returned to his house, and while he threw his washed clothes in the dryer, she started to fix the meal. "Hey, do you mind if I do a load of wash? I was going to do it right when I got home, but then the argument with Oliver happened, and well, I still need to wash the jungle out of my clothes," she called out.

"Sure thing." Huntley was starting the dryer when his phone rang. Fishing it out of his pocket, he saw it was his brother. Everett *couldn't* be checking up on him. Huntley started another load of wash.

"Are you still at the club? Is she still with Oliver? How did it go?" Everett asked.

Huntley nearly laughed at his brother. He was worse than their sister. If Tammy knew Huntley was staying with Melissa, she'd tell their parents. Not that anything would come of this, just like nothing had come of his relationship with Genista. "Melissa is staying with me until she can find a place of her own."

"Hot damn, Brother."

He smiled, then remembered he was supposed to be helping her with the cooking and headed to the kitchen. "It's just a case of an agent helping out his fellow comrade," Huntley said as he rejoined Melissa, though given the sleeping arrangements, he wasn't quite certain what might happen tonight if the two of them wanted something more than just sleep. He knew his brother wouldn't tell a soul that Melissa was staying with him.

"Right, and did that include dancing tonight?" Everett asked.

"A little."

"Is that Everett?" Melissa asked, carrying a bowl of potato salad to the table.

"Yeah." Huntley chastised himself for not helping her more.

"Ask him if he wants me to house-sit his place while he's on his next mission."

Everett laughed. "I heard her. Tell her only if I'm at home. Well, got to get back to packing."

"Be careful when you begin work on this mission, Everett. I know it's a cold case, but you never know when one like that will become dangerous."

"Gotcha. And you be careful too. Sometimes being on leave can be just as treacherous or more so."

Smiling, Huntley said he'd talk later and ended the call.

"So Everett won't tell the whole world I'm staying with you for a couple of days, will he?" Melissa asked, sounding a little worried.

Huntley didn't think her concern had anything to do with who she was staying with. Just that she had broken up so recently. Well, and him too.

"No. He won't even tell my dad. Who would then tell my mother, and she would begin to make wedding plans, with or without you." He set the table.

"I like your mom. She's the life of the party. Not sure about your dad. I heard he investigated both your sister's boyfriend and his brother before he gave the Pattersons his approval."

Huntley hadn't wanted to bring that up. But yeah, his dad would be doing an extensive background check on Melissa if she moved in with him. Like he'd done with Genista. His dad had told Huntley he approved of her. Not that Huntley needed his dad's approval of the girls he dated.

His dad always said he had never done anything but investments. But Huntley and Everett suspected he had been into covert operations—not jaguar shifter, but human ones. He knew too many people who could do investigations on people. Huntley and his brother suspected that some of their dad's jaguar friends also were covert operatives, some of whom were retired now.

Melissa and Huntley sat down to dinner and she said, "I have the perfect show for us to watch tonight if you're game." She began eating her potato salad.

"What's that?" Huntley asked, curious because Melissa was smiling so impishly.

"*Mr. and Mrs. Smith.*"

Huntley laughed. "I swear all of the women in the agency love that movie."

"It shows what good little homemakers we can be while also—"

"Leading a double life." Huntley smiled. "Right. And we do. Between our jaguar-shifter business and the jobs we do."

"Yeah, I agree."

"So, do you wish you used guns more than your jaguar teeth?"

"Nah. It's fun to see the fantasy, but when it comes to

reality, I'm all for the teeth. Don't you feel more invincible that way?" she asked.

"Certainly we can jump farther and take down prey more easily. But if they're shooting bullets, that's bad news. I love that we can discuss missions, though." Huntley finished his potato salad and served himself some more. "Damn, this is good."

"Thank you. I'm glad you're enjoying it. I would have preferred baking my own chicken, but it would have taken so long. The pre-roasted one was okay, but next time, I'm cooking it."

He was surprised when she said so, like this was moving into something more permanent. He could get into dating her for real.

"I couldn't talk to Oliver about the missions," Melissa said, buttering a roll. "Just like I wasn't interested in what he was doing, he wasn't interested in my work. Though I couldn't understand why not. Mine is fascinating."

Huntley smiled. "He might have felt a bit emasculated. You're out swimming with the bull sharks, and he's sitting in an office making phone calls. Hell, if I was doing that and my girlfriend was facing crocodiles, caiman, sharks, and gun-toting poachers, I would feel ball-less too."

She chuckled and her cheeks reddened a little. "True. I tried to talk him into going with me to the Amazon, Belize, Panama, Costa Rica, anywhere that they still have a few jaguars, just to have some fun, but he was completely against it."

"City cat through and through," Huntley said. He had friends who were city cats, and they were as important to him as any others, but he'd prefer to have a mate who'd like to do some of the same things he did, and running as a jaguar in a jungle was one of them.

"True. What about you and Genista? You must have had fun telling each other about what went down on your missions. Each of you would at least understand what the other had gone through."

"Not really. When she was through with her assignment, she was through. She didn't want to examine any aspect of it. Which I could understand. But I like discussing it and getting it out of my system. My brother and I always talked about what went down on a job and how we could do better the next time. Just part of the winding-down process for us."

"That's really nice." Melissa finished eating the food on her plate.

Done with dinner, they carried their plates into the kitchen. "Let me throw my second load of wash in the dryer, and you can do your laundry while I do the dishes. After that, we can start the movie and have some wine or beers," Huntley said.

"Wine, if you don't mind."

"Sure thing."

Before long, they were sitting on the couch, close together. They had finished their glasses of wine, and they'd both removed their shoes. Huntley's sock-covered feet were stretched out on the coffee table, while Melissa's naked feet were tucked to her side as she snuggled against Huntley.

He was watching the show, but he was thinking about holding Melissa close and how nice this was, compared to how he'd started the night when he first arrived home.

Genista gone for good. Him watching TV alone. No one to talk to, just a bag of popcorn to munch on.

When her wash cycle ended, he put away his dry clothes. She put her clothes in the dryer, threw in another load, and rejoined him on the couch.

He could really get used to this.

Melissa said, "He has family in Amarillo."

"Oliver has?" Huntley guessed.

She looked up at Huntley, a smile tugging at her lips. "Jackson, I mean. The poacher. The one who got away from us in Costa Rica."

He nearly laughed. He couldn't believe she wanted to talk more about the mission. And he was all for it. If it hadn't been for being with her, and being…distracted a bit, his thoughts would have drifted that way too. "Yeah, Martin said Jackson had a sister living in Canyon and a mother living in Amarillo."

"Okay, here's a thought I had. Tomorrow, I can spend the day looking for a furnished apartment, and if I find one and it's available right away, I'll move in. We can have dinner out and see a movie after that. *Or*," she said, "we can take a road trip, eat dinner out, and chill out that way."

"Road trip as in drive out to Amarillo?" Melissa was an agent after his own heart. He smiled at her. "You want to go after Jackson."

"Or we can just be on leave and do what normal people do."

"They take road trips." Damn, he was ready to go. Not completing a mission bothered him. If they could get some satisfaction in bringing Jackson down, he was all for it. "You want to call the boss, or do you want me to?"

Melissa smiled. "You know Martin. He's not going to like it that you haven't taken your vacation. I had one fairly recently, so I'm good."

"I'll call him and tell him we're taking a road trip—and vacationing along the way. On second thought, my stuff is clean and I need to pack. Yours is still washing. Why don't you call him, and I'll pack my things."

"Coward."

He laughed. And headed for the closet.

"We'll go first thing in the morning, right?" she asked.

No way did he want to give up sleeping with the she-cat. "Yeah. As soon as we both wake up and are ready to go. No rush. We're on vacation, you know."

"Right. I'll fix us breakfast first thing in the morning, and you can pack the car." Melissa called the boss. "Martin, Huntley and I have decided to take a road trip."

Huntley glanced in Melissa's direction. There was a lengthy pause. She smiled.

"To Amarillo," she told the boss.

Chapter 5

ONCE THE MOVIE WAS OVER, MELISSA FINISHED HER laundry while Huntley made the sofa into a bed. She had never done this before—stayed overnight with a male cat that worked with her. She was afraid that if things didn't pan out, working with him on future missions could be tense. And yes, she was thinking of more than just staying at his place for a couple of days. That's when she realized that being with Oliver had been a way to ensure she didn't have problems with her work relationships.

It had been the same way with other cats she'd dated. No involvement with her in her work, and frankly, she'd had similar problems with them. Not exactly the same—but the issue of her being gone on a lot of assignments did mess up relationships.

She also realized, as she took great care to remove her clothes from the dryer and repack them, that she was feeling both apprehensive and excited, as well as a flutter of panic to think she would be sleeping with Huntley in his bed when she was more than a little attracted to him. She hated to admit it, but she had really been envious that he went home after missions to Genista, an attractive she-cat fellow agent, while Melissa had to go home to sedate, never-do-anything-wild Oliver.

She heard Huntley cleaning the already-clean kitchen and wondered if he was feeling as anxious and unsettled as she was about sleeping together. Probably not.

She heard him use the bathroom, but she still couldn't force herself to go to the bed. She finally took a deep breath, carried her bag to the sofa bed, and set it next to the frame. Did he have a favorite side to sleep on?

Hers was the right side of the bed. Not that it would really matter. She was just a guest, and she could deal with it.

He left the bathroom and smiled a little. She swore he looked as anxious as she felt. This so felt like a first-time one-night stand, when she only meant to sleep here. At least for the night. Then they'd be back on a mission and back to business.

"I'll be right out," she said, not having to use the bathroom again. She'd already brushed her teeth, used the facilities, changed into a tank top and shorts, and was ready for bed. But...

When she came out of the bathroom, Huntley was in bed on her side. *If* it had been her bed.

"Do you want to leave a night light on in the bathroom?" he asked. "In case you get up in the middle of the night and get disoriented."

She smiled at him and turned off the light. "I'll be all right." With her cat's night vision, she would be fine. She made her way to the bed, climbed onto the mattress, and rested on her back like he was doing, except that his hands were locked behind his head as he stared up at the ceiling.

"If I try to take over too much of the bed, just poke me with your elbow," he said, glancing at her. "I'll move over."

"What if *I* try to take over too much of the bed?"

"You're welcome to try."

She swore there was an invitation in his comment. He pulled the covers over them. She felt awkward. It was crazy, really. If she'd been in bed with Oliver, they would have turned away from each other, him fuming that she'd been sleeping with male agents, and her fuming that he thought so. Then after a couple of days, Oliver would make it up to her. At least, that's how it had been after the last few missions. Now she was thinking maybe it hadn't been that at all. Had Oliver been thinking of Chad?

With Huntley, they weren't lovers. This was just a great opportunity for her to have a place to stay until she could get one of her own. She'd been strictly a partner with him on missions, and yet this felt different.

Maybe because they were both free this time. Or because they'd been fighting the attraction since their first mission together. Or it was the dancing, the Singapore sling she'd had, and then the wine they'd drunk. But it didn't feel right to be with him in bed and do nothing more.

"Okay," she said.

He looked over at her. "Hmm?"

Maybe he didn't want anything more to happen between them. Maybe she was just imagining that he might want to, well, kiss her. Maybe he would be shocked at her admission that she wanted to kiss him.

"We…might as well get it over with. Don't you think?" she asked.

He smiled. "If you're…asking what I think you're asking…"

"I…find you…attractive," she said quickly.

"The feeling's mutual."

"I don't want you to think anything more will come of this. We have to work together on missions. I don't want to ruin that for us. I like working with you. You're fun to be with. And I don't want the whole agency to know about this."

"I'll be perfectly discreet."

Then she worried. What if he thought she meant she wanted to have sex with him? She felt her face flush with heat. "We'd better get our sleep."

"Are you sure?"

"Yeah." She didn't know why she was having such a time with this. Maybe because she was so afraid of what others in the branch might think about them. Out with the old, in with the new. And she really wasn't this... impulsive. If anyone else had offered to let her stay for a few nights—like his sister or someone not as hot, someone she didn't like and admire so much and who didn't seem to feel the same way about her but was also available—she wouldn't have had any problem with it.

"Melissa?"

"Hmm?"

"What are you thinking?"

Way too much. "That I should be sleeping. That...we should be sleeping."

She looked over at him. He was smiling. "But?" he asked. His gaze drifted to her mouth.

"We shouldn't," she said.

"We shouldn't," he agreed, yet his eyes stole to her lips again.

"We don't really want this," she said, as if reassuring herself that was the right thing to say and the right way to feel.

"We don't." Only he said it as more of a question. And then he unlocked his arms from behind his head, and she knew she was in trouble. She should have turned away from him and pretended to sleep.

He turned to face her and ran his hand over her hair. She was too far away. Unless he moved closer, or she did... And she knew she shouldn't move any closer.

Melissa was cute. Huntley wasn't really sure what she was thinking. How could he be? He was a guy and what he was thinking was how much he'd like to make love to her. Not just because she was convenient. But because he'd thought about it on and off since he'd first seen her and then worked with her. He didn't think she really was ready to go to sleep. Not the way she was mulling over the situation between them.

He could understand her reluctance to get involved with him—especially so soon after both their breakups. Yet he felt they were so much more compatible than they'd been with their recent others. Melissa needed someone who could enjoy the wilderness with her like Huntley did and who understood what she went through on missions. He needed someone he could decompress with, who didn't shut him out when he wanted to talk about the last mission he'd been on, and who enjoyed working with him on missions.

"You want to talk?" He didn't want the same thing he had with Genista, her not talking and keeping her feelings to herself. On the other hand, he could understand Melissa feeling a little reluctant to be that open with him right at the first.

"What are...you thinking? About this?" she asked, motioning to them and the bed. "About, well..."

"Us?"

"It's probably too soon, isn't it?"

He smiled again. "If you don't think I want this…"

"Just because we want it doesn't mean it would be good for us."

Okay, immediately he was thinking sex again. When he shouldn't be. She might not be thinking that way at all. "Are you trying to talk me or yourself out of it?"

She didn't say anything for a bit, but just appeared to be pondering the notion. Then she looked up at him and said, "Both."

He chuckled. "Come here."

She hesitated.

"We don't have to do anything. Just…sleep."

She let out her breath on a heavy sigh. "You don't want to just sleep." Then she moved in next to him, and he wrapped his arms around her. "Do you?"

"Hell no." He leaned down for a kiss. All he should want was a soft, sweet kiss meant for first dates, but the wine on her lips teased him into wanting more.

He didn't want her to feel as though he was coming on too strong or being too indecisive. When the hell had he ever given this much thought to kissing a woman? When he was worried about how she'd feel.

He kissed her again, a little bolder this time, his hand on her shoulder, everything else forgotten but the way her soft lips met his, brushed his, and sweetly kissed him back. But they were pressuring a bit more, following his when he pulled slightly back. He went for it again. A little more force, a tad hotter, and then she did what she should never have done if she hadn't wanted more. She darted her tongue out and licked his mouth. A teasing, playful gesture that made his blood roar with need. Already his erection was pressing for release.

When he tried to gain entrance to her sweet mouth, she let him, moving her body against him and rubbing his arousal, flaming his blood.

His tongue penetrated her mouth, swept in and conquered, his body sliding on top of hers, though he was barely conscious of having taken over so quickly.

Her hands stroked his hair, her fingernails grazing his scalp in a sexy, intriguing way, and he was suddenly between her legs, pressing his cock against her mound, rubbing and ready to come in his boxers.

Their tongues tangled as she shifted her hands to his buttocks and stroked him through the cotton. And then, coming to his senses, though he sure as hell didn't want to, he kissed her lightly against the mouth, ending the kiss but dying to fulfill his raging needs.

He moved off her, saw the way she was smiling at him wickedly, and wasn't quite sure how to take it. Which is why he couldn't do this. He thought she might not be ready to jump into a new relationship. Hell, he wasn't sure he could do it—and he blamed it all on how much he enjoyed working with her and didn't want to ruin a good thing.

"Thanks," she said and kissed his cheek. "I... needed that."

"I needed more," he said quite honestly.

She grinned at him. And he was glad he could tell her that he wasn't turning away from her because he really wanted to.

"But I think that's all I can handle...for now." Then he smiled back.

And she sighed. "Totally works for me."

Then, to his surprise, she snuggled against him. "If I make you too hot, just push me away."

"Not on your life," he said, wrapping his arms around her. "I'm prepared to suffer."

She chuckled and he smiled. He wouldn't be able to make the same concession the next time they were in bed together like this.

<hr />

The next day, after driving three hundred and fifty miles, Melissa and Huntley arrived in Amarillo. Well, the outskirts. They hadn't left the suburbs of Dallas as early as they had planned. They were making this a vacation of sorts.

"So Martin approved the job and is paying expenses?" Huntley asked Melissa as they looked for the perfect hotel that would be their home base.

"Yep. Said if we couldn't just have fun on our leave and had to look for this Jackson character, he'd take us off leave. But he added to have fun while we're at it."

"He's a great boss," Huntley said, carrying his bags into the hotel. Then he checked his weapon. Loaded and ready, just in case.

"Yeah, he is. When I started working for him four years ago, I didn't quite get his humor. I would have thought he was joking about this. But not him."

"No, not him."

"So none of our men have tracked Jackson down, Martin said." Melissa checked her own weapon. "Because of the trouble he was in, he might have had a time getting out of Costa Rica."

Huntley shook his head. "The bad guys can slip across borders without any trouble. It's the good guys who have more trouble. He knows his way around. Are you ready to take a drive out to the parents' place?"

"Who's going to call them? You? What's the cover story?"

"I'll be his military buddy. More of a likelihood."

As soon as they found the one-story yellow, boxy house, Huntley parked. Vehicles were sitting along the curb, dogs roamed the street, and no one was out and about. School-age kids were in school, so it was quiet.

Huntley called Jackson's parents' number and got the poacher's mother.

"Hello, Mrs. Jackson? I was in the 1st Cavalry Division with Tim Jackson, and he said to look him up, if he happened to be staying with you. I was just passing through Amarillo on my way to see my folks in Florida. I wondered if he was in and maybe we could get together, if he has time."

"He's not here right now," the older woman said.

Huntley couldn't tell if she was glad or sad about it. "Oh? I could have sworn he said he'd be visiting you about this time of year. My mistake."

"Maybe he's at his sister's place. He hasn't been in touch with us for a couple of years."

He listened for signs of whether she was telling him the truth or covering for her son. No telling with family. "Okay. Well, thanks, ma'am."

"You're welcome. And if you see him, well, tell him…"

Huntley waited, hating this part of the business. It

was too easy to see the black and white of a situation. But no matter how low a person went, usually someone still cared about the lowlife and would be devastated to lose him. It did sound like Jackson's mother hadn't seen him in a while, though.

"Forget it," she finally said. "Take care, young man. We appreciate you men who serve in the military."

"Yes, ma'am. Good-bye."

He turned to see Melissa studying him. "He hasn't returned to see his mother in a couple of years. But she said he might have dropped by his sister's place. I think she's telling the truth about not being in touch with him."

"Sounds like they've all had a falling-out. Okay, we've still got the sister in Canyon. You're doing well with the old army-buddy ploy. Might as well use it on the sister, don't you think?"

"I agree."

Still, they stayed near the parents' house for a few more minutes to ensure that Jackson didn't suddenly leave the place. When they didn't see any action at the house, they drove to Canyon, fourteen miles south of Amarillo.

"You said you went to West Texas A&M. Did you ever run as a jaguar out here? There are only scrub trees, no real place to hide."

"Lots of wilderness out there," she said. "Red canyons, lots of live oak, cedar, pinyon pine, and rocks. I saw a puma once, a couple of coyotes, jack-rabbits, roadrunners. A wolf, even. Though I thought that was odd since supposedly the last wolves in the area were caught or killed in 1970. That was it. No people. Though I must admit, I didn't run as a jaguar much out there. Only at night. Just when I had to let off steam."

"You?"

She smiled. "You don't want to see me when I'm crotchety."

He laughed. "I've seen you when you're aggravated. Doesn't bother me."

"Yeah, but not with you. Then you might feel differently."

He chuckled. Somehow he didn't think so. It was Genista's silence when she was annoyed that had bothered him. He'd rather know when someone was irritated with him and not have to guess about it.

When they reached the development where Jackson's sister, Eloise Struthers, lived, they parked a few houses down from her house. Martin had called them with a few details on the way there—the sister was currently living with some guy, divorced twice, no children. Currently unemployed. The guy she was living with was a security officer at the university and most likely would be working. Huntley made the call to Eloise.

"Hello, Ms. Struthers? I'm an army buddy of Tim Jackson, and I talked to his mom about getting together with him. She said he wasn't there, but that he might be visiting you. I was just passing through the area and thought I could drop by and say hi."

"He's not here," Eloise said abruptly. "We haven't seen him in a couple of years."

Huntley immediately concluded that either she was angry with her brother for not getting in touch with the family, or she wanted to protect his butt because he'd been there recently or was still there.

"So you wouldn't know how I could get in touch with him."

"When my parents moved back to the States, Tim hated it. He joined the service, and we heard he went back to South America when he got out. We don't know what he does down there, and we don't care."

Which sounded to Huntley like the family knew what was going on or strongly suspected Tim was into illegal stuff.

"I'm sorry if you're an old army buddy of his and wanted to see him, but we can't help you." Eloise hung up on him.

"She says he's not there."

"How much do you want to bet she knows more about him than she's willing to admit?" Melissa asked as they waited and watched the house.

"Yeah, my thoughts exactly." He studied the house, hating this part of the job.

After twenty minutes, they were ready to move on.

"I knew it was a long shot," Melissa said, "but worth checking out. Martin said they checked here for Jackson, but that was three months ago. Martin still believes he's in South America."

"Never hurts to be thorough." Huntley started the car and was about to leave when the front door was opened by a redheaded woman who matched the photo they had of Jackson's sister. She stalked out to her car, dropped her keys on the driveway, and hurried to retrieve them. Then she climbed into her car, backed down the driveway, and sped off.

"Maybe she has a hair appointment or she's just going shopping or something. Although she looked a little rattled, didn't she?" Melissa asked.

"Yeah, I was thinking the same thing." More than a little rattled. She'd fumbled with her car door even after she retrieved her keys, and she'd nearly dropped her purse as it slid off her shoulder. The purse almost hit the pavement before she caught it.

They followed her to a trailer park a mile away and waited down the road as she drove into a gravel drive in front of a beige mobile home with stairs leading to a tiny wooden deck. She climbed the wooden steps in a hurry while Melissa and Huntley rolled down their windows and listened.

Melissa was already on the phone with Martin. "Did Jackson have any other connections in Canyon?"

"Not that we are aware of."

She gave Martin the address of the mobile home in case he could ID the person who owned the place and maybe tie him in with Jackson. Maybe Jackson was even there.

Eloise knocked on the door, then wrung her hands. She glanced nervously around, but she wasn't wary enough. She didn't pay any attention to Huntley's black car, the tinted windows making it hard for her to see them at the distance they were parked from the mobile home. Though Huntley was good at tracking and keeping his distance.

Then someone opened the door and spoke to her, and she shook her head.

The woman threw her hands up in a gesture that appeared to say she didn't know.

"I just realized you didn't give your 'army' name to her," Melissa said.

"She didn't ask. Best-case scenario."

Martin called Melissa back, and put the call on speakerphone.

"Phil Gorsman owns the place. He has a rap sheet two miles long. Mostly petty stuff. Lots of theft. Drug possession. Illegal gun possession. What's going on?"

"As soon as we called Jackson's sister, she denied he'd been here for the last couple of years, same with the parents, but then she took off and arrived at this house. She's having an angry conversation with someone inside, though she's still standing on the front stoop. We're not close enough to hear what's being said," Melissa said.

"I've got men on it, searching to see when this bozo was last out of the country. Wait. Looks like he was in Venezuela just last month."

They watched a man's hand stretch out, grab the woman's arm, and drag her into the house.

"Rescue mission," Huntley said, whether it was or not. He wasn't taking any chances. Jackson's sister might be up to her eyeballs in criminal stuff herself and just hadn't gotten caught yet. But Huntley didn't want Phil Gorsman to take matters into his own hands.

Chapter 6

HUNTLEY WAS OUT OF THE VEHICLE IN A FLASH WITH Melissa right behind him after telling their boss what they were doing. She had turned the phone off speaker, and Huntley could just imagine their boss having a conniption. Not that they weren't trained for this kind of action. But Martin still worried about his agents like a she-cat mother.

"Yes, we're armed," Melissa whispered to her boss as they reached the trailer.

Huntley motioned for her to go around back, while he went to the front door and rushed up the steps. Only one way to do this. Knock on the door, pray Phil didn't shoot at it, and then if he didn't open the door, break it in.

Okay, so this wasn't exactly what Melissa had in mind on this mission. Tracking Jackson down, yes. But taking down bad guys here? She really figured they'd be back to rainforest duty before they knew it.

As soon as she heard Huntley knock on the front door, nice and loud and manly, she heard the back window slide up.

She took a deep breath and let it out. The game was definitely in her court.

Two gunshots rang out. Damn it!

Then a scrawny man tried to scramble out through the

window, but Melissa was on him. Despite being in her human form, she still had a cat's agility and pounced on the bastard as soon as he landed on his feet.

"Back here!" she shouted to Huntley, not wanting to shoot the man, but having difficulty throwing him to the grassy ground the way he was fighting her.

Phil was wiry and seemed to be high on something. Melissa was struggling with him so hard that she didn't see Huntley jump out the window. He slammed a boot into Phil's leg in an attempt to break it, but she didn't hear a crack. Still, Phil cried out, dropped his weapon, and fell to the ground. She kicked his gun away from him while Huntley handcuffed the creep.

"The woman?" Melissa asked Huntley.

"She'll need a doctor."

Melissa was on it, running into the house and calling her boss, who called 9-1-1. Martin would handle the situation by using the cover story that his Golden Claws were an undercover DEA unit that had heard a gunshot fired and had to go into rescue mode. It had always worked before. They would flash their badges, help the real police where they could, and then disappear before the real agents showed up. Even if they didn't manage to slip away in time, they were with the special unit, which said it all.

Inside, the place smelled like beer. Empty cans were sitting all over a coffee table that had one leg broken and propped up on telephone books.

Melissa had to wade through fast-food trash scattered on the floor to get to the woman who lay on her back, clutching her chest with blood all over her T-shirt. Her face was ashen, and her green eyes stared up at Melissa in a kind of a haze.

Melissa grabbed the quickest thing she could find—a filthy pillow off the couch—and held it against the woman's chest. "The ambulance is on its way. You'll be okay. Just hang in there. Did Phil work with your brother?" As much as she hated to interrogate the woman now, she had to or lose any opportunity to catch him.

"What's he done now?" Eloise asked, barely able to get the words out.

So the sister, at least, was well aware that Jackson had been in trouble before.

Sirens wailed in the distance.

"He's got himself into real trouble in South America. Has he got in touch with you?" Melissa asked.

"Get off me, man!" Phil said beyond the trailer.

"Talk, damn it," Huntley said. "When was the last time you spoke with Tim Jackson?"

Jackson's sister coughed up blood. "Ever since we were little, he was in trouble." And then she took a last breath and her heart stopped beating.

The EMTs rushed through the door, and Melissa quickly relinquished her job to them, managed to secure the woman's cell phone, and headed outside. She showed her ID to the police who were just pulling up, verifying that she was one of the agents that Martin had vouched for before she joined Huntley. Another couple of police officers were taking Phil into custody for attempted murder. If the EMTs couldn't revive Jackson's sister, Phil would be charged with murder.

"Are you okay?" Huntley asked, seeing the blood on Melissa's shirt as he led her back to their vehicle.

"It's Eloise's, not mine. Her heart quit beating, and I didn't have time to revive her before the EMTs arrived."

She hated this part of the job—when someone innocent, who was most likely trying to protect her brother, got in the way.

"Did you get anything out of Phil? He'll be going away for a while. Either Eloise didn't know anything or she didn't want to squeal on her brother. She asked what he had done this time."

"According to Phil, Jackson's still in Costa Rica. He was looking to put a team together and wanted Phil on the job. He was supposed to be leaving on a flight tomorrow."

"Great."

"Yep. And you won't believe it, but Jackson is doing business in Costa Rica again. Not even going to another area to conduct his operations. He must have the right setup where he is now."

"He's not going to the same park, is he?" Melissa asked.

"Yeah, he is."

"Why?"

"Maybe he's trying to prove he can do the job without losing his catch—and his men—this time. Maybe he's got a buyer lined up and the deal is too good to back out on now. In any event, I called Martin and he's got us on a flight back down there later tonight out of Amarillo. He'll have our car picked up and left off at the Dallas airport when we need it for the return trip home. Like us, he never thought the man would be fool enough to try the same thing twice or Martin would have just left us down there."

"Maybe that's what Jackson thinks too. That no one would suspect he'd return that soon. Are you ready to go back to the rainforest and end this?" She smiled up at Huntley.

He wrapped his arm around her shoulders and walked her to the car. "Hell, yeah. Best place in the world for a couple of jaguars to take a vacation. Don't you think?" He handed her a cell phone. "Phil's. See if you can get anything on it."

She waved Eloise's phone at him. "Working on hers first."

She got into the car and Huntley drove them back to the hotel in Amarillo so they could pick up their bags, check out, and get on a flight.

"Why did Phil shoot Eloise?" Melissa asked.

"Maybe he suspected she might have led the police to his doorstep?"

"Maybe. He shot her after you knocked on the door. You could have been anyone, but he was high on something and probably figured you were the police. But he was thinking coherently enough if he thought to eliminate someone the police could interrogate."

"Because she knew something about the crimes her brother is involved in? I bet you anything that she's not squeaky clean, even if she doesn't have an arrest record," Huntley said. He turned the vehicle around and headed back to Canyon.

"Where are you going?"

"We've got some time before our late flight. We'll drop by her place and check it out. See if we find any clues about her brother's illegal operations there."

"What if their mom and dad are also involved?"

"Could be," Huntley said. "Either just covering for him, or involved in the operation themselves. I remember a case where a mother of three older teens who was on welfare had no trouble with the law—until police discovered that her sons were selling drugs and Mom was depositing the drug money in her bank account. She had a couple of million dollars. She was the sweetest woman. No one suspected a thing. Though a couple of million red flags should have caught someone's attention."

"Could be." Melissa called Martin and gave him a heads-up about their next move, figuring the police would be investigating Eloise's place next.

They arrived at her house a few minutes later, but the police weren't there yet.

"Do we go in or wait for the police and then show them our badges?" she asked.

"Here's a car coming now."

They left the car and showed their badges. After half an hour, Melissa and Huntley finished their investigation and left.

"Did you find anything?" Huntley asked on the way to Amarillo.

"Hair dye. Black. Eloise is a natural redhead. The description of her boyfriend states he's a redhead also. I'm betting Jackson used the hair dye. He's a blond, but his scent was all over the bathroom and on the used-up vials dumped in the trash. Bloodied cotton balls smelling of hydrogen peroxide were also in the trash. Bandage wrappers. A few blond chin whiskers in the sink. But best of all? Jackson's scent on the beard shavings. Wonder when or how he got injured. But it shows she was lying about when she saw him last. What did you find?"

"Men's clothing in a spare bedroom, smelling of

Jackson. Couple of Glocks and one tranquilizer gun. Police confiscated them."

"Hmm. Do you think he managed to come here while we were still looking for him in the rainforest?"

"Looks recent, so I'd say that was a good probability."

"Then he got in touch with Phil, and they were going back out on the job. When you called his parents, they probably called his sister's place to either warn him or learn if he was there. He was and took off."

Huntley let out his breath. "Yeah, sounds like it."

Melissa updated Martin on what they'd found at the sister's place. "He might be flying out today."

"I'll have a team look into it," Martin said, sounding exasperated.

"Hey, boss, if he's planning on flying the coop again, he might not get word that Phil shot his sister. Maybe we can get the hospital and the police to give out the story that she's in critical condition, if the EMTs were able to revive her. Maybe Jackson would come back to see her."

"Or to kill Phil for it. All right. I'll make some calls."

"Okay. I was checking through her phone's text messages and emails. She was supposed to get in touch with a guy named Monty. But there's no last name, no number for him. Jackson told her he had a job for Monty in CR."

"Costa Rica."

"Huntley got Phil's phone. Let me check that really quick." She looked through the texts. "Yeah, Jackson said he'd see him. Nothing about locations or anything, but we kind of figured that would be too easy."

Chapter 7

"So what made you go into the JAG?" Huntley asked Melissa as he drove her back to Amarillo. It wasn't just small talk. He'd heard she and her sister had joined the organization because of some past history with the JAG, but he didn't know what that entailed. He didn't think it was because she'd been getting into trouble when she was a teen. But he was curious.

"Martin. When we were thirteen, he rescued my sister and me from a hostage situation."

Now *that* Huntley hadn't expected to hear. He wished he'd been there to help the girls. He would have been sixteen and ready to tackle as many of the men as there'd been, all on his own.

"They picked the wrong house to burglarize," Melissa continued. "Dad and Mom were at work, and Bonnie and I were in the kitchen doing homework—we were homeschooled. We were working on creative writing. After that, we both rewrote our stories."

He smiled at that. "About the break-in…"

"Yeah. Anyway, the three men thought everyone was gone. When they saw both my mom's and dad's cars had left, they broke the back door. They didn't even bother to knock to see if anyone would answer. I grabbed the phone off the dining-room table and called my dad, but we didn't wait around. My sister and I ran for the front door, but one of their men was standing on the front porch. He caught us as we threw the door open, probably waiting for his friends to unlock it for him. He looked as startled to see us as we were to see him. He waved a gun at us, and we were afraid they'd kill us because we saw their faces."

Huntley ground his teeth. He couldn't even imagine how frightened the girls had to have been. He would have been ready to kill if his sister, Tammy, had been home alone and three men had broken into the house.

"I'd managed to get through to my dad, but I wasn't able to speak with him yet. I just screamed at the men, 'Why are you breaking into our house? Don't shoot us! Ohmigod, there are three of you!' I hoped they didn't figure I was talking to someone on the phone. They must have thought I was hysterical. I hoped my dad wouldn't talk and give us away and that he could use another line to call for help. He did and contacted his fishing buddy, Martin. He wasn't the director of the branch yet. He was just a highly decorated field agent and had known us since we were little." She smiled. "He even read us bedtime stories a time or two."

"Martin did?" Huntley chuckled. "I can't envision it. What did he read to you?"

"He made up his own version of 'The Three Little Pigs,' only the big, bad wolf had to face three little jaguar shifter cubs who made the wolf think twice about huffing and puffing and blowing their house down. The moral of the story was that we didn't need to take any guff from any bad wolves. When the break-in occurred, I think he was glad we hadn't taken him to heart and tried to fight the men on our own. Martin immediately called for reinforcements, but he didn't even wait for them."

Huntley smiled a little at that. "He tells us never to go into a situation without someone to watch our backs."

"Yeah, that's probably why he says that. It probably got him into trouble a time or two. Anyway, he headed straight to our house to rescue us. You can't know how good it was to see his scowling face. He killed one of the men before the man even knew what hit him. Martin was getting ready to take down another when three of his fellow agents burst into the house."

"Thank God for that."

"I agree. We had thought of shifting, but our parents drummed into us that we couldn't do that ever, or we'd cause real trouble. If we had turned in front of them, they could have shot and murdered us before we had a chance to kill them. And can you imagine what a mess it would have been if we had killed them? Though Martin and the other agents did kill the men. But not as jaguars. They took care of the mess, and Martin and another man stayed with us until our parents could get home. They were both on their way as soon as they knew our house had been broken into, but they had a forty-five-minute commute. My sister and I made a pact then that when we were old enough, we would be just like Martin and make a difference for our kind."

Smiling, Huntley shook his head. "You're a lot prettier than Martin, so you could never be quite like him. And it turns out you did become the jaguar shifters in his version of the story."

She chuckled. "What about you? Have any earth-shattering reason for joining the force?"

"Nope. Our signing up was just the way it was supposed to be. My dad didn't want us to work for anyone else. Said that he wanted us to work for our own kind. So my sister ended up in one branch, and my brother and I ended up in the JAG. It's kind of like talking to a kid about when he goes to college—not if, but *when*. When we joined the Service, the only thing left up to us was which branch we would choose."

"Why did your sister, Tammy, pick the Enforcer branch?"

"She's sweeter than us?"

Melissa laughed. "Okay, so what does that say about me?"

He grinned at her. "Hell, Melissa, you're totally hot, unpredictable, and a lot of fun. Beyond a doubt, JAG material."

—◆◆◆—

It was almost midnight when Melissa and Huntley arrived at their tropical resort near the park in Costa Rica. They were glad the manager was so agreeable about them getting in so late. Martin had made sure their accommodations were a place surrounded by rainforest for privacy but with a view of a beach. And he'd paid the manager to have groceries bought so Melissa and Huntley would have a stocked fridge despite arriving so late.

Melissa definitely appreciated that. They would be spending a lot of time in the rainforest, but they would take protein bars and water and leave them with their camping gear like they had done before. Having a cooked breakfast before they left and dinner tonight would be most appreciated.

The owner of the resort, Raina, offered to provide

fruit from the resort gardens, homemade coffee, and even sugarcane juice they made. But Melissa declined, saying she and Huntley would be up and about before dawn. They'd head out before first light to begin watching for Jackson and his men right away. They had to catch the bastards before they grabbed any more exotic animals to sell.

Raina had offered for them to drop by anytime and feed their pet pacas, which looked like very large guinea pigs with stripes and spots covering their coats, square heads, small ears, and barely visible tails. Jaguars— not the shifter kind, but their cousins—found pacas a tasty meal.

Bags in hand, Melissa and Huntley climbed the wooden steps to the deck. As soon as Huntley unlocked the door, he said, "I know this is moving kind of fast, but…"

She raised a brow at him and wondered if he was thinking about what had happened between them last night. She suspected that he wasn't going to want to stop at kissing this time. "You're needy?"

He laughed. "Okay, if you want to put it that way. The cabana does have two bedrooms. But I thought we might…share the same one."

"You don't think it's too soon?"

He followed her into the last bedroom. "No."

She chuckled. His answer was so adamant that she figured if she'd said she wasn't sure, he'd try to talk her into believing she was.

"So…we're just having a little lighthearted fun, right?" Melissa asked, unpacking her bag in the room, where the double bed sported a yellow comforter with a couple of towels folded into the shape of elephants sitting on top.

She smiled at the sight.

"Yeah, I'm good for it."

Hearing the huskiness in his voice, she glanced up to look at him.

He smiled at her, his blue-green eyes swallowing her up like aquamarine pools of warm water, beckoning her to get closer.

"I know what this is about," she said, closing the drawer, straightening, and poking her finger at his chest.

He took her hand and kissed it, then wrapped his arms around her, pulled her close, and held on tight. "Oh?" He brushed a kiss lightly over her forehead and again at one temple, and then swept his warm, appealing mouth across her forehead and kissed her other temple.

"Yes," she said, running her hands up his T-shirt. "You like my cooking."

He laughed. "And your sense of humor. I mean, yeah, I love your cooking, but there's a hell of a lot more to you than that."

"Good to know."

And then he leaned down and kissed her. It was different this time—not so needy, but more of a willingness to get to know her, inside and out.

"You keep kissing me like that, and I'm going to think you want something more than just friendship."

He smiled and kissed her again.

What the hell. Life was all about risk, wasn't it? Anytime they went on a mission, they might not come back. She realized now why she'd taken up with Oliver. He was safe, and she didn't have to worry about him being hurt. Not in his line of work. But what if she really got interested in a JAG agent? The dynamics would change between them, wouldn't they?

She sighed, put on the brakes on this time, and said, "Let's get ready for bed." She meant to sleep. The way he gazed at her just a little longer, using his cat senses to analyze her, told her he hoped she meant otherwise.

"I'm going to get some water while you take a shower," she said when he didn't move to get ready for bed.

"Okay." He was in the bathroom in a flash. Only this time, he didn't shut the door.

Feeling like a schoolgirl, she stalked out of the bedroom and down the hall. Once he'd finished with his shower and climbed into bed, she showered separately and then joined him. She swore she felt like this was last night all over again. She wasn't sure why the thought of sleeping with him made her feel so…anxious. She didn't recall having any trouble like this when she started seeing Oliver as more than just a friend.

The lamp next to Huntley's side of the bed was still on. At least that seemed to be his side of the bed since he always chose to sleep there. He was in the same position as before, arms behind his head as he looked up at the ceiling, though he glanced in her direction and gave her a small smile when she climbed into bed.

"I don't want you to think I do this," she said, motioning to the bed and him, "all the time."

"You mean you don't change lovers at the drop of a hat?"

She chuckled. He was so cute that she couldn't help it. With that sexy body of his and liking him just for who he was and the way he teased her so sweetly, she wanted this. Probably before he was ready for her. She had to admit she was impulsive sometimes if it meant she didn't have to overthink something. She moved over, sliding her leg over his, and said, "Yeah, like that."

Then they were kissing again, only this time his hands cupped her head as she pressed her mouth against his, her pelvis rubbing against his growing erection. She realized another difference between Huntley and Oliver: Huntley's body seemed more attuned to hers, much quicker to respond. She'd had to really work hard to get Oliver to this point with her, so she was thrilled that her body could do that to Huntley's. Or maybe he was like that with all women—with Genista even.

She closed her eyes and took in his scent, the way his minty tongue stroked hers, and the feeling of his hands shifting down to her back. Then he slid his roughened hands beneath her tank top and up her bare skin, making her tingle with delight. He smelled like one hot, turned-on jaguar. Her pheromones were just as hot and helping to build the mutual attraction.

She slid against his boxers and enjoyed the feel of him growing harder as she moved against him.

He broke free from the kiss, his eyes heated, lust-filled. She was wondering if he meant to cool it between them again until he said in an ultra-husky voice, "This is not *just* going to be another good-night kiss, is it?"

She chuckled, then leaned down to kiss him again, not wanting to talk. She didn't want to consider that what they were doing might be a mistake. Not that this was wrong, but the circumstances weren't ideal.

And then he slid his fingers down her mini-boxers,

cupping her bare flesh in his hands, and she didn't care. For the moment, all that mattered was this.

When she rubbed seductively against his cock, he slid his hands back up to her top, snagging the bottom of it, and pulled it up and over her head and tossed it to the floor.

He feasted on her breasts for a moment before he cupped and massaged them. Then he moved her onto her back and began to kiss one of her breasts, his mouth on the tip, his tongue licking her hard nipple. Her senses were reeling, her blood in flames as he stroked her other breast with his hand, and she was already wet with wanting.

This was *so* not the way to accomplish a mission, she thought as she slid her hands down his back and began tugging off his boxers. He glanced up at her, and she wasn't sure if he was shocked, not ready for this, or what.

She was. He'd have to get used to it.

His surprised expression quickly turned into a big cat smile, right before he yanked off his boxers and then, without hesitation, removed hers.

Now he rubbed his cock against her swollen sex. The heat and friction—and his mouth doing wicked things to her nipples—triggered that cataclysmic state that she'd never managed to reach before. She felt the whole world move for her—the bed, him, her—until she cried out in surprise and exaltation.

She couldn't believe it. Okay, she was keeping him. Even if he wasn't sure of this being right for him, she would convince him it was. Because hot damn, he was right for her.

"Are you—" was all he got out before she was tugging at him to enter her so that he could feel the earth-shattering pleasure she'd experienced. She hoped that she'd come apart all over again, only this time when he was deep inside her.

Huntley wasn't asking any further. "I need to get a condom."

"I'm on birth control."

"Okay." If they regretted this later, they'd deal with it. He was too stoked not to finish now, not when Melissa was encouraging him. More than encouraging him. He swore she looked like she'd bite him if he didn't follow through.

That had him smiling, right before he leaned down to kiss her. Their tongues tangled as she ran her nails lightly down his back, and then she pressed her hands against his buttocks, pressuring him to finish this.

He slid into her tight sheath and felt the way her strong inner muscles held him firmly as he pushed deeper. She felt heavenly, wrapped around him with a warm, wet grasp. He pulled out slowly and then began to thrust as she stroked his skin, her nails doing wicked things to his back and buttocks. He loved the feel of her scratching him like a cat with claws, giving him just a taste of their wicked intent.

She was moving her hips to match his thrusts now, and he slowed down, gyrating his hips in a circular motion. She smiled before he began thrusting again, their bodies connecting, sizzling. He felt the end coming and leaned down to kiss her again as he came, wanting that connection, the complete joining, his tongue in her mouth, his cock deep inside her.

He came, exploding, felt the heady completion, and continued to thrust until he was finished—but she wasn't. He could feel and smell her tension, so with them still joined, he reached between them and began to stroke her to the end.

She quickly succumbed, her face etched with pleasure and need, her fingers clenched around his waist. "Yes!" she said, her voice a whispered exclamation.

They were two satisfied cats, he thought, as he rolled off her and then pulled her into his arms.

They said nothing, just rested together like that: her head against his chest, her hand on his shoulder, her breast pressed against his skin. He stroked her back for a long time, feeling satiated, and she appeared to be just as boneless.

She wasn't sleeping, and he worried about what was going through her mind. That she wasn't sure about this? About them?

He shouldn't ask. Best to leave the subject alone, let them get some sleep, and deal with it tomorrow. Still, he was reminded of Genista and how she never wanted to talk about anything. He'd much rather clear the air. If this was not going to work for Melissa, he'd have to live with it. As much as he loved what had just happened between them.

But then she lifted her head, pressing her chin on his chest, and looked at him with half-lidded eyes, appearing as happily tired as he felt. He continued to stroke her back, waiting for her to say what she had to say.

"Usually…I like to sleep through the night, or day, depending on the mission I'm on," she said, toying with his nipple.

Already she was making him think her "sleeping" with him wasn't going to be conducive to sleeping.

"But if you wake up and are feeling…needy…"

He smiled. "Damn, yeah."

She smiled at him then, kissed his chest, and rested her head against it again. "Good," she said, circling her finger around his nipple. "I might be too."

He hoped their mission would work out as well as their relationship was going right now. He really wished that this was just the beginning for the two of them.

And he was hoping she felt the same way.

She sighed. "I should have told Oliver that I was going to the rainforest again and wasn't able to pick up my things. And that I'd still need time to find a place of my own."

That shot down the notion she was moving in with Huntley right away. Why had he thought otherwise? Because they had something that was special, he believed. The way they worked together, the way they thought, the way they played together, and sex? Mind-blowing.

He sighed. "He wouldn't dare throw your stuff to the curb before we return," Huntley said. "Or he'd have to face me."

That had her smiling against his chest. "He wouldn't dare do it or he'd have to face *me*."

———

Somehow, Melissa and Huntley managed to get a few hours of sleep, though as hot as they had been for each other last night, he was surprised that they had awakened at the crack of dawn this morning and not slept half the day. Even so, they'd meant to leave before this.

Melissa tried to throw together a quick, hardy breakfast, but forgot to put the water in the coffeepot. She put the toast in the toaster and forgot to turn it on, while he was busy packing their gear for the rainforest. He had to smile when he joined her in the kitchen and saw her wondering why half of the breakfast wasn't ready.

She gave him a sideways glance, as if to tell him he'd better not say a word. He chuckled and turned the toaster on while she filled the coffeepot with water.

"Wait until we get into the rainforest and bed down for the day," she warned.

"What? You think I'll have forgotten something?"

She smiled at him, a devilish look that said if he had, she'd rib him for it. He loved it.

He was worried she might not be able to last long with as much as she was dragging. He wanted to offer to carry her pack, though he was carrying the tent already, but when he turned to ask her, she gave him a dagger of a look that said he'd better not ask.

He just smiled. "No extracurricular activities for you when we bed down in the tent today."

She snorted and he chuckled.

———※———

Once inside the park, Melissa and Huntley trekked for miles, not seeing much of anyone or anything, not with the way the rains were coming down in torrents in the steamy rainforest. They hadn't found any sign of Jackson. Just a few hikers, hardier than most, who endured the rains and mud to see glimpses of wildlife here and there. When Melissa and Huntley finally set up camp for the night, she felt wet and miserable. And she couldn't believe how Huntley looked like he could go on for several more hours when she was totally beat.

She should have regretted not sleeping more last night. But making love to him was what she'd needed. Not that she thought anything permanent was likely to come out of the relationship.

Just the same, she'd needed to feel sexy and wanted and loved. Huntley gave that to her and more. So when he'd wanted more, she just couldn't say no, despite knowing that she needed a good seven hours of sleep to feel normal the next day.

She was thinking of Jackson and how he had slipped away from them the first time. She hoped they'd find him soon. Then gunshots fired off in the distance.

Her heart skipped a couple of beats.

"We don't have time to take down the tent. Do we go as humans or jaguars?" Huntley quickly asked her.

She loved that about him—how he always included her in the decision making. "If they're rangers or police, I want to go as humans. Even if they're poachers, I think we'll be safer if we look like we are 'tourists.' We can always shift when we get there if we need to."

"Sounds good."

At least they were armed with tranquilizer guns this time. They headed into the rainforest with their machetes. Many locals carried them around for all kinds of uses—from cutting down vegetation to cutting a piece of tape. So it wasn't unusual to see people armed with them.

They moved deeper into the rainforest as quickly as

they could, traveling off any beaten human path. Though they were quieter than most humans tromping through the underbrush, they still made more noise than if they were in their jaguar forms. And the going was rough. They had to be careful they didn't hurry too quickly and step on a poisonous snake or twist an ankle in the dark.

Melissa's heart was beating hard as she and Huntley made their way through the rainforest, trying to reach the area where they had heard the shots fired before the men and their prey were gone, if that was the correct assumption. And at dusk? She assumed that a poaching attempt was the only thing it could be.

She thought they were close to the river, but she couldn't be certain because of how hard it was raining. Had the poachers beached a boat on the riverbank instead of planning to trek to one of the ocean beaches? Then she saw headlamps moving through the rainforest. The men were moving as fast as they could, carrying a heavy burlap sack between them.

Instantly, her heart went out for the animal. A male jaguar. But something way worse. A shifter. She smelled a light cologne and his jaguar scent. Though he appeared to still be in his jaguar form, from the looks of the shape of the body in the bag. She and Huntley had to rescue him before the men got him on a boat.

Then something else happened. She heard another report from a rifle. More men. Shooting at something else about a quarter mile away. She looked at Huntley. "I'll go after them," she mouthed.

He didn't look like he wanted her to. But there were only two men here and they were busy carrying the jaguar. If Melissa and Huntley waited until all the men gathered together and dropped their loads into a boat, he and Melissa would lose the advantage of a surprise attack. Besides, it was way too dangerous for their kind in captivity and they had to do something now.

He nodded to her, then went after the two men while she tore off in the direction where she'd heard the other shot fired.

She wanted desperately to strip and shift. She was in such a rush that she nearly stepped on a fer-de-lance, a large, poisonous viper that caused more snakebite deaths in Costa Rica than anything else. Like so many of the creatures of the rainforest, he was looking for something to eat at night. His tail began vibrating. Large, long fangs filled with highly toxic venom quickly struck at her.

She leaped out of the snake's path, managing to get around a tree. Other vipers would leave in the face of danger. Not this kind. They had an edgy disposition and would strike first. Out of his path, she raced off again, breathing hard, her heart still pounding because of concern for another animal the men were shooting at, the snake that had nearly bitten her, and the toil the hot and steamy rainforest took on a body running through it.

Not to mention that she'd stumbled so many times, she'd lost count.

She was still rushing when she came upon fifteen to twenty white-lipped peccaries foraging for roots, palm nuts, and grasses. She came to an abrupt stop. The wild pigs were the most dangerous kind and would charge any enemy in their midst. She didn't want to tangle with them. She tried to move out of their sight and circle way around them. She prayed she'd reach the man who had fired the weapon quickly and not have any more obstacles in her path. And that Huntley was all right.

Then she heard another shot fired, this one in the vicinity of where Huntley was.

For a second, her heart nearly stopped. Again, she didn't move, just listened. She was torn between returning to him and going forward. Hoping she was making the right decision, she had to go after the other poachers that she had headed for initially. She was closer to them now.

And the shot fired in Huntley's area could very well be Huntley taking one of the two men down.

The sound of the waves crashing along the beach maybe an eighth of a mile ahead of her warned her that she didn't have any more time to lose. As soon as she reached the trees at the edge of the beach, she heard the sound of a motor taking off.

No!

She bolted out of the trees and saw the boat crashing through the waves as the men made their escape with their bounty. She could have screamed she was so angry.

There had been four men, and she could identify each of them by scent now, if she could locate them again. She had to. Now her main concern was Huntley. Her heart beating triple time, she ran back toward the place she had left him, hoping to avoid any more encounters with peccaries or vipers.

She didn't find him. She knew he had to be here. Right here. She was not going to panic. He hadn't followed the men to the beach. She sniffed the ground and smelled blood. Huntley's?

Trying not to be alarmed, though she couldn't help

the dread that pooled in her belly, she attempted to locate his scent. All she could sense was the one trail, the one that they had created in getting here. She stared in the direction of the path that would lead her back to the campsite and sprinted for their tent, hoping that Huntley was all right. That the blood wasn't his.

She whipped out her cell phone and called him. His phone would be on vibrate—so she wouldn't be able to hear it ringing if he was close by, but if he was all right, he'd answer her. When the call went to voice mail, she continued to follow the path, calling him and hoping he'd answer. She heard and felt the vibration of Huntley's phone when she was nearly standing on top of it. She found it buried in leaves and searched around for any sign of Huntley, her worry level escalating.

His scent had stayed near the path so she hurried along it, praying he was all right and had returned to their camp to wait for her. Though she couldn't imagine him doing so unless he was badly injured. Otherwise, he would have come looking for her.

She kept recalling the second shot that had been fired at his location, worried he was injured terribly. Yet she hadn't found a lot of blood. And he hadn't collapsed anywhere around there. Plus, he'd had enough presence of mind to continue toward their camp.

She seemed to take forever to reach their tent, where she heard two cubs snarling and crying inside. She stared at the tent for a moment, knowing what she was hearing, but not believing it. She was so worried Huntley could be dying and…

This didn't make any sense.

She approached the tent with her tranquilizer gun

drawn. She slowly lifted the tent flap and found Huntley passed out on his sleeping bag, his forehead bleeding, and a couple of two- to three-month-old spotted cubs sitting on his stomach, blue-gray eyes staring back at her, wide-eyed and curious.

Chapter 8

HUNTLEY FELT LIKE SHIT. HIS HEAD WAS BURNING where the bullet had grazed his forehead, and his skull was pounding like someone was trying to get out. Worst of all, he had lost the men who had taken a jaguar shifter. The pain was so great that he couldn't open his eyes. He wasn't sure how he had managed to get back to the campsite.

He cracked open one eyelid, only to find two cubs on his sleeping bag that were now kneading their small fishhook claws into his belly, their nails digging straight through his T-shirt as they cried for their mother.

And hell, they were shifter cubs! He could smell a faint hint of baby powder on them. He'd tried to call Melissa on his way back to the tent, but he'd lost his phone in the rainforest and hadn't been able to find it.

He hoped like hell Melissa was all right. If he had been trying to rescue these cubs' father while the other men were after the mother, he prayed that Melissa had managed to free her.

Then he smelled Melissa and turned to see a very shocked-looking Golden Claw agent, her mouth agape as she stared at him and then at the cubs.

"They're not mine," he managed to say, and then the lights went out...*again*.

Holy hell! Melissa had never had a mission that had turned her world as upside down as this one had. She always had a plan. Maybe not a great one, but she always had some notion of what she was going to do next. *This. Was. A. Disaster!*

Not only was she feeling highly agitated and concerned about the jaguars the poachers had taken off with, but she was also worried how they'd care for a couple of baby jaguars. Their parents had to be the ones taken. She didn't think there could be many shifters in the park at one time.

And Huntley. What an all-around catastrophe, though she was thanking God that the cubs were all right and that she and Huntley had been here to take care of them in the interim. And that Huntley would be fine. She hoped.

The mother had to have smelled that jaguars had slept here, known they were shifters, and hoped they'd take care of her cubs. The problem was that the babies would be nursing, and jaguar cubs weren't fully weaned until around four to six months of age. She and Huntley had to get the babies back to their lodge. Then Melissa had to get milk for them pronto, even though mother's milk would have been much preferred. Shifter babies could handle any kind of milk, thank God. But she was certain that finding formula nearby would be a real challenge.

Melissa was so rattled that she had begun to take care of Huntley's head wound out of instinct. Having cleaned it, she administered an antibiotic and bandaged his head before she even knew it. She called her boss right after that.

"Martin, we've got a terrible problem." She explained

everything that had happened, and as worried as she was about Huntley, the cubs, and the parents, she felt chilled to the core.

What if any park rangers came across them and found them with the cubs? The rangers would take the cubs away from her and Huntley and then take them to a facility. And she and Huntley could be arrested for trying to poach the jaguar cubs. What if the mother shifted, which would cause the cubs to shift, and they were suddenly two human babies? No matter where their mother was in the world, the cubs were tied to her shifting, a way for the mother to control their actions until they were old enough to know when to shift and when not to. Melissa could just imagine Mom in the grocery store with her twin human babies, and all of a sudden they turned into jaguar cubs. Total catastrophe.

Their kind needed to be able to shift when little though, so they could learn to vocalize like other jaguars, just as human babies had to learn human speech from early on. The same went for hunting and playing as cubs or learning to socialize as human babies. It was a necessary part of their lives. But if their mom died, she would change back into her human form, and the babies would also remain in theirs until they were older. When they could shift on their own was different for each child. Just as some matured quicker and could walk or talk faster, the same was true for shifter children who could turn on their own at an earlier age.

This was a real nightmare of epic proportions.

"Okay, Melissa," Martin said, and she didn't realize he'd been speaking to her for some time when he said, "Melissa?"

Breaking through the fog in her brain, he repeated her name and this time she said, "Yes?"

"Listen to me. I'll have a team there within thirty-six hours to track down the mother and father, if the ones taken are the mother and father."

What if they weren't? What if the mother and father were somewhere else? No, they couldn't be.

"Your mission, and Huntley's, is to get the cubs to your cabana. Keep them hidden and safe. Feed them. Nurture them. Protect them at all costs. Watch Huntley. Make sure he's all right. If his condition deteriorates—"

"He's unconscious!"

Silence. Then the cubs began to snarl again as if *she* could feed them!

She felt Huntley's cheek, but his temperature was fine and his breathing normal.

"Yes, but we heal quickly. If that changes—if he begins to get feverish or shows any other sign of infection—let me know at once. You should pack your gear and move to the cabana tonight."

"Huntley's unconscious!"

A pause.

"Yes. Melissa, listen. You *need* to move the cubs under the cover of night. You've *got* to get them out of the park before anyone sees you with them. You've *got* to get them to your cabana before morning. I hear them in the background. They're hungry. They're going to give you away if anyone's about. I also hear it raining. Good cover. For now. It won't last, though."

She stared at Huntley, who was still dead to the world, and the cubs looking up at her as if waiting for her to take care of them.

"Melissa? You can do this. You have to do this. I've got eight people dropping their missions immediately to track down the parents. All right? Concentrate on the cubs."

"It was Jackson," she said, feeling numb as she wiped some dribbles of blood off Huntley's neck. "He had black hair—dyed, but I smelled his scent. He was responsible for this."

"We'll get them. You take care of the cubs."

"All right. I've got to go. I need to revive Huntley and pack the gear."

"Okay, call me when you can."

"Will do."

She tucked her phone back in her pocket and began to pack their bags. This was going to be some job. She rolled up her sleeping bag. She could fit one of the cubs in her backpack—at this age, they were about thirteen pounds—and Huntley could carry the other. She was trying to think positively, but it was a stretch. Carrying their regular gear was a hardship in the rain, heat, and humidity, but adding another thirteen pounds to each of their packs when Huntley was also injured?

"Huntley, wake up. We need to leave."

He opened his eyes and she frowned at him.

"Can you see me?"

"Two."

Great. He was having double vision.

"All right. I called Martin. He's ordered us to return to our cabana."

She moved the cubs off Huntley and then offered her hand to him. He was like deadweight. His eyes rolled back in his head, and he was out like the proverbial light. Again.

"Huntley," she tried again, "Martin said we have to go." She figured if anything would sink into Huntley's semiconscious brain, it would be the director's order to conduct a mission in a certain way. "You need to wake up." She was firm but gentle. She thought of being rough and tough with him, anything to get him to wake, but she couldn't. He wouldn't be that way with her. He'd probably try to carry her out of here with the cubs and leave the gear behind.

"Huntley," she said in a sultry voice.

He opened his eyes.

She smiled brightly at him. Although she wasn't feeling the urge, she was trying to convey something that would get him in the mood. "Will you take me to bed?"

"Will you think less of me if I tell you I have the worst headache?"

She chuckled, loving his sense of humor no matter the dire circumstances. "Okay, I'll take a rain check. Let's just get you up and on your feet. We may have to leave some of our gear behind if we can't carry all of it in addition to the cubs."

"The cubs," he said, and she knew he still wasn't all right.

"Yeah, one for each of us. Two little females." She helped Huntley to stand, felt him sway a bit, and held on to him tight. "Are you going to be all right? I guess I could take the cubs with me, barricade them in the small kitchen of our cabana, and come back for you and the rest of our gear. But I really don't want to leave you alone."

As it was, they'd take several hours to reach their cabana, and the day would be dawning. Luckily, as before, the day would be gray and the resort was mostly empty, with each of the cabanas shielded from the others by thick vegetation. The problem was getting past the ranger's station without the ranger suspecting something if the cubs started to squirm or cry.

"No," Huntley said. He sounded so weak that she felt bad for him. "We stick together. Safer that way."

"Good. I'd prefer it that way. So here's the deal. If you start feeling really woozy, we'll stop, and you can rest. If you can't make it, I'll erect the tent for you, continue on with both cubs, and come back for you. At least we'll be closer to home. All right?"

He grunted.

She smiled. "You can be all tough JAG material another day. I just want us all to get out of here without getting caught."

Not that they wouldn't have problems after they reached the cabana. Someone could discover at any time that they were caring for two motherless cubs. And then they'd be in some kind of mess.

She propped Huntley up against a tree until she could take down the tent. He always insisted on carrying the extra weight, but she had to have him on his feet, so she'd carry the tent this time. If she could have carried both cubs, she would have. She put the more golden cub in his backpack and the darker one in hers, then helped him on with his pack.

"I'll take the tent," he said.

"You stay on your feet." She finally managed to get her pack on. With the tent and the cub and as tired as she was, she was having a time of it. "I'll lead the way. You hold on to the strap of my bag. I don't want to lose you and not realize you've fallen behind."

"All right."

She knew he had to be feeling poorly if he agreed to everything so readily. "Okay, let's go."

She trudged through the rainforest, trying to take the most direct path back, but the mud sucked at their boots. Huntley's pulling at the strap on her bag indicated he was having trouble and that practically unbalanced her too. He either was swaying to one side or the other, or pulling back on the strap as if he was losing his balance or consciousness.

The only good thing was that the cubs had gone to sleep in the bags, the rocking motion and confinement comforting them, so they were no longer crying for their momma.

"Are you doing all right?" she asked Huntley for the fifth time since they'd started the interminable hike back to their cabana.

"Yeah," he grunted.

"Okay." She didn't dare look back at him. She couldn't look over her shoulder because of all the gear she was carrying. She also was afraid of turning around because he was holding so tightly onto her backpack strap that she might throw him off balance and he'd go down.

How far was it? The trip back seemed to be taking four times as long as it should. Which it probably was, considering how slowly they were moving.

"So, they seem to have bonded with you," she said. She didn't want to waste her breath, but she wanted to make sure he didn't pass out on her. If talking helped, she would do it.

He grunted.

She smiled. "I saw the way they were kneading your shirt."

"Belly," he said.

She chuckled. "Yeah, they have sharp little claws."

"Yeah, got the wounds to prove it."

She laughed. "Sorry. I'll take care of you when we get to the cabana."

"How far is it?"

"Not sure. Maybe another five miles. We were in fairly deep."

"About four more hours then."

"Yeah. Can you make it?"

"Yeah." He didn't sound like it to her. "You?"

Every inch of her hurt. Especially her back and shoulders. She needed a back rub for certain. "Yeah. I'm fine."

"Tell me what happened."

She sighed and told him how she'd only managed to reach the beach when the men tore off in the boat with the jaguars. "And you were shot."

"Real bullets. Not tranquilizer darts. Only I was damned lucky and moved so quickly that the bullet only grazed me. It still feels like I was hit with Thor's hammer, and I must have passed out. Or else they'd have made sure I was dead."

"Then you went back to the camp because you'd been injured."

"The only thing that came to mind was for me to return to the tent and wait for you. I knew I couldn't manage locating you on my own the way I was feeling."

"Good thing too. And then you found the cubs."

"Hell, that was a shock."

"For me too. Not only was my partner out for the count, but he had two cubs…bonding with him."

He chuckled.

They had only made it maybe another mile when they heard voices. She came to a dead halt. They were using a trail to make the trip back easier. Even so, the path was strewn with tree roots and vines. But given Huntley's condition and the extra load she was carrying, using a trail would help to get them to where they were headed quicker.

She began to move off the trail, hating to take even one step away from the direction they had to go. Then the worst possible thing could happen. Her cub began crying and growling.

No, no, no.

She moved deeper into the thick vegetation and stopped, hoping that whoever it was wouldn't come searching for the crying cub.

"Hide," she told Huntley.

"What?"

"I'm going to shift. You take my cub with you and hide. I'll pretend to be the mother hunting, and if they get anywhere near where you are, I'll growl and show a whole lot of teeth."

"If they're poachers?"

"I'll take them down."

"I don't like it."

"You don't have to. Huntley, you're not in any shape to shift. And you're responsible for taking care of the cubs."

Boots tromped through the leaves, drawing closer. "Do you hear a cat crying?" a man said.

"Big cat. Not a domestic," another said. "Cub."

"Yeah, over this way," a third man said.

There were at least three of them.

"Hey," a fourth said. "If its mother is out hunting, we're screwed. Let's go away from the sound of the cub crying."

Great advice! If the others would heed it... But they didn't.

The other men headed for where Huntley was staying behind a tree with the cubs. Once the one cub started fussing, the other began to also.

Melissa hurried to strip off her clothes. There was only one way to discourage the men from getting any closer. She shifted. And waited in she-cat mode protecting "her" cubs and their "father."

"This way," the one guy said.

She growled softly, letting him know before he even got close enough to see her to turn around and head the other way. The cubs quieted.

"Wait," one of the men said.

All of them stopped crashing through the woods, their flashlights sweeping across the dripping wet vegetation, the rains quieting down to a light shower, as they searched for any sign of the growly jaguar. She wanted to tell them how dangerous it was to approach a protective mother cat.

She remained quiet, hoping they'd just move along, but then one of the cubs began to cry again. One of the men moved in her direction, slower this time, but his boots were just as noisy as he broke twigs in his path.

She growled. This time he swung his flashlight in her eyes and she crouched, ready to pounce.

"Okay, it's okay. I'm not going to hurt you," he said, trying to sound reassuring, his voice trembling a little as he moved backward slowly. The light was blinding her, but he was pulling away until he tripped, swore, and landed on his back, his light suddenly shining on the canopy above him. She wanted to laugh.

The other guys hurried to help him up.

"Hell, man. You don't want her to think you're her next meal for her cubs, do you?" said the guy who had warned the rest of them to leave well enough alone. "Just keep the light in her eyes. It'll blind her until we can move far enough away from her and the cubs."

They continued to back away from her, keeping their lights on her, though they were fading so much that they would be out of view shortly.

"I just wish I could have gotten a picture," the man who had tripped said.

"I did."

"Me too."

And then they were gone. Relieved, Melissa came around the tree to see why the cubs were so quiet now, expecting them to be sleeping in Huntley's arms, but he and they were gone.

Chapter 9

HIS MIND CLEARING ENOUGH TO RECOGNIZE THE danger to the cubs and to all of them, Huntley moved away from the tree to keep the cubs quiet and give Melissa a chance to look scary and menacing to the park visitors.

He was hoping he was far enough away to keep the cubs from causing more trouble when Melissa came out of nowhere, as quiet as a jaguar, and nearly gave him a heart attack when she roared at him. She was cute when she was pissed. At least he was feeling better. Not a hundred percent, but better.

And at least he saw only one pissed-off jaguar and not two of her now. He followed her back to her clothes, and after she shifted and dressed, he helped her on with her backpack.

The sky was getting lighter, despite the gray clouds, so they would arrive at the cabana in broad daylight. It couldn't be helped.

Scarlet macaws took flight when they smelled the jaguars in their midst. Huntley and Melissa were close to the cabanas now. They could smell the food cooking in some of the cabanas and at the lodge. Time for breakfast and Huntley was actually hungry. Which was a good sign. His headache had lessened. Had he really told Melissa that he had to beg off on going to bed with her because of an excruciating headache?

"About the headache," Huntley said. "It's nearly gone."

"I'm so glad," she said with heartfelt relief.

"Yeah. That means I can take you up on your rain check."

She didn't say anything as she trudged along, looking like she was ready to collapse the way she was putting the effort into moving one foot ahead of the other.

He chuckled.

"I'm glad you're feeling so much better," she said seriously.

"I am. And I'm serious about taking you up on the rain check."

She laughed, then groaned. "I'll be so glad to get this backpack off my back. And get cleaned up."

"And sleep."

"Yeah, but now that we have a couple of babies, I can't go to sleep right away."

Then they reached the ranger's station. Looking bedraggled, they smiled and were about to head for their cabana, hoping to clear out in a hurry before the cubs did anything to give them away, when the ranger said to Huntley, "What happened to you?"

"Tripped and fell and bloodied my head," Huntley said, trying not to look as anxious as he felt. Melissa had forged on ahead.

Afraid the cubs would wake at any moment and that if she even tried to stop, she'd never get up the momentum to move again, Melissa kept trudging back to the cabana, praying Huntley would get past the ranger before they had more trouble.

"Make sure you get it looked after," the ranger said to Huntley.

"Sure thing." Huntley soon caught up to her, and she again couldn't believe he could have any energy, especially after being wounded.

Then she saw the trail to their place and sighed with audible relief. "We made it."

She looked at the daunting steps to the deck that she'd need to climb to reach the front door.

"I'll take the tent," Huntley said when she hesitated.

"No, I'll manage." She didn't want him to have to carry anything more. She knew he had to still be feeling poorly.

He lifted her pack as she began the climb the steps. She couldn't believe he could manage.

She unlocked the door and went inside. He followed, helping her off with her backpack. What a relief. Then she quickly did the same for him. What she wouldn't give for a hot tub or masseuse right now!

Huntley rolled his shoulders and groaned a little.

"I feel the same way." She was glad he wasn't so macho that he tried to hide the fact that his muscles ached like hers did. She headed for the kitchen and considered how open it was to the breakfast nook and living room. "We're going to have difficulty no matter how we manage this. I was thinking we could put them in the kitchen, but there's no good way to do that."

"Bathroom or the bedroom."

"Bathroom. I'll need to make up a cat litter box for them. I can get some sand from the beach." She fished his phone out of her pocket and handed it to him.

"You are a treasure. I'm so glad you found it. I

figured I'd have to go back out there and search for it as soon as I could," Huntley said.

"Glad I discovered it. I kept calling your number, hoping I'd locate you. Really had me worried when I found your phone and no you."

"Don't blame you there."

"Why don't you wash up and go lie down? I'll join you after a while."

"Are you kidding? You think I'm going to let you take care of our first kids all on your own?"

She laughed. She appreciated a man who still had a sense of humor under these circumstances. "You have been wounded. Don't act all he-man on me. What if you collapse again?"

"Then you can give me mouth-to-mouth resuscitation and revive me. And while you're at it, you could give me that rain check."

Smiling, she shook her head. "We have babies in the house now. I'm going to try to feed them."

"I'll help. What do you want me to do?"

"We'll have to show them how to lick up the milk from a bowl. They'll probably get it, if they're hungry enough."

"Easier than if they were human babies," he said, watching as she poured milk into a bowl and then set it down on the floor.

She poked her fingers in the milk and let the more adventurous of the two cubs lick it off her fingers. "Yeah, but don't even mention the baby part."

The cubs were making a mess and not really drinking much. Huntley got on his cell and put it on speakerphone. "Mom, I've got a question. Melissa Overton and I are on a mission in Costa Rica, and well, how do you feed a two-month-old jaguar cub if you don't have mother's milk?"

"What?"

Melissa chuckled while she continued to try to get the cubs to lap up the milk. It wasn't working. The one with brighter gold fur stepped in the bowl. The other chewed on the edge.

"Poachers captured the mom," he said quickly. "We're trying a bowl of milk on them, and it's not working out very well."

His mother began laughing.

Melissa smiled. She liked his mom.

"I'm sorry. It's not funny." Then his mother started laughing again. "Okay, okay, it is funny. They need baby bottles just like a baby. And after they've fed, you put them over your shoulder and rub their back and pat them to burp them."

"You're kidding, right?"

"I raised three of you kids. And I still have a day care. Don't you think I know how to do it?"

"Wait, if we were jaguars, you'd have to have been a jaguar and not needed a bottle."

"Right, but some of the mothers run in their jaguar forms and don't want to take their infants with them, so when they leave their babies with me, I have to feed them bottled breast milk. Just get some baby bottles, and though the milk won't have all the nutrients the cubs need, it'll be good enough until the momma can take care of them again. At that age, they should drink nearly all of a bottle." She started laughing again.

He smiled at Melissa. "Thanks, Mom. We're off to see if we can find some baby bottles."

"Love you, Son. You and Melissa will do fine with them."

"Yeah, love you too." He pocketed his phone and looked at Melissa.

"Baby bottles. It might take me a while. If you can watch them, I'll run to the store and see if I can also find something to use as a litter box. And get some more milk. Will you be all right?"

"Yeah. Just be back really soon. Okay?"

She smiled, then patted his stomach. "Fatherhood suits you. Call your mother back if you have any trouble."

Then she slipped her passport and some money into a small bag and left, praying no one would drop in unexpectedly and cause even more problems for them. She got into the rental car and headed for the small store ten miles away, which was a long way on these roads, considering the potholes and boulders in the road. She called Martin to let him know they were safely back at the cabana and that Huntley was doing much better.

"Good. I've asked all the branches to put out a search to see if we can discover who the jaguar shifter parents are and where they were staying. I keep telling everyone we need a database with all of our people listed for this very reason."

"Right, but everyone would have to voluntarily sign up to be monitored, and you know how that goes over with some folks," Melissa said, turning off the windshield wipers as the rain finally subsided.

"I agree. But if these people had told us that they were jaguar shifters and going to be in the park at a certain time, we'd know about it."

"Right. Would it be possible to send a nursing

jaguar-shifter mother out here to at least nurse the cubs?" She was certain he'd say no, but it was an idea.

"Can't. Not only do we not have a database to know such a thing, but a nursing mother would have babies of her own to care for."

"Yeah, but she could shift if anyone began snooping around. All they'd see would be a human woman with a baby or babies of her own."

"And two cubs that she stole from the park."

"Got it. But what if these cubs' mother is incarcerated and it takes weeks to locate her and free her? Huntley and I can't stay here all that time."

"We're working on a way to get the cubs back to the States. You might have to move to another location where we can send in a plane or a helicopter. It's going to take some time, though. Do the best you can in the meantime. We'll keep you informed."

"All right." She knew Martin would have all the resources he could working on this problem, as well as the other branches pooling their teams to aid them. Anytime that a shifter was captured in his jaguar form and imprisoned, it became a case of extreme concern for all shifters. But even more so when the imprisoned jaguar left behind cubs. If the mom died in captivity, she'd turn back into her human form, and the cubs would too. Then they'd have two babies to take care of.

Melissa tried several stores but came up empty. After more than an hour, she walked inside another small store and nearly had a seizure. Two men dressed in park ranger uniforms were buying some items. She hoped she didn't look as worried about seeing them as she felt.

She searched everywhere for something she could

use as litter boxes and finally found a couple of plastic tubs for storing stuff. She bought both, just in case one cat wouldn't use the same "litter box" as the other.

One of the rangers was buying chips and magazines while talking to the clerk, mentioning about gunfire in the park but being unable to reach the site fast enough to catch anyone. That had her listening. No details. They were only searching for any evidence that someone had been shot.

The other ranger was looking at cold medications. He grabbed a couple of packages and headed for the checkout counter.

Melissa picked up some more milk, not sure how much the cubs would drink. She kept trying to think of what else she might need. Milk, litter box, four milk bottles, and a couple of towels to let them sleep on. That was it.

The rangers left, and she paid for her purchases and drove back to the cabana.

She tried calling Huntley, but there was no answer. She could envision the cubs not drinking much of the milk, stepping into it, spilling it, and then making puddles on the tile floor. So maybe he was cleaning up after them. She smiled a little, glad she had this job instead, though she worried again if he was feeling all right.

When she finally arrived at the cabana, she saw toucans snacking on the papaya trees near the deck, and spider and howler monkeys making a ruckus in some trees farther away. The scent of orchids perfumed the air as she made her way up the steps. She hurried inside with her supplies. She was about to call out to Huntley to let him know it was just her when she saw him on the floral couch sound asleep, the cubs curled up on his stomach and watching her.

"The two of you have made a buddy, I see." She put the milk in the fridge, then left the cabana to get some sand from the beach for each of the litter boxes. Exhausted, she didn't think she'd manage to climb the steep wooden steps to their place again. She was glad Martin had chosen this cabana because it had such a nice view of the ocean and more privacy—and sand for litter boxes.

She finally managed to get in through the back door with the two containers of sand. No one had budged from the couch.

She fixed up the sandboxes in the bathroom and then used a towel to create a bed for the cubs. She took her shower, then threw on a tank top and shorts and walked into the living room, almost wanting to leave everyone where they were because they all looked so angelic. Well, Huntley did. The cats were watching her, like any wild animals would that were wary of their surroundings. The cubs could make a mess of things if they decided to jump off Huntley's stomach and do some exploring on their own while she and Huntley slept.

And she needed to feed them. She filled two baby bottles with milk and then warmed them. Then she set the bottles down on the coffee table, took one of the cubs, sat down on a chair, and began to coax her to drink from the bottle. It was not as easy as Melissa had thought it would be. The cub wasn't sure how to get the milk out of the bottle and was gumming the nipple. Then she finally figured it out and began to suck. The other was watching from Huntley's stomach. She was much mellower, really sweet, with blue-gray eyes that were a touch browner. Sweetpea, Melissa would nickname her.

When the first cub had finished nearly all of the bottle, Melissa did what Huntley's mother suggested. She put the cub over her shoulder and stroked her back, then patted her. The jaguar finally burped and Melissa smiled. Okay, so that wasn't so hard.

Then she took the cub into the bathroom to use the litter box. Her fur was a brighter gold than Sweetpea's, so she thought Goldie would suit her. She had darker lines under her eyes and whiter fur fringing the inside of her ears, but otherwise the cubs' markings were very similar. The pattern on top of their head was different, however. More of circular pattern like a halo on Sweetpea's head. Goldie's pattern was narrower.

First, Goldie just sniffed at the smells of the sea on the sand in the box, then she used the box. Thankfully, felines were so much easier to litter train—at four weeks old or even younger—than human babies were to potty train. Melissa carried Goldie back to Huntley and let her curl up on his stomach again. Then Melissa fed Sweetpea.

After that one finished feeding and Melissa burped her, she carried them under each arm as she talked to them. "Time for your new bedroom. Litter boxes for the two of you. And your bed." She set them on their towel bed and they curled up together, their blue eyes watching her.

"Nighty-night," she said, closing the door. It might be daytime, but for her, it was way past time to sleep.

She thought about waking Huntley so he could go to bed with her, but she didn't want to wake him in case he couldn't get back to sleep afterward. When she entered the bedroom, she found him in bed, waiting for her and smiling.

"I didn't expect you to be in here," she said. "How did you all do with one another?"

"They made a real mess with the milk and both puddled on the kitchen floor."

Smiling, she shook her head.

"And if you smell milk on them, it's because they both took a couple of nosedives into the saucer of milk. Were we ever that little?"

She laughed, pulled the covers aside, and climbed into bed with him. "I'm sure we were. But we probably always had our mother's milk when we needed it, and I guess bottles when that wasn't a viable option. We didn't have to resort to drinking out of a bowl."

"I guess we're getting submerged in a quick study of Jaguar Shifter Parenting 101. Did you get bottles?" He pulled her against him and she smelled tropical spice on him. He had to have taken a shower while she was gone.

"Yeah, and once they got the hang of it, they drank a lot. Good thing your mother told us what to do. We would have been starving them."

He began stroking Melissa's shoulder and she wanted to purr. "They're cute. I didn't ever think I'd be saying that about a couple of cubs while on a mission," he said.

"They're cute, all right. But if they start raking their claws down the couch or urinating where they ought not to, not so cute." And worse, if somehow any of their neighbors caught sight of them, Melissa and Huntley would be in big trouble. "We have to ensure they don't get into any of the windows and peek out. Probably no one would see them, since we are a distance from the beach and have the vegetation all around us. But we often have squirrel or howler monkeys swinging on the balcony, and I can just see someone glancing up with a telephoto lenses, taking pictures of the cute monkeys, then seeing the jaguar cubs clawing at the glass to get to the cute monkeys."

He chuckled and ran his hand through her hair.

"Are you really okay?" she asked, still concerned.

"Yeah, feeling much, much better. Just still tired. How long were you gone?"

"Two hours. No place close by had baby bottles. It's a good thing all we have to worry about for now is taking care of the two cubs—and not getting caught." Then she closed her eyes, luxuriated in the feel of his hot, hard, virile body, and hoped the cubs would be all right on their own so that Huntley could cash in on his rain check.

But only after they had a good, long catnap.

Chapter 10

SNUGGLED AGAINST HUNTLEY'S WARM, HARD BODY, Melissa was dreaming about running through the rainforest in her human form, half knowing it was a dream when she heard a baby cry out. Still drowsy, she was annoyed that anyone in the area had a baby and that the cabana's walls were so paper thin that she could hear that baby cry.

She took that thought into the rainforest as she drifted back into her dream, now as a jaguar leaping into a shark-filled river. She was paddling across the water as quickly as she could when she felt a hand brushing her arm. She opened her eyes and looked up to see Huntley smiling at her.

"Headache all gone?" she whispered, not quite ready to join the living. A soft rain pattered on the roof, and she was enjoying being wrapped up in Huntley's arms like this. She wondered how she'd feel if she began really dating him and he had to be on a mission with another female agent. She'd be jealous. Funny, she'd never given a thought to Oliver working with other women or going to office parties thrown by his workplace when she was out of the country. Then again, she'd never considered that he might be interested in his next-door neighbor. But with Huntley, she was quite certain she would be jealous.

It was dark out and when she glanced at the clock,

she saw that it was two in the morning. Good. They had slept for six hours.

"Headache's all gone," Huntley said, his voice already sounding husky.

She thought that if she could wake up mornings like this, she'd be raring to go. As long as she had a solid amount of sleep during that time.

His hand slipped under her shirt and caressed her bare skin. She smiled and licked his nipple. He was starting to lift her top off when she heard a baby cry out, and then another. And then silence.

"Ohmigod, the cubs," she said, realizing that the baby's cry she'd heard earlier was *not* from a neighbor's cabana, but their own.

She threw off their covers, fearing the worst. If the cub's mother had died, the woman would shift into her human form. Melissa scrambled to get out of bed.

Huntley was right behind her as they rushed down the hall to the bathroom. The babies were quiet as she carefully opened the door, not wanting to hit them with the door if either had managed to get near it. She flipped on the light and saw two blue-eyed cubs staring back at her—and then they snarled as if she'd scared them.

Confused about what she thought she'd heard, Melissa crouched down to greet them. "You did hear babies crying, didn't you? Human babies?" she asked Huntley. She wondered if she'd only imagined it.

The cubs were all over her, trying to get her attention and growling in their cute little cub way.

"I thought I did. Maybe they just sounded like babies." He crouched down next to her, and they began to climb all over him, excited to see him too.

"No, I don't think so." She was sure of it, in fact. "Make sure they used the litter boxes. I'll warm up some milk for them."

"All right."

She was about to leave him when he rose and took her in his arms and kissed her thoroughly as one of the cubs scratched at the sand in the litter box. "We have unfinished business to take care of after this," Huntley said.

She smiled. She could really get used to this. She kissed him back. "It's a deal."

Then she hurried off to get the baby bottles ready so she and Huntley could put the kids back to sleep and return to more pleasurable adult pursuits.

She had just finished warming the bottles when she heard a ruckus in the living room. She grabbed the bottles and left the kitchen to find Huntley on the floor with the two cubs. He was pulling one of their towels around as they pounced and dug their claws into it, growling as he dragged them around.

"Don't wake them up too much," she warned.

"I'm wearing them out," he said, winking at her.

"I sure hope so." But she wasn't certain that would work. Wouldn't they be all excited and keyed up and not be able to sleep?

When the cubs saw her with the milk bottles, they instantly knew what that meant. Both ran to her and clawed at her bare legs.

"Hey, manners," she said to the cubs.

Huntley quickly scooped Goldie up and took a bottle from Melissa, then sat down on the couch. Melissa lifted the other cub into her arms and sat on the chair and began feeding her.

It was fun watching the cubs drink from the bottles, knowing that she and Huntley were taking care of them in the best possible manner.

"Much better than a bowl of milk, isn't it, Dragon?" Huntley said, looking like he was the cub's father.

Melissa raised her brows. "Dragon?"

He shrugged a shoulder. "She has the pattern of a dragon on her forehead."

Melissa chuckled. "Goldie, because her fur is a brighter gold than the other's. You can't call a cute little female cub 'Dragon.'"

He smiled at her. "And the other?"

She noticed he wasn't venturing another name. "Sweetpea. She's lots calmer and has a halo on her head."

He laughed.

She wondered then if her father had ever fed her like this. "This is so much better. And this way we know how much each is really eating."

"Agreed."

After a moment of watching her own "baby" drink her milk, sucking away at the nipple, paws grasping the bottle as if she could hold it on her own, Melissa glanced at Huntley to see if Goldie was nearly finished.

He was watching Melissa and Sweetpea, and smiled when she caught his eye.

"You're a natural at this," he said, his voice full of admiration.

"You're not so bad yourself. My first thought when you were playing with them was that they'd get so excited that we'd never get them back to bed. But now that their bellies are filling up, they're looking drowsy, and I think you had the right idea."

"Yeah. I never thought I might energize them by playing with them. Just wear them out. But we could try it your way next time—just keep them calm and sleepy and see if it works."

She hoped they wouldn't have a lot of next times. That Martin would come through for them and ensure that the cubs were safely on their way home soon to the States.

"Looks like they're about ready to return to bed, don't you think?" Huntley asked, looking hopeful.

Both had finished most of their bottled milk and were curling up to sleep on Melissa and Huntley's laps. Melissa wanted to cuddle with Sweetpea for a little while longer, but when Huntley smiled at her as if knowing that was what she was thinking, she rose from the couch and carried her charge back to the bathroom.

Huntley had snagged the spare towel he'd used to play with them and added it to the other to make more of a bed. Luckily, as soon as they put the cubs on the bed, they sat down, looking up at them.

"Litter boxes need to be cleaned," Melissa said, wrinkling her nose at them.

"I'll take care of it before first light."

"Good." She would help, certainly, but if he didn't mind, the job was all his. "I'll join you in a second." She brushed her teeth, and he nodded and closed the door.

She used the bathroom, then said, "Nighty-night," to the cubs, who were watching her, their eyes half-lidded as they curled up against each other. They sure were cute. She closed the door and rejoined Huntley in bed. She just hoped the cubs would sleep long enough so that Huntley and she could finish what they'd started—but the reminder that the cubs had to have shifted into human babies weighed heavily on her mind.

As if knowing what she was thinking, Huntley said, "They'll be all right." He pulled her close. "The cubs and the mom and dad. Martin will make sure of it."

She thought of Martin rescuing her and her sister when they were teens and prayed Huntley was right. Then he was kissing her, stroking her back, and trying to take her mind off their troubles that they could do nothing about.

And she was kissing him and rubbing against his erection, working him up and thinking—if it wasn't for the serious problem with the cubs and their parents, she could deal with this part of the job in a heartbeat and love every minute of it.

Genista had to be crazy not to want this. Was Huntley hiding something from her? Something that had made Genista want to slip away without even talking it over with him first? Melissa liked her as a fellow agent but didn't know anything about her personally.

She sighed, realizing she was overthinking this again, and went with the flow. She slipped her hand inside his boxers, wrapping her fingers around his erection, loving the feel of him in her grip, and sliding up and down over his rigid cock. She loved the way his eyes grew heated and he groaned with intense need.

His mouth was on hers then, claiming her, his hands cradling her face as he tasted her and she tasted him right back. So virile—hardness to her softness, spiciness to her sweetness, maleness to her femininity; his kisses hungry, penetrating, eager.

He reached down to pull up her tank top, forcing her to let go of his arousal. But he seemed too pumped to wait any longer and tossed her shirt. Then he slid her boxers down her thighs and stopped. Eagerly, he began rubbing her clit, arousing her and making her bud swell to his touch, the erotic sensation undoing her. His mouth was on hers as he maneuvered her onto her back and kissed her slowly and tenderly, while his fingers dipped into her wet sheath.

Now *she* groaned with intense need, wanting all of him penetrating her, the joining, and the heat and passion that were Huntley and her combined. He sensed when she was about to come, anticipated it, and provoked it with his skillful strokes. He was with her every step of the way, teasing her into ecstasy and pleasuring her like no man had ever done.

She felt the rising need building, then the sharp thrill of the climax as it hit, sending shards of pleasure streaking through her. Sinking into the mattress, she luxuriated in the feel of her inner core as it thrummed with pleasure. Before Huntley could do anything else, she jerked off his boxers and freed his cock. He quickly slid her own boxers the rest of the way down her legs until they were on the floor, and she and Huntley were skin to skin. Then he drove into her, not gently, but like a big male cat with a mission—wanting, craving this, having to have her. And she loved the sensation of knowing he needed and wanted her this badly. Just as much as she needed and wanted him.

His eyes were dark as midnight, his cock plunging into her, his mouth hot on hers as she traced her fingers along his back and tangled her tongue with his. For the moment, all she cared about was this—him inside her and the physical and emotional connection they shared.

Huntley slowed his thrusts, burrowing deep and taking in her woman's fragrance of peaches and sexy cat. He loved the way she touched him, the way she moved her hips to meet his thrusts, the feel of her skin soft against his. She was wild and unpredictable, and he couldn't get enough of her.

He licked her neck and nuzzled his face against her skin like a big cat courting a female—affectionately and looking to mate. Her face was flushed and radiant, her reddish-brown hair spread out over the white pillow like a jaguar goddess, her green eyes shuttered. Her knees were bent and spread, opening her to him, and her heart was beating as wildly as his.

And then he came, thrusting into her, the hunger for her finally quenched—for now. But he knew it wouldn't last.

After making love, they cuddled and Huntley wasn't too surprised when he and Melissa both fell back to sleep for a few hours. He was feeling great, his head no longer hurting and his other more primal needs met—and hers as well. The rains had stopped, and he was enjoying the feeling of Melissa's light breath on his chest and her hair tickling his skin. Then the cubs began snarling for something to eat.

Before the cubs woke Melissa, he gently slipped out from underneath her, threw on some boxers, and headed for the bathroom. Thankfully, the shower had a glass door so the cats didn't have shower curtains to play with—and shred. They'd used both litter boxes. That beat having a bunch of messy diapers.

He grabbed a couple of milk bottles, warmed them, then took the cubs into the living room and sat down on a chair to feed them. He really thought it would be easy. It wasn't. While he was trying to feed Sweetpea, Goldie was attempting to grab the bottle with her paws and biting at the bottom of it. He chuckled. He still thought she should be called Dragon.

Man, this was harder than it looked. Somehow, milk had splattered on Sweetpea's face and head. But she was drinking just like a baby, her paws clinging to the bottle as her sister tackled her. He could see where it helped to have two people to do this.

When he wouldn't feed Goldie, she grabbed hold of his arm with claws extended, trying to get him to pay attention to her and feed her. *Little monster.* She was already showing how strong even a baby jaguar cub could be. Once Sweetpea was finished, he took her back to the bathroom, hoping if she had to go, she'd use the litter box while he fed the other one. Handling one was so much easier.

Once Goldie had finished feeding, he left the two in the bathroom, or planned to, so he could take one of the litter boxes outside to clean. Everything was a chore. Both cubs wanted to go with him and were winding around his legs and getting underfoot, while he was trying to keep them in the bathroom and both hands on the box. He finally managed to slip his arm under the box, cradle it, and quickly shut the door without closing it on a tail or a foot.

After taking care of the box, he returned with the clean litter box and found Melissa in the kitchen, yawning as she pushed the hair out of her eyes and gave him a sleepy smile.

"This mission isn't anything like I thought it would

be," she said, washing her hands and preparing ham and eggs. "Glad you're taking care of the kids."

He chuckled. "Hey, if you're cooking, I'm good." He returned to the bathroom and found the cubs sleeping on their towel bed. He exchanged litter boxes, then closed the bathroom door. "I'm glad my mother told us about the bottles because I'm certain they wouldn't have gotten the hang of lapping up milk from a bowl."

"I had a kitten when I was little, and I fed her from a bowl. So that's why I thought it would work for a jaguar cub. Even so, it would help if we had a regular cat or dog dish that didn't tip," she said.

"Yeah. Not that we would find anything like that here." He headed outside with the second litter box.

When he returned, she asked, "Did they use the boxes okay?"

"Yeah, they were good. Although I managed to get milk all over their faces—don't ask me how."

She chuckled.

He cleaned the cubs up, then returned with two wet cats and a towel, and set them on the kitchen floor near the table. At least jaguar cubs loved the water. The whole cabana was tiled, so no problem with cleanups if they were needed.

The cubs were sniffing at the aroma of the ham and eggs.

Melissa smiled down at them. "You two are too little yet. Later, you can eat big-people food. I think." She looked at Huntley for confirmation.

Huntley started to agree but then said, "Let me call Mom."

Melissa smiled.

Huntley went to put on some jeans and a T-shirt, and did a search on the Internet to learn when jaguar cubs began to eat meat, but he wasn't certain if the same rules applied to jaguar shifter cubs. He returned to the living room with the phone in hand and called his mother.

"Okay, another question. The cubs look like they're dying to have some meat while Melissa's cooking ham and eggs. I did a quick Internet search, and one of the sites said the mother takes them to a kill site and they begin to eat meat as young as seven to nine weeks of age. But human babies can't even eat pureed food at that age, can they?"

"No. But when they're jaguars, they have all the needs of a full-time jaguar. So, yes, they can eat meat. They'll eat just what they need, so try them out on a little bit of it. Not anything too spicy," his mother said.

"Okay. Thanks. We have ham and eggs this morning. Do you think smoked ham would be all right?"

"Soak it in water and that will take out some of the spicy flavor. If you have some raw hamburger, that would be even better. Just feed them a little bit."

"Okay. Thanks, Mom." He poked around in the fridge. "Got some. Got to go. I'll call if we have any more questions."

"Good luck to the both of you. Any luck with finding the mother?"

"Not yet. Soon, we hope." Then they said their good-byes, and he separated a little bit of the hamburger for each of the cubs. "A little bit of raw hamburger, Mom said."

He sat down on the floor to feed them to get them

out from under Melissa's feet. Immediately, both cubs scrambled onto his lap and tried to get to the meat. He parceled it out to each of them, both licking at his hands with their small sandpapery tongues. Then they began to nibble at the hamburger. He looked up to see Melissa watching him and she smiled.

The cubs finished the meat and began rubbing their heads against his shirt, then clawing at him.

"No claws," he said, and Melissa chuckled.

"You're going to have to get visitation rights after their parents are returned to them," she said.

He heard the lightness in her voice, then saw the worried frown etching across her face right afterward.

"We'll get their parents free, and the cubs will be with them before long," he assured her.

"Martin said that he's working on a way to fly the cubs out of here using a private plane or helicopter."

"Good. That would be best for all concerned."

She served up the breakfast. "They also have all the branches working on trying to identify the parents."

"With no real database, that won't be easy. They can't put a bulletin out asking if anyone knows of a couple with twin babies that went to Costa Rica recently. Then the police would get involved. It would be a mess."

"I agree. They'll only be able to have everyone in the branches ask everyone they know, and try to put the word out just among our kind. Did you talk to Martin this morning while I was still snoozing?" she asked.

"No, I've been too busy with the cubs. They're a handful." He set them aside and washed his hands, then joined her at the table. "I'm not really good at sitting still on a mission. I want to do something. Like go out and free the parents and kill the bastards who captured them."

"Yeah, but there's not much we can do about it. We can't even just go out and have fun. Attempt snorkeling or horseback riding or boating. Not without worrying about the babies," she said.

He laughed. "Do you realize that overnight we became an old married couple?"

She smiled and felt her cheeks burning. She figured they were having too much bed sport for that. She looked down as Sweetpea stretched her paws onto her lap, looking up at her and wanting to curl up on her lap. They were just so adorable. "No, not right now, baby. You get more milk. No other food. I'll play with you in a little bit."

After Melissa and Huntley ate and cleaned up, they noticed the cubs were curled up with each other on the towel, watching them.

"I'm going outside to cut some vines."

"All right." She raised her brows.

"So we have something we can play with them."

She smiled. "Like I said, total dad material."

"We've got to be prepared if they wake up long enough to want to play. Besides, it's important to teach them to hunt and play like wild cats when they're little or they won't be able to handle it. Which is why the parents have them down here so young."

"Right. I'm calling Martin to see if he's got any updates." Like real mission stuff.

"All right. I want to listen in." Huntley thought she'd be disappointed because Martin would have called first thing if he'd learned anything.

She put the call on speakerphone and asked, "Have

any word on Jackson's whereabouts or the parents' or who they are? Or when you can have someone pick up the cubs?"

"No, on all accounts. We've got everybody on this that we can. Everyone who knows any shifter has spread the word that a couple has been taken into captivity. We've sent out the word that we've got a couple of agents taking care of the cubs for the time being."

She glanced at Huntley.

Hell, yeah, if Martin hadn't said which two agents were babysitting, he'd bet a year's worth of salary that everyone was dying to know.

"But some of the jaguar-shifter couples are loners and don't associate with others, which might be the case with the parents. So far, everyone that anyone knows with cubs has called in to let us know they're all accounted for. One had triplets that they knew had gone to Belize and they were concerned they might have made trip changes, which had us worried that one of the cubs was missing, but the family was found safe at one of the resorts in Belize."

"What…what if there *were* more cubs than just the two?" Melissa asked, appearing stricken.

Huntley said, "I doubt it. The tent was zipped up when I got there. The mother made sure that the cubs couldn't slip out. They were sleeping on my bedding when I arrived. So I really don't believe that there were any more of them. Besides, I only smelled the mother and the two cubs. The father hadn't even been anywhere near the tent."

Melissa let out her breath. Huntley pulled her into his arms and rubbed her back.

"We're searching everywhere for their identity and their current location. We'll keep you posted on that. In other news, the EMTs were able to revive Jackson's sister before they took her to the hospital. She came out of surgery, and she's going to make it."

"Thank God for that," Melissa said.

"Yeah, but Phil Gorsman was released on bail."

"Great. What's wrong with the damn judges?" Huntley asked.

"That's what I say. Apparently, when they were processing him, they made a mistake and released him on bail bond. Okay, if you've got everything under control there for the moment, I'll call back later when I have anything more."

"Talk later." Melissa ended the call and was about to speak to Huntley when her phone rang in her hand. She looked at the caller ID. "Oliver, great." She swiped her finger across the screen and said, "Oliver, I'm sorry I didn't pick up my things and move them out of your place yet, but—"

"Where are you?"

"Back in Costa Rica. We had to track down the poachers and—"

"You and Huntley Anderson?" Oliver sounded suspicious, as if he thought she'd planned it this way. "You were supposed to be on vacation."

"Yes, but then we had a lead." She wondered if he'd decided to be with Chad and now wanted her out of his place sooner rather than later. "We had some problems right away."

"*Figures*." He couldn't guess the half of it!

"Yeah, well, the poachers captured a husband and

wife who are jaguar shifters, except that they left two cubs behind in the rainforest."

Oliver was silent for once.

"Are you still there?"

"Yeah."

She thought he sounded a little shocked. "So we're trying to find a way to get the cubs safely back to the States. In the meantime, we've got to take care of them."

"Hell, Melissa. This is why I didn't want you to be working in that job any longer. What if anyone finds you with the cubs?"

He sounded like he still cared about her safety. She appreciated his concern.

"We'll be in a lot of trouble. So it might be a while before I come get my things." When he didn't answer her, she said, "All right?" She hoped he didn't just decide to dump them.

"Do you know who the parents are?"

"No. Our director has some of our people trying to determine their identities, and he's also asked the other branches to look into it."

"I'll check my records."

"For what?"

"Some shifters have signed up for life insurance policies with me. I'll check and see if any of them are out of the country—in particular, on vacation in Costa Rica. I doubt I'll find the right couple, but I'll look into it."

Shocked to the core but glad for his help, Melissa said, "Thanks, Oliver."

"Don't worry about your stuff. I'll…just move it to the guest room and you can pick it up when you return."

"Thanks. I appreciate it."

"Take care of yourself and I'll be in touch." He sounded really concerned, which was more like the Oliver she really had liked.

"All right," she said and ended the call.

Huntley must have gone outside to cut some vines while she was talking to Oliver because now he was playing with the cubs, sweeping a couple of vines about the room. The cubs were chasing after them, catching them with their claws and then being dragged a couple of feet as they bit at the vine. Half the time, they ended up tackling each other. They didn't have all their teeth yet, but their claws were wicked enough.

Huntley caught her eye. "Everything all right?" He sounded like he was trying to remain neutral, but he looked hopeful that she wasn't having trouble with Oliver.

She smiled. "Everything's fine. He's just going to move my stuff to the guest room where I can pick it up when I get back." She sat down next to Huntley and swept one of the vines across the floor for the cubs, but they had tired out.

They climbed onto her lap to sleep. She stroked their fur. "They don't last long, do they?"

"No. They eat, stay up for about an hour, and then they conk out again."

They heard voices below their cabin and then footfalls as two people climbed their wooden steps. Huntley and Melissa were both on their feet in an instant. "I'll hide them and the litter boxes. You speak to whoever is at the door," Melissa said.

Huntley began stripping out of his clothes.

"What are you—"

"Making it look like I just got out of bed, or we were making love or something."

She hurried into the bedroom and put both cubs under the bed. It was like a cave underneath the bedspread, and she hoped they'd stay put. Then she ran to get the litter boxes, clamped the lids on the tubs, and moved them to the bedroom closet.

A knock on the door sounded and her heart skipped a beat.

Huntley went to the door and saw two policemen in uniform. Not good. He waited a couple of heartbeats, then opened the door, dressed only in his boxers.

"Are you Huntley Anderson of Dallas, Texas?" the shorter of the two men asked, glancing at Huntley's attire.

"Yes, sir."

"And Melissa Overton? Is she here?"

"She was taking a nap. Well, we both were."

"We would like to speak to both of you."

"Certainly. Melissa?" Huntley called out, not making a move to allow the men in. "The police want to talk to us."

She shut the door to the bedroom, then strode into view, yawning, her hair tumbled. "Yes, officers?"

Chapter 11

ONE LITTLE SQUEAK FROM ONE OF THE CUBS WOULD BE all Huntley and Melissa needed to cook their goose, Huntley thought as he tried to appear friendly and not like they were trying to hide anything in front of the police.

"May we come in?" the taller of the two policemen asked.

"Sure," Huntley said, wanting to say no. But if he did, he figured they'd believe he was guilty of some crime and arrest him on the spot. Then they'd arrest Melissa and find the cubs, and Martin would have an even worse mess to clean up.

Huntley should have said he was going to put on some pants, but he figured he had only one option. Fleeing was out of the question. Shifting and killing the men wouldn't work. They undoubtedly had told higher-ups—or higher-ups had told them—they'd be here questioning Melissa and Huntley. Turning them? He'd never known anyone who had been turned before his half sister changed a human, so he wasn't certain it would always work. Or how they'd managed to do it.

That was the only thing he was leaning toward, and it was a bad notion all the way around. The men had to have family. How would they be able to hide what they were from them and their police force?

Huntley took Melissa's very cold hand and led her to

the couch. They took a seat there while the men sat on the two chairs across from them.

"I'm Alvarez Mendez, and this is my partner Pantepi Cato. We're looking into poachers who have been trying to steal our cats from the park. You've been in the park recently," the shorter of the two men said, frowning at them.

"Yes. And if this is about calling the park rangers concerning the cougar and the two cubs those guys tried to poach that you caught up with on the beach, yes, we called you. Melissa and I are both undercover," Huntley said, winging it. Hell, what else was he to say?

Melissa was watching him, her lips parted slightly.

He shrugged at her. "We *were* undercover." He said to the men, "We work for an agency called the JAG, and we bring down poachers whenever we can. We don't take them in. We just report them to your own forces so you can mete out their punishment when we find them. Not just here, but all over. We want these people to be examples of what happens when they try to steal from your parks.

"The poachers we were after are U.S. citizens, and we had men investigating them when they arrived in Costa Rica. One of them got away, returned to the United States, and came here again. He formed a new crew. They were trying to capture a jaguar this time. I tried to stop them, and they shot at me. The bullet nicked my forehead and knocked me out, and I was damned lucky it didn't kill me. Then Melissa tracked them to the beach, but they had already taken off in a boat."

"Did they get a jaguar?" Alvarez asked.

Huntley shook his head. "Not that we could tell."

"You didn't call it in to our rangers that time?" Alvarez asked, though it was more of a statement of fact because he must have known darn well that neither Huntley nor Melissa had.

Huntley shrugged. "There was no evidence to prove they'd done anything illegal. The first time we called your authorities, the poachers were caught red-handed with the weapons and the cougars in the burlap sacks."

"What's to say you aren't part of this team and lying about all of this? That you were there, but heard us coming and got away?" Alvarez asked.

So Alvarez was one of the men who had arrived at the scene of the crime. "You can verify it with our boss. We have badges and everything, if you'll permit Melissa to get them to show to you."

"Who's to say that your 'boss' isn't the leader of a bunch of poachers, and he's got the same cover story in case we questioned you?"

"If we were the bad guys, we wouldn't stay at a resort here. We wouldn't have called the authorities to let them know we had found the poachers, or knocked them out so that you could get there and take them into custody. We wouldn't make reservations to enter the park."

"Yet you're undercover," Alvarez reminded him.

"Right, as in we were after the poachers, not knowing if we'd find them or not. Do you think a cougar, one that was drugged, could have taken all those men down at the beach? Even if she hadn't been drugged, she couldn't have knocked them out cold." Only jaguars could do that. A cougar would have torn into them with her teeth. "And who called you to inform on them then? How would anyone but us know about making the calls? I used one of the men's phones while all of them were unconscious."

"Why not your own phone?"

"We were supposed to be undercover."

Alvarez looked at his partner as if checking his take on it.

"We used our martial arts training to knock the men out. Unfortunately Jackson, the ringleader, got away. He had fallen behind. According to his men, he had become ill. He must have reached the camp at some point, seen what had happened to his men, and taken off. If we had been working with the rest of the poachers, we would have taken off in the boat—with the cats."

"So after you knocked them out, you called us and then left?" Alvarez asked.

"We watched over the she-cat and her cubs. Asleep, they were vulnerable. So we made sure only the police and park rangers discovered them. Then when the mother and her little ones were awake, they took off, and we did too."

"But…we didn't see any sign of you."

"We were—"

"Undercover," Alvarez said.

"Right."

"Okay, let's see that ID. But I'll go with you," Alvarez said to Melissa.

Huntley prayed that the cubs stayed hidden and didn't fuss, and that Alvarez didn't start poking around in the bedroom. Melissa rose from the couch, her face pale, totally ill at ease. Where were the cubs? Hell, what if they were sitting on the floor by the bedroom door?

"You have to admit this is all hard to believe," Pantepi said.

"I understand. That's why we have been conducting these undercover missions. We can't catch the bastards in the United States. By then, they've already sold the animals somewhere else. This is the closest we've ever gotten to them. Our job was to catch them in the act with all the evidence present and turn them over to you. Then you could handle the matter. You'd make them serve a sentence in jail here, the cats would still be living in their home, and all would be well."

Huntley was getting ready to shift if he heard any indication that Alvarez had discovered the cubs in the bedroom.

But then he heard Melissa and Alvarez's footfalls on the tile floor in the hallway and glanced in that direction, barely breathing.

Alvarez had their badges and passports and her cell. He handed the badges to his partner. Huntley felt a modicum of relief that the officer hadn't seen or heard the cubs, but Huntley and Melissa weren't out of the jungle yet. Not until the police officers were satisfied and left.

"I'll call the director and we can put it on speakerphone, if you like. You can ask any questions you want of him. All right?" Melissa asked. "If he hears a man on my phone he doesn't know, he's going to think I ended up in the hands of the bad guys. Like you're unsure of our identities, he wouldn't trust yours."

"All right. Call him." Alvarez gave her phone back to her and passed off the passports to his partner.

Huntley prayed this would work.

"Martin, this is Melissa Overton."

Using her full name would clue the director in right away that Huntley and Melissa were in trouble. He would know who she was from his caller ID. Martin was smart and waited to hear what she had to say.

"We're afraid we had to break our cover with a couple of Costa Rican police officers. We had to tell them about the cougar and her cubs that we rescued on the beach. I have this on speakerphone so they can ask you questions."

She handed the phone back to Alvarez. "Hello, sir, this is Alvarez Mendez with the police here in Puerto Jimenez. We found a tranquilizer dart in a tree and assumed that whoever had fired it was poaching animals at Corcovado National Park. And we found a round of ammunition below that. We've gone over records for those visiting the park, and Huntley Anderson and Melissa Overton were listed as having made reservations during both the time when we caught the first poachers and the second time when shots were fired and we discovered the tranquilizer dart and round."

"Yes, and the poachers would not be making reservations at the park," Martin said. "My people obey the restrictions. If we need to get into the park, we call ahead of time and ensure we have the necessary approval."

Alvarez studied Huntley, then Melissa. "Yes, it seems that was all in order. But why didn't you tell us why they were there in the first place?"

"They're special agents who are highly trained to track these men and take them down without killing them."

"But one got away, and according to Mr. Anderson,

he returned to poach again. And got away," Alvarez said, sounding annoyed.

"That couldn't be helped," Huntley said. "After they shot at me, I was out for the count." He had to let the boss know that's what he'd told these men. "Melissa was on her own, and if she'd called the police, then what? They wouldn't have had any evidence against these men. Just her word that Jackson had been at the scene of the first crime. But no real evidence."

"Right," Martin said. "We take the crimes against the animals seriously. The two agents have worked countless missions fighting against these kinds of people. Both Melissa and Huntley are biologists who have worked extensively with big cats—in particular, jaguars—all their lives. They know them as you would know your own family members. All of us at this branch want the same thing—to protect wildlife in their native habitat. We're on the same side in this. Give me the name of your superior and I'll speak with him."

Alvarez gave Martin the number. "I'll call him and he can talk to you," Martin said.

Huntley knew Martin would do so immediately. He had to be as worried as they were that one of the cubs would let out a hair-raising snarl that meant she was hungry. They seemed to need to be fed every few hours, so he hoped that they would continue to sleep as long as the police officers were here. He had heard Melissa close the bedroom door, so at least the cubs couldn't get up and just wander down the hall.

"Would you like something to drink? Tea? Coffee?" Melissa asked as the police officers waited to hear from their boss.

They both shook their heads, thank heavens, and handed the passports and badges back to Huntley. Then they turned Melissa's phone over to her.

They waited what felt like forever, but only a few minutes passed before Alvarez's phone rang and he answered it. "*Sí. Sí.*" He looked at Huntley. "*Sí.*" He raised an objection in Spanish, then tried to explain why they'd come here, while glancing back at Huntley and Melissa. Then he said, "*Sí.*"

Huntley fought smiling. From his expression and reactions, the guy appeared to be in hot water with his boss. Huntley wondered what Martin had said to the police officers' supervisor.

Alvarez quickly rose to his feet. Pantepi joined him, looking concerned.

"*Sí.*" Then he pocketed his phone, wrote a number on a piece of paper, and handed it to Huntley. "If you need to enter the park, just call this number and arrangements will be made right away," he said to Huntley and Melissa. "No reservations needed."

A baby began to cry in the bedroom, and then the other started to wail. Everyone glanced in that direction as if they'd never heard a baby cry, *ever*. What was really bad was that Melissa had just taken the one officer into that same bedroom and there had been no sign of any babies.

Nobody made a move for an instant. Huntley and Melissa's hearts were beating triple time.

"Feeding time," Melissa said, but then waited as if to see if the police officers were done with her.

Huntley could just imagine her bringing out the babies, wrapped in towels, no less, and then all of a sudden they would shift into jaguar cubs.

"Good day," Alvarez said, looking really surprised, just as much as Huntley and Melissa were, that they had a couple of babies on a mission—*undercover*.

Huntley and Melissa weren't just surprised, they were horrified. The mother had to have shifted to cause the babies to shift again.

Alvarez made a beeline exit for the door. "Have a nice day."

Pantepi said in Spanish, "What did he say?"

"We are in trouble. He wants us to report in right away. These people are not to be bothered again under any circumstances or we lose our jobs," he said, also speaking in Spanish as they headed down the stairs.

Huntley hurried to lock the door as Melissa raced to the bedroom.

He stalked down the hall to help her, and when he reached the bedroom, Melissa was holding one of the two naked babies wrapped in a towel. "Here, take Goldie." She handed him the baby, her hair in dark ringlets. And then Melissa picked Sweetpea up off the other towel, her hair darker and straighter, and swaddled her. Both were still crying.

"Their mother," Melissa said, trying to fight tears.

"She might not be dead," Huntley said, holding the baby away from his body, not sure how to handle it. A cub, no problem. The baby was totally dependent on him to keep her safe. "The mother could have just shifted."

"Hold her close, so she doesn't feel like you're going to drop her," Melissa said, frowning at him. He did what she did then, cradling the baby in his arms and then they left the bathroom to feed them, not sure if that's what they needed this time. "Why would the mother shift?" she asked.

"Maybe intending to do what we would do if we were in that predicament. Unlock the cage she must be confined to and escape." At least that's what Huntley hoped had happened. "The husband might have already done so, but we wouldn't have a clue because only the mother's shifting corresponds with her baby's shifting."

"Okay." Melissa had to trust that was the case. She didn't want to believe the cubs had shifted for any other reason, but she was damned glad the police officers had left. "I have to go back to that store. It's the only one I found that had baby articles. They'll have diapers. I should have gotten some at the time, but I didn't think the cubs would shift."

"I keep thinking that the family had to be staying somewhere near the park. If we could locate their rental unit, we could find their passports and baby stuff, and learn who they are."

"That would take time. We know they're not at our resort because ours are the only jaguar scents around here. Most of the places I looked up on the Internet are hotels, and I'm certain this family wouldn't have been running as jaguars through a hotel. So it would be someplace like this that's more of a single unit, isolated from the rest and close to the park." She handed her baby to Huntley, and she swore he was going to panic, not certain he could juggle two squalling babies at once.

She hurried to warm up the bottles of milk.

"They might have had a tent in the rainforest, like we set up," Huntley said, bouncing the babies slightly in his arms to soothe them.

She smiled at him. He was a natural dad. "I thought we were going to be found out when the police officers were here. Did you see the looks on their faces when not one but two babies began to cry?"

"Yeah, I'm certain they were trying to figure that one out—how we could be on a mission and managing two babies at the same time. They were probably dying to ask about that. I couldn't believe that calling Martin worked."

"I just want to know what Martin said to their supervisor." She set the warmed-up bottles on the kitchen counter, relieved Huntley of Goldie, then grabbed a bottle and headed for the living room. Huntley followed her, sat on the couch, and began feeding Sweetpea. But she wasn't feeding. Still, Melissa smiled when the baby looked content to be sitting on his lap. Maybe they'd just been startled by the change into their human forms and needed to be held. "You look like you know what you're doing."

"Might as well get in some practice. When my half sister, Maya, has hers, I might be called on to do baby-sitting duty."

She smiled at him. "I would never have imagined you offering. What would your brother say?"

"Everett would be laughing his head off. My sister? Tammy would be the same way. Of course, I'd have felt the same about my brother if he'd been in my situation. Tammy babysat when she was a teen so she would be ready for it."

"Not me," Melissa said, glancing down at Goldie. She was just mouthing the nipple, not sucking, but like her sister, she seemed happy just to be held. "I figured I wouldn't be handling babies until my sister had some."

"I didn't know that she's seeing someone seriously," Huntley said, surprised.

"She isn't. But when she does, she'll have kids. She's always wanted them."

Melissa's phone went off. "How much do you want to bet it's the boss, and he's going to be just as concerned as we are?"

"Just a tad."

She managed to get to her phone while holding on to the baby, but she set the bottle down because Goldie didn't seem to want to feed again so soon. Melissa decided she wasn't half bad at this.

"Yeah, Martin, the cubs turned into babies."

Silence. Melissa knew that her boss was thinking the worst-case scenario: that in death, the jaguar had shifted in front of human onlookers who just happened to be Costa Rican police officers.

She took a deep breath and let it out. "Are you still there? I just pray the mother is fine. That she just shifted and the babies turned with—"

The babies suddenly shifted from their human forms into cubs.

"Oh, thank God," Melissa said. "They're back to being cubs. At least I hope everything's all right. That the mother wasn't found out. The babies cried when the police officers were here, unfortunately, but they didn't question us about why we had babies on the mission. Just wanted to let you know." She couldn't manage Goldie, who was squirming to get out of the towel. "I'll call you right back." She unwrapped the cub from the towel and carried her into the bathroom so she could use the litter box. Then Melissa remembered that the litter boxes weren't in the bathroom but in the bedroom closet.

She went to retrieve one, then set the cat and box in the bathroom. Then Melissa quickly called Martin back. Huntley joined her and set his charge on the floor, then wrapped his arms around Melissa and hugged her tight. She smiled up at him. This was turning out to be some wild mission.

Melissa put her cell on speakerphone and said, "Martin, what did you say to the police officers?"

"We gave them a million dollars last year to help fund more rangers for their park."

Feeling a bit shocked, she didn't say anything.

"Did we?" Huntley asked.

"Hell yeah, we did. It's the least we can do to help save a habitat where our people can still enjoy the wilderness in our jaguar coats. And your father, Huntley, footed a fourth of the bill. Which I also told the police officers' supervisor. I was down there when we handed over the money, so Gonzalez knows exactly who I am and how important this is to us and to our organization."

"You could have told us," Huntley said.

"We preferred remaining anonymous. Tell one person, and the word gets out. But when we need to use it for leverage, we will. Even so, if the police had found the cubs in your possession, I couldn't have helped you. If they were truly jaguar cubs, you would have handed them over to authorities to care for. Since they aren't, my ploy wouldn't have worked to get you out of that trouble."

"Gotcha. So now what do we do?" Huntley asked.

"Sit tight. Are the cubs doing okay otherwise?"

"Yeah. They're eating well and playing with us," Melissa said. "And as long as no one discovers them here and reports us, we're okay."

"Good. Hold on." Martin talked to someone in the background. "Okay, great." He said to Melissa and Huntley, "Just got word that we have a plane flying in tomorrow at noon. We need you to drive to the private field—figure on three hours to reach it—and we'll get the cubs back to the States. We should be good to go, as long as the two of you don't get caught on the way there. You can come home that way too."

"Wait. What about Jackson and his men?" Melissa asked, wanting to get the bastard. She definitely didn't want to go home until they helped find him and freed the parents.

"We've got teams on it. Okay?" Martin asked. It wasn't a case of getting their approval. He made the rules.

"All right," Melissa said, but she didn't agree with the plan, and she was fairly certain he could hear the irritation in her tone of voice. "Are you going to have someone come along to take care of the cubs?"

"I thought you were doing a great job of it." She heard a hint of a smile in Martin's words. "Yeah, of course. I'm sending a couple of Guardian agents. Brother-and-sister team. They'll take care of the cubs until we can bring the parents home."

"Good," she said, totally relieved because she had other plans.

When they ended the call, Huntley said, "I know you have something in mind. Why else would you ask if someone else was coming to take care of the cubs? What are you thinking?"

"We're here already. We return to the park as jaguars and stay there, living off the land until we can track Jackson down, if he returns to the rainforest. Let him take us to the couple. If he hasn't already sold them off."

"That's damn risky and there are a lot of ifs," Huntley said. "Discounting any trouble, we drop off the cubs with the pilot and the Guardian agents, and then return to the cabana, leave our gear, and head into the rainforest that night? We'd have to let Martin know, just in case we don't make it back. It would be bad if four of us needed to be rescued and no one had any clue where any of us were taken, and then we were separated and shipped off to God knows where."

She nodded. "We have to do whatever we can to return the couple to their cubs and take down Jackson at the same time. We're here and too close not to see this through. I don't understand why Martin would want to pull us from the task."

"Maybe he thinks we're too close to the situation. Too emotionally tied to it." Huntley shook his head. "Hell, Oliver thought you were in danger on these missions? *You* are dangerous."

She smiled up at him. "Is that a problem for you?"

"Hell, no. I'll grab the other litter box out of the bedroom." Once he was done, he said, "We need to make sure that we have a more foolproof way to ensure Jackson returns to the rainforest."

She straightened out the towels for the cubs, then closed the door to the bathroom so they'd go back to sleep. "We've still got Phil and Eloise's phones. What if we have 'Phil' text him? Say he arrived late because he got into a fracas with the police. Tell Jackson that he plans to meet him at that beach late that night. And you and I are there instead—as jaguars. Jackson wouldn't be able to resist capturing us."

What if when Phil was accidentally released from jail, he came down here? What if he wants the money for the job of poaching some more animals, and Jackson doesn't know anything about his sister?"

"Lots of ifs, Huntley. If Phil is down here, we'll grab him too."

"What if I am the only one running as a jaguar, and you call it in?" Huntley said, sounding suspiciously like he didn't want her to go with him on that part of the mission.

"Call it in to the rangers? Ha! By the time they got there, Jackson and his men would have taken off with you. Same if I called Martin. It would be way too late."

"There's no way for Martin to track us either. That would be the best way to go about this," Huntley said.

"Okay, so we let him take both of us, because we have a better chance of rescuing ourselves if there are two of us. We're highly trained JAG agents, after all."

"What if Jackson thinks Phil's call is a trick?"

"He'll probably arrive there early."

"Or he won't come. We need to have someone watching our backs," Huntley said. "We need to have a team down here ready to free us if everything goes bad."

"Okay, so who's down here now?"

Huntley got on the phone to Martin. "We have an alternate plan."

Chapter 12

"MARTIN CAN'T SAY NO," MELISSA SAID TO HUNTLEY later that afternoon as they made a lunch of casado, a traditional Costa Rican meal of rice and beans, meat, salad, tortillas, and plantains.

They were still pondering how they would allow Jackson to capture them as jaguars in the park. One thing Melissa loved about her boss was that he was always willing to listen to suggestions from his field agents. She and Huntley were in the field and well aware of their capabilities and limitations. They knew that this job came with a lot of risks. But they had to do something. Every hour that went by meant Jackson could be moving the jaguars and selling them off. And then tracking them down could be a real nightmare.

Some places that bought the big cats didn't care for them properly, and the cats could die. If that happened? A shifter dying in a cage in front of a bunch of onlookers and then turning into his human form, unable to keep his jaguar form in death, would be a disaster. Not to mention that a pair of cubs could lose their mom or dad.

"We'll do it, Melissa. We just have to come up with a plan that Martin can live with. He doesn't want to lose us." Huntley carried the dishes to the small wooden kitchen table and they took their seats.

"And if we can't come up with a plan that works for him?"

"Then we do it our way. But I still believe we need

to nail down how we're going to carry this out without getting ourselves into a fine mess. What if other poachers grab us instead? We would be nowhere near rescuing the other shifters, and we'd have a time rescuing ourselves," Huntley said, digging into his casado. He took his first bite and looked like he was in heaven.

She smiled, loving that he enjoyed her cooking and that he enjoyed letting her know it.

"Okay, so what if some of our teams spread the word that jaguars have been spotted at the beach where Jackson and his friends tried to escape with the puma and her cubs? We could have someone with the agency say that he is looking to buy a male and female jaguar he assumes are courting. That he has witnessed the cats three times on the same beach. And he knows they've claimed the territory. He could give them all the facts about jaguars, showing he's a real expert in the field, so that's why he knows what he's talking about. At dusk, we could put on a jaguar courting show on the beach, acting all lovey-dovey, in the event Jackson comes to check out the agent's story."

"I could really get into that role." He gave her a sexy wink, then ate more of his meal.

She chuckled. She had never imagined a mission where she would pretend to court a jaguar in the wild for the benefit of poachers. "Jaguars that are mating also stay together during the female's pregnancy. So the agent, acting as the buyer, states that he assumes that the female might already be pregnant with one to four cubs. She wouldn't be having them for ninety-five to a hundred-and-ten days, but he doesn't know how far along she is, if she's pregnant.

"Breeding big cats in captivity isn't very successful,

and he could let Jackson know this. I read about one pair that has been bred successfully three times in captivity, which is really rare, and they sell the cubs each time—once they're old enough. So we could have an agent posing as a buyer, looking to get a pair of jaguars that are courting in the wild and see if they will have a better success rate at breeding them in captivity. Not to mention that this courting couple of jaguars—us—might already have a litter on the way."

Huntley smiled at Melissa. "I think we've got our plan. Then when Jackson goes to sell the jaguars—us—to the buyer, the agents swoop in on him and his buddies, and if our mom and dad shifters have already been sold, we force Jackson to tell us where they've gone."

"With any means available to us."

"You got that right," Huntley said.

They finished eating lunch and Huntley said, "You call Martin with the new plan of action. I'll clean up the dishes."

She pulled out her phone, gave Huntley a kiss on the cheek, and called Martin.

"Okay, here's our new plan."

And he'd better damn well like it. She feared time was running out to catch up with the parents before real disaster struck. If the couple was trying to rescue themselves and got caught, what would the poachers think? Not that they'd caught a couple of shape-shifting jaguars, but that they had two naked humans who, for whatever crazy reason, had let their jaguars go—and then? The poachers would kill them.

Tomorrow, after they left the cubs with the Guardians who would care for them on the flight home, Huntley and Melissa had every intention of heading back into the rainforest. They didn't want to risk waiting for the word to get out and hoping Jackson heard that a buyer was looking to pick up a male and female mating jaguar pair that frequented one of the beaches. That said buyer had witnessed them and wanted to have them captured because he didn't have any way to do so himself. Melissa and Huntley hoped that if they visited the beach at night, the word might get back to Jackson that way.

Martin wasn't happy about their plan, but he didn't have a better one. He said he'd have men accompany them. The agents would arrive on the plane carrying the Guardians who would pick up the cubs.

Now, there wasn't anything to do but wait for tomorrow morning.

Huntley gathered Melissa up in his arms and said, "Martin went along with our plan, at least."

"Very reluctantly. I'm certain he's worried about us," she said, kissing his lips.

"Hell, yeah. *I'm* worried about us," Huntley said, then kissed her back, tongue in her mouth and exploring, his body pressed against hers, his arousal growing.

She smiled, ready to take this back to bed.

Then her phone rang, instantly stoking her ire. "Our boss better not be changing his mind." She answered it and heard Oliver's voice instead. She was so surprised that she said, "Oliver?" As if it couldn't be him, and she had to verify it.

Huntley immediately frowned at her, like he believed her ex-boyfriend was trying to make up to her. More likely, he wanted to remind her to pick up her stuff soon.

"I think I might have found your couple." Oliver sounded excited.

Melissa's heart skipped a beat. "Wait, let me put this on speaker." She couldn't believe it!

Oliver paused and she was afraid he didn't want to share the information with Huntley, but she wanted her partner to hear the same thing she heard.

"Oliver?"

"Well, I wasn't sure it was them. But they took out a life insurance policy for their kids, and the twins are two months old. They were adamant that if anything happened to them, they'd have money set aside for their baby girls."

Melissa barely breathed. "Yeah, go on." *Get to the bottom line*. He was always this way when talking about insurance and his clients, and it drove her nuts.

"Okay, so I called their house. I got an answering machine. I tried to text them. No response."

"Wait, I wonder if they camped in the rainforest and their stuff is still out there," she said. Not that they could go searching for it and leave the infants behind—or take them with them and risk running into trouble.

"That might be," Oliver said. "Okay, so I'm still not certain it was them. I called the man's sister, who also came in and signed up for a policy, and told her that I learned a couple had disappeared at the park and that you were taking care of their babies."

Melissa took a deep, calming breath.

"She broke into tears. She said she knew it was too early for them to take the babies to the Amazon. That they should have had a bunch of family members go with them to watch their backs."

"Wait. Amazon?"

"Yeah, wrong rainforest."

Huntley was grinning.

Melissa could just strangle Oliver. She punched Huntley in the shoulder. Not hard, but jeez. This is what drove her crazy about Oliver. He had to tell her every detail of whatever he had been doing before he ever got to the point.

"So the sister verified that they had taken a trip to Columbia, not Costa Rica."

"Airlines? Everything?" Melissa asked, still wondering if they'd changed their minds and booked a flight and made reservations in Costa Rica instead.

"Yes. They were on the flight, got there fine, and they're headed back today."

"I thought you knew who they were." She was so exasperated that she might have growled.

Huntley took her in his arms and rubbed her back.

"Okay, yeah, the sister was angry with me for upsetting her unnecessarily, but then she realized that another couple was out there and in danger. She said that her brother's daughters stayed at a day care sometimes—jaguar shifters only. And so she gave me the information. I called the day care and spoke to the owner. I told her the bind the JAG branch was in while trying to determine who the missing parents were."

Melissa held her breath again. "Tell me you got the right names this time."

"I did. Avery and Kathy Carrington. The girls' names are Jaime and Jenny. The woman at the day care said that the girls wouldn't be returning until the end of next week. Kathy had told the woman that they'd be at the same park as the shifters were taken from, and they would have been there at the same time as their disappearance. She was horrified, of course, and wished you all the best and offered to do anything she could to help."

"Ohmigod, thank you so much, Oliver. You're a godsend," Melissa said, smiling. "I've got to call my boss. Thanks so much, and…I'll let you know when we have some resolution." Melissa loved Oliver for having helped them on this mission. She immediately called Martin.

"Oliver Strickland, my ex-boyfriend, called to tell me he believes Avery and Kathy Carrington are the cubs' parents. The girls are Jaime and Jenny."

"Amen to that," Martin said. "I'll have agents right on it. Call you back ASAP."

"Thanks!"

Melissa hugged Huntley. "I can't wait until the cubs are home safely."

"You and me both."

She was going to ask Huntley what they should do now when Martin called back again. "We have the location of the family's bungalow. It's five miles from where you are. I need one of you to pack up their belongings and store them at your place so that when the plane comes tomorrow, their things can be shipped off with the cubs."

"Okay, will do."

When she ended the call, she said, "I'll run over there."

"Wait. Don't you want more time to bond with the kids?" Huntley asked, sounding like he really hoped he'd get out of cub-sitting duty for a while.

She grinned at him, patted his chest, and reminded him, "Maya will likely have her kids before my sister does—since she doesn't even have a steady boy-friend—so you'll need all the practice you can get."

He kissed her thoroughly. "Don't get caught."

"I won't." Then she headed out with every intention of doing what Martin had asked, pronto, hoping she wouldn't run into any trouble with the management there when she tried to remove the Carringtons' things.

Huntley hadn't wanted to make a big deal of it, but he was concerned about Melissa, just as he knew she'd be concerned about him if he had left her alone with the cubs. Anything could go wrong, as they were learning on this mission. He was glad to have a partner who was as flexible as she was and could handle a crisis effi-ciently, though. He still admired her greatly for how she had managed to get him, the cubs, and their gear all back to the cabana in one piece when he'd been half out of it.

Then the babies began to cry, not snarl like they should have if they were cubs, and he nearly lost it. Sick with worry about their mother, he rushed to the bath-room to take care of the babies. He paused midway to the bathroom and realized he needed to get the bottles first. They hadn't eaten the last time they'd turned, and it had been about four hours.

He wanted to call Melissa, but he couldn't worry her about the mother when she had a job to do. Man, he wished he had insisted she stay home and be their momma while he took care of the family's personal effects.

He called Martin as he stalked into the kitchen and began warming up the milk. "Hey, boss, Melissa's on her way to get the Carringtons' things, but bad news. The cubs turned into babies again."

Chapter 13

WHEN MELISSA ARRIVED AT THE CARRINGTONS' resort, she explained to the manager at the lodge how Mr. Carrington's boss, Martin Sullivan, had sent her to pick up their things and ship them home due to a sudden family illness. Of course, Martin wasn't Mr. Carrington's boss, but that was the only way they could get the Carringtons' personal belongings. Thankfully, Martin had already called the management and the police to ensure things would go smoothly. She loved how Huntley hadn't tried to talk her out of switching places and just smiled knowingly at her.

The cubs would probably sleep until she got back anyway. Though it was getting to be about feeding time again.

The manager was grateful because Martin hadn't asked for a refund for the rest of the family's time at the resort. Keys in hand, she headed for the correct bungalow and thought she heard rustling inside. At first, she believed someone had broken into the place. Her second notion was more hopeful. The couple, or at least one of them, had made it safely back to the bungalow.

She made lots of noise as she approached the front door—better to let thieves know she was coming and give them a chance to run off, or if it was one or both of the parents, to give them a heads-up that she was paying them a visit.

It got really quiet inside, then she heard a window open on the backside of the bungalow. She told herself if it was thieves, she'd let it go. She wasn't here to apprehend anyone. On the other hand, her agency training prepared her for any eventuality. Letting the bad guys go wasn't part of her psyche *or* her agent teaching. Passports were one of the biggest income makers for thieves, and who knew what else they might have grabbed at the Carringtons' bungalow. The couple had already had enough of a time of it, and she wanted to thwart the burglars for that reason alone.

She raced around the side of the bungalow through the thick foliage and saw two men wearing field packs as they dove into the vegetation. She wished she had on her jaguar coat. Then this would have been a really easy task, though catching thieves in a resort in her jaguar form wasn't the thing to do. At times like these, she wished the rest of the world knew that jaguar shifters existed and accepted them for what they were.

She ran to catch up to the first man trailing behind and leaped on his back, throwing him off balance. He fell sideways and hit the ground. With a swift kick to the head, as effective as if she'd been a jaguar and sliced at him with her wickedly strong forelegs, she knocked him out. Then she dashed after the other man who was still running through the vegetation, breathing heavily under the weight of the stuff he'd stolen—maybe from several bungalows, not just the one.

She was nearly upon him when he turned and saw she wasn't his comrade in crime, but only a woman. He had the nerve to cast an evil smile at her, as if he thought he could take care of her quickly and be on his way. She had to admit that she didn't like it when he went for a knife in the sheath at his belt.

Not waiting for him to withdraw it, she grabbed his shoulders and brought her knee up hard into his groin.

His body was bent over as he clutched his crotch, groaning. She slammed her knee into his nose and heard a crunch, breaking it. Last time he'd ever think any girl was an easy target.

He was holding his nose when she did the sidekick to the head that meant lights out.

She rolled him over, yanked off the bag he was carrying, unzipped it, and found maybe a dozen or so passports, credit cards, cash, a couple of iPods, and four cell phones. Nice haul. She quickly searched through them and got the Carringtons' credit cards and passports and other items that she could smell belonged to them, then checked the other bag. More stuff—iPods, watches, a couple of gold bracelets. None of that belonged to the Carringtons. Everything else, she left in the bags to turn over to the manager.

She hauled the bags to the Carringtons' bungalow first, knocked—as if anyone would be home, but it was a case of habit—then unlocked it and went inside. The place had been left undisturbed, and the thieves seemed to have tried to hide the fact they had been there. She left all the Carringtons' things on the kitchen table, locked up, and headed over to the lodge to turn over the bags.

She hated to do anything but pack the Carringtons' stuff up and leave, but she had to let the manager know about the bad guys and turn over the rest of the stolen merchandise. As she entered the lodge, he glanced up from reading a paper. "*Sí?*"

She plunked the two bags on the counter and explained that two men had tried to steal all these things. She was an agent with a special U.S. unit and had managed to knock the two men out. The manager stared at her like she was crazy.

She started pulling out the passports in one of the bags. "Some of your guests'?"

He started to compare the names with his guest list and then got on the phone immediately to notify the police.

"I have to go. I've got to pack up the Carringtons' things and leave." And Melissa had to get back to poor Huntley. She imagined the cubs were ready to feed, and trying to take care of two at once was cumbersome. As soon as they realized the bottles meant milk, neither wanted to wait for the other to get her fair share.

"No, no, you must stay and talk with police."

Great. They could take forever to get there. "I'll be at the Carringtons' bungalow packing their things then." She called Huntley as she headed back to their place. He didn't answer the phone until the third try, so she assumed he was having a time of it.

"What's taking you so long?" he asked, sounding totally frazzled.

She heard babies crying in the background.

"*No*," she said, entering the bungalow and shutting the door. Every time the cubs turned into babies, she feared the worse for the mother. "I…had to take down some thieves. They were in the Carringtons' bungalow. Now I've got to wait on the police before I can leave."

"You're okay, not injured, right?" He sounded like

he needed help—poor guy. But he also sounded really concerned that she might have been hurt.

She was glad she was here and not there. "Yeah. I'm fine. The men I took down aren't." She sighed. "But I'm going to be here for a while longer. Can you manage all right?"

"Do I have a choice?"

She smiled as she began to pack up the Carringtons' things. "Sorry," she said again.

"Next time, I want the easy job," he said.

She chuckled. Then she heard a cub snarl and sighed with relief. "I found diapers and more bottles, baby clothes, and other baby supplies. We'll be all set if they shift again."

"Only if you're here with me."

She laughed. "I don't know. They might have to put this on your résumé at work. If anyone needs a rescue that includes cub- or babysitting, you could be…"

She paused as she looked through one of the drawers filled with socks and boxers.

"What's wrong?" Huntley asked, his voice dark.

"There's something stuffed in a sock. Wait a minute." She set the phone down on the dresser and dug into the sock, having a hard time pulling whatever it was out without using both hands. She grabbed her phone. "It's a badge."

"Badge," Huntley parroted.

"Yeah." She stared at it in disbelief as she flipped it open and read the name and branch. "Says he's one of us."

"We don't have a Carrington in our organization that I know of."

"Not with our branch. He's an Avenger." They were like jaguar-shifter assassins and took out the trash, meaning they were sent in after the bad guys and they never took prisoners. Highly trained Special Ops. "Calling it in to Martin. They lead double lives, so this might be an alias."

"With a couple of kids? And a wife?"

"No telling. I'll call it in." She was about to hang up on Huntley when she heard a car pull up and peeked out the window. "Ah, hell," she said as she saw the police car park outside the bungalow and the same two police officers who had grilled her and Huntley before. "The police—our buddies—just arrived. I'll be home soon."

"You take care of yourself, Melissa," Huntley warned, sounding like he'd fix her good if she got herself into a real mess that left him dealing with the jaguar-shifter babies on his own for the duration.

"Yeah, talk later. Good luck." She quickly called Martin, "Can't talk but had to call. Carrington is with the Avengers branch. Got to talk to the police. Call back as soon as I can."

As soon as she hung up, she realized she hadn't had time to tell him why she had to speak with the police. She sighed, then pocketed her cell phone, tucked Carrington's badge into her pocket, and greeted the police officers outside. They looked horrified to see her, probably having thought she was some sweet little American woman who had run into thieves, not the agent who had helped Huntley take out five poachers. She smiled brightly, trying to lessen their fear that they'd be in trouble with their boss again because they had to speak with her *again*.

She explained what had happened as she led them to where the two men were beginning to regain consciousness.

The police quickly took the thieves in hand. Then she asked if she could go.

"These two were some of the poachers you were after?" Alvarez asked, frowning at her.

"Not that I know of. They were just stealing from a bungalow and I caught them at it. The bags with the evidence in them are with the manager of the resort."

The police officers exchanged looks and appeared to want to ask her more questions, but then maybe thinking better of it—after their boss had chewed them out the last time—they let her go. She hurried to finish packing the Carringtons' bags, then loaded them in her rental car.

As soon as she got on the road, the rain started again, and she hoped she wouldn't have trouble getting back to Huntley. Most of all, she hoped they wouldn't have any trouble getting the kids back home.

When she reached their cabana, she called Martin, but he was still having a talk with the head of the Avengers branch. She'd have to check in with him later, but she let him know she'd gotten all the stuff from the Carringtons' bungalow and explained why the police had wanted to talk to her. When she entered their bungalow, Huntley was mopping up his T-shirt in the kitchen. She noted small tears in the blue cotton fabric and no sign of the cubs.

"Asleep," he said, anticipating her question.

"Good. Did they get *anything* to eat?" she asked as he went outside in the rain and helped her with the rest of the Carringtons' bags.

He cast her an amused look.

"You appear to be wearing quite a bit of *their* milk," she said, in case he didn't get her point as she eyed his shirt again. It was dripping wet from the rain now too, but she could still see the splotches of milk. And the little tears in his shirt? Jaguar-cub claw tears. Guaranteed.

He shut the door to the cabana, dropped the bags on the kitchen floor, and locked the door. She saw the glint in his eye, and before she could prepare herself, he pounced. All she managed to do was drop the bags in her hands onto the floor. In one giant step, he grabbed her up. She squealed, never expecting anything like this, and laughed. She loved it.

He tossed her over his shoulder and stalked back to the bedroom.

"What do you think you're doing?"

"I've had enough babysitting duty. It's time for some grown-up action."

An hour later, Melissa and Huntley were half dozing, feeling blissfully sated, and she was again wondering if it could work out for them in the long run when Martin called Melissa. She figured he was calling her instead of Huntley on this mission because she was nearly always the one calling him. "Did you learn anything about Carrington?" she asked, climbing out of bed and snagging a T-shirt, then turning the phone on speaker.

Huntley threw on a pair of boxers, joined her in the kitchen, and took the phone from her while she looked in the fridge to fix them dinner.

"Yeah, he's definitely one of the Avengers. No one

knew he was at the park. He was on vacation with his family, as far as we know. Here are pictures of his family in jaguar form so you can identify the parents when you reach them and not let the wrong jaguars out of their cages if Jackson has any more locked up."

She released the fridge door and joined Huntley to look at the pictures. "Is the Carrington name an alias?" she asked.

"No, that's truly his family," Martin said.

"Okay. We're all set for tomorrow? Kids get picked up, and then Huntley and I hit the beaches as jaguars?"

"Yeah, not that I like the plan. I'm still worried some other poachers will attempt to pick the two of you up. The word has gone out to all the small villages and towns about your sightings to let anyone who has done this before know to get in touch with the buyer. But he insists on someone with experience and references. No new guys who could end up killing the two of you by accident."

"Nothing doing," Melissa said. "If the wrong guys come for us, we'll take care of them. We know what Jackson looks like and what he smells like." Not that she liked the idea of getting shot, even if just by a tranquilizer dart. The wrong amount of tranquilizer could kill either her or Huntley.

"If I could, I'd have one of my men insert GPS implants under your skin. But until they come up with the technology, that's out. GPS collars would be highly suspect. All we can do is watch your backs and help you take out anyone who might try to grab you and is not affiliated with Jackson. And call in the particulars about the boat and the direction it takes when they carry you off. Hopefully, and that's a big hope, Jackson will be the only one who will make the effort to grab you and transport you to where he's got the other cats. Then you can free them and take the bastard and his cohorts down."

"That's the plan," she said, hoping to hell it all worked. They ended the call. That night, she and Huntley ate dinner, played with the cubs, fed them, and figured they would miss the little tykes after they sent them on their way. They planned to get a good night's sleep because the next day and that night, they wouldn't have any time. Sleep. That's all. At least that *was* the plan.

"Are you awake?" Huntley asked before dawn, kissing Melissa on the top of her head.

"Hmm, yeah. Going to be a long day and a longer night."

"Yeah. Are you ready for it?"

The cubs began to "rawl" in the bathroom. She chuckled. "As ready as I'll ever be. But first things first. Time to feed the munchkins."

Still, he kissed her again before releasing her, and she didn't want to let him go any more than he seemed to want to let her go.

They were heading back into danger, and her worry about getting caught while transporting the cubs to the airport, and then the next phase of their mission, made her want to enjoy this special time with Huntley a little longer.

With reluctance, they both got out of bed. After dressing, feeding the cubs, and having a big breakfast to sustain Huntley and herself for the day, they packed the rental car in the pouring rain with all the kids' stuff and the rest of the family's things before loading the cubs into the car.

"Are you ready?" Huntley asked as they made sure one last time that they had everything.

"Yeah." She felt a little sad that she'd have to see the cubs go, but she also was really apprehensive that they still might get caught with the cubs in hand. Then *they* would look like the poachers.

Huntley embraced her, then kissed her. "Okay, let's do this. Then we can rescue Mom and Dad."

True. Until they had their hands free of the cubs, they really were stuck there.

It was still dark out, the rain coming down in buckets, and—Melissa realized—getting the cubs to the airstrip was going to be a job. They didn't have a cage for them. "Okay, who gets to sit in the backseat with the cubs?" She figured that was the best way to handle this.

"I'll drive," he said, smiling, then carried Sweetpea outside to the car while she took Goldie.

She was fine with it, preferring to play with the cubs while he drove in all this bad weather.

Once she was in the backseat, he handed Sweetpea to her, then shut the door.

They had filled all the bottles. The Carringtons had a small ice chest that they must have used to keep the bottles of milk cold on trips. Huntley had filled it with ice that he had made the night before for their trip home. She'd thought to grab towels to dry the cubs off and to cover them in an emergency.

"Quit biting," Melissa said, laughing.

"Are they giving you a hard time?" Huntley asked, a smile in his voice as he drove onto the rutted road.

"I'm trying to dry them off and they're biting me, the towel, and each other. They're just too cute. Who would have ever thought a simple job would be so much work. Oh, darn," Melissa said.

"What?" Huntley asked, worried they'd forgotten something of grave importance.

"I meant to grab the comforter."

"It would have gotten soaked."

"To cover these two in case we ran into traffic on the road when it gets a little lighter. I can see them popping their heads up in the window and getting us both in real hot water."

"Will the towels work?"

"Some." She rustled around in the backseat, pulling off her rain jacket. "I'll use this too. They're rambunctious this morning and not ready to settle down."

"All right. I'll warn you when I see traffic coming."

To their advantage, it poured the entire time they drove to the airstrip. They couldn't risk going to a big airport, and he hoped the plane could manage on this field, given the bad weather.

The car had slid on the wet, rough roads a number of times, and the craters were tricky to navigate in the dark and rain. He could both sense and smell Melissa's anxiousness. Though he was glad she was in the back with the cubs, noting that she had given him the choice and didn't object when he had wanted to drive. She was laughing and playing with them still, enjoying their antics, and he knew she needed this special time with them to say good-bye.

He realized just how much he enjoyed seeing her like this and was glad his brother, Everett, hadn't been here with him instead. He could imagine the two of them fumbling through this. Besides, pretending to be courting Melissa as a jaguar would appeal to Huntley, if locating the jaguar-shifter parents wasn't the reason they had to do it.

They'd driven about an hour when he realized it was finally quiet in the backseat. He glanced back and saw Melissa stretched out, her eyes closed as she slept, and the cubs sleeping on her stomach, the towels half covering them. He smiled a little at her. Yeah, this wasn't anything like he'd expected. Then he sobered. The worst wasn't over yet.

Two hours later, they finally reached the airstrip and then had to wait. Rainforest surrounded them except for the road to the airstrip and the runway for the planes. As soon as Huntley parked the vehicle, the cubs stirred.

Melissa groaned and sat up. "We've got to get the litter box for them."

"I'll open the trunk and let them use it in there. They might get a little wet, but better than us trying to do this in the backseat of the car."

"I almost wish they were babies wearing diapers about now," Melissa said, stroking the cubs.

"Each form has its advantages and disadvantages." Huntley opened the trunk and the lid of one of the litter boxes, then returned to take Goldie, the more awake of the two cubs, from Melissa. "Don't let her sister do anything before I come back for her."

Huntley and Melissa knew the cubs' names now, but not which was which, and calling them by their real names hadn't helped them identify them either. Both answered to either name. So they stuck to the nicknames.

Melissa snorted. "Maybe we should switch roles, and you stop a cub from having to go to the bathroom. Just tell yours to hurry up."

He chuckled with Goldie in hand and took her to the trunk. She quickly used the litter box, and he returned her to Melissa and traded off.

After that, Huntley joined Melissa in the backseat and they took the opportunity to feed the cubs, holding them, talking to them, laughing, and playing with them one last time. He loved this incredibly unusual time he'd spent with Melissa and the cubs, and tried not to worry about what would happen if anyone caught them with the cubs before they were airborne.

Over the sound of thunder and the rain, they finally heard the rumble of the plane.

"Yes! Thank God," Melissa said.

Their salvation. Until they got themselves into the next mess.

The plane landed, taxied, and finally pulled to a stop fifty yards away. Huntley and Melissa waited, burying Jaime and Jenny in the towels and their rain jackets. The cubs settled down to sleep between them as if this was their new den.

Neither Melissa nor Huntley wanted to approach the plane. What if it wasn't the right one?

Melissa's cell rang and she fumbled to get it. "Yes?" Melissa put it on speakerphone.

"I'm Katrina Sorenson. My brother, Matt Sorenson, and I are here with the Guardian branch. We see your vehicle. Are the cubs all right?"

"Yes, we just fed them. We have litter boxes for them too," Melissa said.

Huntley suspected the Sorensons had everything ready for the little ones and wouldn't need anything Melissa and he had brought with them. But the towels would go with them, kind of as security blankets, the smells of Huntley and Melissa on them to reassure the cubs on the flight back to the States. Melissa had thought to bring out some of their mother's and father's clothes to let the cubs smell the scents on them, but she'd been afraid that they might start crying for their parents. Huntley had agreed.

Now he thought she looked sad, her teeth clenched a little like she was fighting tears. Like she was giving away her daughters and all their belongings to perfect strangers. She might say her sister was next in line to have children, but he thought Melissa was ready for them.

Katrina said, "You stay there in the car where it's dry. We're coming to you."

They watched as three men and a woman got out of the plane. They stalked through the rain, the two men, blonds, the couple both dark haired. The two men must have been the ones sent to watch Huntley and Melissa's backs.

Katrina reached into the driver's side of the car and popped the trunk lid. Huntley was about to help the men haul the stuff to the plane, but Katrina said, "They've got it. We'll give the cubs the best of care, and you can bring their parents home to them."

"Yes," Melissa said.

"Jason and Luke Whittaker are here to watch your backs. They wanted to be the ones to take down

Jackson once they learned that their fellow Avenger agent and his mate were taken hostage, but Martin has the lead on this because he's worked the case all along. All the branches are working together, though," Katrina said, looking from them to the cubs, who were poking their heads out from under the towels and jackets, curious who the new voice belonged to.

"You've both done a remarkable job with them." She gave Melissa and Huntley a bright smile. "I don't think we've ever had a case quite like this. Your boss has been keeping all the branches alerted with updates. When you learned who the cubs belonged to, cheers went up all over the Guardian branch headquarters."

"I bet that happened at all the branches," Melissa said.

"Yeah. There will be even more when we get these babies home—and their mother and father too," Katrina said.

As soon as Katrina's brother joined them, they were ready to take the cubs.

One of the other men closed the trunk lid, then the two Whittaker brothers stood on either side of the car, waiting for instructions.

After hugging Jaime and Jenny one more time, Huntley and Melissa handed them over.

"Let us know how they're doing, Katrina," Melissa said as she pulled on her rain jacket and Huntley grabbed his and did the same thing.

They both got out of the car, making way for the two Avenger agents to climb into the backseat.

The woman glanced at Huntley as if she understood how Melissa was feeling, but Melissa and Huntley had other priorities and the cubs were now under the Guardians' care and going home safely.

"As soon as you're off the mission, I'm sure they'll love to see you," Katrina said. Then she and her brother said good-bye and headed to the plane with the cubs.

Huntley should have returned to their cabana immediately because they needed to grab their gear, let the Whittaker brothers dump whatever they didn't need, and then hike into the park. But he couldn't. He was certain Melissa also wanted to see the plane take off for home before they returned to the cabana.

Jason and Luke Whittaker were blue-eyed blonds, sitting quietly in the back. He sensed their tension, wariness, and anger. He could understand how they felt. He felt the same when any of their kind was harmed in any way. Having a father and a new mother with infants involved made it all more difficult.

As soon as the plane disappeared, he heard Melissa sniffle. Huntley turned and saw the tears cascading down her cheeks. "Ah, honey," he said and tried to take her into his arms to give her a hug, but the console made that difficult. "They'll be just fine. They'll be so much safer back home."

"I know," she said, her words choked with tears. "But...I'll miss them."

"Yeah, me too, but don't you ever say I said so to anyone in the branch."

In the backseat, the Whittaker brothers chuckled. They were so quiet that Huntley had nearly forgotten they were there.

Melissa smiled a little at Huntley, then frowned. "Let's get their parents back and get rid of some poachers."

"I'm all for it."

They talked about the rain and what they would do if one scenario happened or another. Both the brothers were eager to kill a bunch of poachers, but Huntley reminded them, "We have to ensure that we don't kill Jackson and his men. We need to be taken to their compound. If we have trouble, you can't kill anyone else either. Call the park rangers and they'll take care of it. Knock the bad guys out, handcuff them, and that's it."

"That's not in our mission statement," Jason said.

Yeah, Huntley knew all about the Avengers' mission statement. Kill 'em dead. No second chances for scum like this.

Truth be told, Huntley suspected that's how this mission would end for the poachers anyway. He wasn't taking any chances with Melissa's or the Carringtons' lives just to protect the men who had endangered all their kind.

Chapter 14

Melissa and Huntley decided they would take two tents into the rainforest, along with some of their gear. The Whittaker brothers would leave the rest of their possessions at Huntley and Melissa's cabana. And if all went as planned, the Whittakers would pack up Melissa and Huntley's stuff in the rainforest, return it to the cabana, and wait to learn where they were being taken once they were captured as jaguars. Then they would help provide them transportation out of there.

The guys really didn't talk much, and Melissa was glad to have them at their backs, but their presence bothered her somewhat because she enjoyed her private time with Huntley more and more.

She didn't think that would have concerned her so much before, when she and Huntley were each seeing someone else. Everything was different now between them. She hoped that wouldn't cause problems on the next phase of their mission.

Packed and ready to go, Melissa and Huntley led the way, remaining in human form while hiking to the park. When they reached the ranger's station, the park ranger immediately contacted his supervisor to tell him that the JAG agents had returned with a couple more agents to back them up.

Then the ranger offered to send assistance.

"One of us will call you if we catch any more

poachers," Melissa said before anyone else spoke. She was glad that the Whittaker brothers stayed in the background and let them take the lead. Either the boss had insisted, or they realized that Melissa and Huntley had gone down this road before and knew what they were doing.

When the ranger looked like that wasn't the answer he wanted to hear, because this *was* their jurisdiction, she said, "We might not come across anyone for a few days, if ever. Could all be a waste of time. Plus, the more of us there are, the more likely they will see us before we see them. If they're spooked, none of us would catch them in the act."

The ranger nodded then, agreeing, and she hated that she spoke the truth. That they might never catch up to Jackson or his men.

It was dusk when they reached the beach where she and Huntley would roam as jaguars. The rain had stopped earlier in the afternoon, and they'd grabbed a quick bite to eat then. Huntley and Melissa made up their tent. Inside, they hugged and kissed each other one last time before they ditched their clothes. Melissa could smell Huntley's apprehension. She didn't think it was because he was concerned about being captured, but about her being hurt. She worried just as much for both of them.

She rested her forehead against his, their bodies pressed tight. "Let's do this," she said softly.

"Don't take any unnecessary risks," he said, looking down into her eyes with such concern that she sighed and hugged him again.

"Ditto, Huntley."

And then they released each other and shifted into their jaguar forms. They waited a moment, listening to make sure that no humans were approaching their location. Satisfied no one was, she and Huntley left the tent. She leaped into a nearby tree and Huntley joined her. They watched while the Whittaker brothers packed their stuff and hid all their gear in another tree while Melissa and Huntley waited, ever watchful and wary, listening for sounds of other humans while the monkeys howled, the insects buzzed, and the birds chattered.

Now the Avenger agents knew what Melissa and Huntley looked like in their spotted coats. She figured the two of them would be easy to recognize anyway. There were not that many black jaguars. And even if Huntley had been a golden color, they would stand out for the courtship reason alone.

She and Huntley leaped down from the tree and loped the short distance to the beach. As soon as they left the rainforest, they began to explore the beach, looking and listening and smelling for any signs of Jackson and his men. Wearing green camo gear, Jason and Luke stayed hidden in the vegetation bordering the beach and watched them at all times.

She felt apprehensive, unable to shake the fear of being tranquilized and hauled off to God knew where. Even though she wanted to do this, and would do anything that would help them to free the Carringtons as soon as possible so they could return to their babies, she felt fearful that nothing would go as planned.

Huntley brushed up against her and she looked to see what he wanted to tell her. He grinned a little. She smiled back. He was courting her as a male jaguar would. But she didn't think he was just pretending.

She liked that he would. She hadn't had anyone court her in jaguar form since she was younger. Oliver wouldn't shift no matter how much she had coaxed him to give it a try. Both sides of her being were equally important to her. And she realized just how much so when Huntley showed her this side of himself with her.

Her mind back on business, she roamed the beach with Huntley for hours until she was so tired that she wanted to lie down and go to sleep on the warm sand. Which would look unnatural for a jaguar. A jaguar would return to the rainforest and sleep hidden among the trees.

Huntley looked as worn out. He nosed her cheek, then turned his head toward the rainforest, indicating he wanted to return to where their stuff was hidden. She was totally agreeable. It was about a quarter of a mile up the beach and time to get some sleep. They loped along the sand, leaving big-cat pug marks in the wetter stuff. He tackled her all of a sudden, shocking her and tickling her. She played with him, mouthing and biting him in a way that wouldn't hurt. Just playful and fun-loving. Their skin was so loose and stretchy in their jaguar form, unlike a human's, that they didn't hurt each other.

After he pinned her down, she kicked at him with her back feet, trying to push him off, not because she wasn't having fun, but because that's how the game was played. Next time, she'd get the best of him—when he was unprepared. He was heavier than her, and no matter how much she tried to get him off her, she couldn't. He gave her a wickedly evil and toothy grin. Then he licked her nose and jumped off her. She got to her feet. Then they shook off the sand and raced up the beach. Besides having a bit of jaguar fun, they were letting any poachers watching know for sure the two big cats were courting.

After they had gone a little of the distance, they dove into the rainforest to hide from sight, if anyone was observing them.

They saw the Whittaker brothers then, both nodding to them as if to acknowledge they knew Melissa and Huntley were headed back to sleep for a while. They continued to run through the rainforest to reach the tree where they'd wait until the Whittaker brothers arrived. They finally found it and Melissa jumped up there. And found a boa constrictor coiled up on the branch. Before Huntley joined her, she jumped right back down. She could kill the snake, but she didn't want to.

She found another tree and leaped onto a branch. Huntley waited for her to jump down again, as if she was looking for the most comfortable spot and often checked out branches as a trial run. She roared at him to get his butt up there. He showed off his teeth, grunted, and joined her.

Luke got their gear from the other tree and began dumping their tents and field packs down to Jason. Melissa appreciated that the brothers quickly got to work erecting her and Huntley's tent. She had to do it herself before.

Jason tossed Melissa and Huntley's backpacks inside, and then he and his brother set up their tent nearby.

The brothers didn't say anything to them or to each other, and she suspected they were just as disappointed that Jackson hadn't taken the bait and arrived to capture Melissa and Huntley to sell them.

Melissa and Huntley leaped down from the tree and shifted inside the tent, and Huntley zipped it up. Naked, they laid their sleeping bags together, then sat on them and each ate an energy bar. Then they cuddled.

"It's going to work," she said, more to assure herself than Huntley.

"You know it will," he said and kissed her forehead.

"They sure are quiet."

"The brothers?"

"Yeah."

"I think it's part of their training."

She snorted. "Glad I'm not with that branch then. I mean, I don't talk nonstop or anything, but that would drive me nuts, not to be able to talk…ever."

Huntley chuckled. "I couldn't see myself in that branch either. We'll sleep for most of the day, eat, and then try again when dusk falls."

She never thought in a million years that she'd be hoping she'd be shot with a tranquilizer dart, captured, and hauled off to be sold to some buyer.

Huntley couldn't quit thinking about the end of the mission, not wanting to waste time worrying about how this would all end. He needed to resolve some things with Melissa before they had to deal with them again. "I want you to stay with me when we return home," Huntley said, kissing the top of her head and running his hand over her arm in a light caress.

"It won't work," she said.

He didn't feel that she was reluctant and pulling back from him, so he wondered what was up. He wanted to get to know her better and, if he was going to be blunt about it, lay a claim to her so other cats would know she wasn't available. "I want to give it a shot."

"My sister stays with me when she visits. Three on your sofa bed would be awfully crowded."

He smiled.

"I need to get a place with a guest room."

Relieved that was the problem, Huntley took a deep breath and let it out. She smiled up at him.

"Then that's what we'll do." He went back to stroking her arm.

"You want to vacate your place to get a two-bedroom apartment just so my sister can stay with me occasionally?"

"Or get a condo. I have some money saved up. And I had been thinking about it."

"You have?" She sounded skeptical.

Hell, yeah. Once Genista left and he was enjoying the time with Melissa on and off the mission. Maybe that's why Genista had wanted to leave. Not enough space. Anyway, he wanted to set down some roots, and even if things didn't work out between Melissa and him, he wanted a bigger place.

"If you get a condo and I stayed with you, does that mean I don't have to pay any rent?"

He chuckled. "No rent. I wouldn't object too greatly if you wanted to make the meals. And I'd take you out to eat whenever you didn't want to cook."

"Hmm."

"Agreed?" He was about to list all the reasons her staying with him could be a good thing. Financially, she could save a lot of money. When one of them was gone, the other would at least be there to watch the place and enjoy it for the mortgage he would be paying. Not to mention that he wasn't a loner and would love the company. *Her* company.

"I could live with it, I suppose…for a while," she said, brushing her fingers over his arm.

He stroked her cheek with his thumb and then began kissing her. He wanted this intimacy between them with the rainforest sounds all around them, despite the Whittaker brothers being so close by with cat's hearing that would pick up sounds that humans might not. This might be the last chance for Melissa and him to be together—if anything went horribly wrong.

Not that he needed any reason for making love to her, other than she wanted this as much as he did. "You know, you're getting in a lot deeper with this," he said, wanting her to know that he wanted more with her. Not just a roommate or a friend with benefits.

She smiled up and said, "Tell me about it."

"As long as we're thinking along the same line." And then he began to kiss her, wanting to show her how much she meant to him.

He started lightly on her mouth, his hand stroking under her chin and down her neck, loving the softness of her skin against his fingertips and the way her mouth sought his in a tender kiss. Not hard and wanting, but gentle and accepting. And he couldn't help but feel that he was truly falling in love with Melissa—this fun and daredevilish woman and she-cat rolled up in one.

He moved his hand to her breast, cupping, massaging, and feeling the nipple peak between his finger and thumb. She lifted her leg between his, teasing him by gently rubbing her thigh against his balls. He was already hard as steel, as he was any time he began to kiss her or see her naked or touch her—or when she eyed him with interest or touched him. She ramped up a fire inside him way before they got close like this.

The jungle was hot and humid, but kissing and touching her was making his temperature skyrocket as the palm of his hand massaged her breast, and she began to rub her mound against his thigh. Her mouth on his, she sought entrance and forced the kiss to deepen. The passion built, her scent musky and sweet and triggering his need to claim her. He'd never made love to a she-cat in the jungle before, but this felt right—the two of them wild, free, willing, and loving it.

Forget the notion that it would be too hot or buggy or humid to make love there like this. Anywhere with Melissa would be the right place. She became more aggressive, her hands stroking his hair, her body arching to connect with his thigh. He kneaded her sensitive nub to help her reach the pinnacle before he satisfied his own growing need.

He returned his mouth to hers, muffling her whimpers of need, her little growls of pleasure, and his own groans of craving. "Oh, oh, God, I love you, this, everything," she said, arching against him one last time, and he was shocked to hear her say so. Did she mean she was in love with him for everything that he was, or just how he made her feel right this moment?

He hoped he made her feel as special as she did him. He pushed the tip of his cock into her sheath, looked down into her green eyes swimming with lust, and drove home.

Melissa felt almost embarrassed about the words she'd said to Huntley, afraid he'd pull away, worried that she was getting interested in marriage, a home, the cubs, the whole deal, when all she meant was he was so perfect for her—at this time, in this place, there with her now. He made her feel beautiful and needed. He made her reach for the moon and collide with it and burst into a million stars.

He made her "feel" the rainforest in a different way— truly special, a memory she would hold dear forever.

He was kissing her again, his tongue dancing in a heated way with hers, his cock pumping into her as she moved her legs so he could really penetrate her deeply. Her declaration of love seemed to have encouraged him to take over.

He held his breath for a moment and held himself still—as if he was trying to hold to the end, trying to extend the high—and then he thrust into her again and she felt him come deep inside her, the rush, the tension in his expression easing. And then he kissed her eyes and nose and cheeks, ending in one long, lingering kiss on her mouth before he pulled away from her and encouraged her to sleep against him. Close, hanging on to the memory, keeping the connection.

"Beautiful," he whispered against her hair as he stroked her back.

"Hmm," she said, her body boneless and more than satisfied.

She loved the way he made love to her, the way he thrust into her while she was still feeling the afterglow of her own orgasm. The way he kissed her to muffle her sighs and growls and any other noise she couldn't contain so that no one else would hear them, much. The way he was eager to make love to her like this before another night of trying to offer themselves as cat bait. The way he smiled at her when she told him she loved him—his eyes dark and lust-filled. She didn't know how she would feel in the long run, but in this moment, she loved him. Just in case, she'd be careful before saying it again.

If they continued to be like this toward each other— then yes! She would love him like this forever.

—∿∿—

They slept most of the day, after having been up all of yesterday and most of the night. So after they made love, they were out for the count for hours.

Much later that afternoon, Huntley woke as Luke said outside the tent in a hushed voice, "Anyone still alive in there?"

Huntley chuckled. "Yeah," he said, his voice low so as not to disturb Melissa.

"We're going to scout the area and search for signs of anyone that we need to look for. Be back in a while."

"All right. Thanks, man."

"Sure thing."

Huntley listened as the two men trudged off into the rainforest. He had every intention of chilling out with Melissa and waiting for dusk to fall. For the last several hours, it hadn't rained. Tonight, they would be well rested if they ran into Jackson's men.

Melissa was still dozing on the sleeping bag beside him. Huntley got on the phone to Martin, his arm around Melissa. "Any word that our man met with him?"

He didn't mention who "he" was just in case Jackson came across them and heard his name being mentioned.

"Not that we know of for certain. We didn't want to have our man ask for him specifically, afraid that might spook Jackson into thinking this was some kind of a setup," Martin said. "He could have gotten word of the jaguar pair and be planning to check them out soon. Or maybe he just had to gather up some men to accomplish the job."

"Wish he'd hurry it up."

"Me too. The two of you hanging in there all right?"

Huntley looked down at a sleeping Melissa. She was beautiful, her curls caressing his chest, her breathing light and steady.

"Yeah, boss."

"You be careful, both of you. Don't take any unreasonable risks."

Sometimes Martin had a dark sense of humor.

"You got it. Talk later." He settled down with Melissa and fell back to sleep, but a couple of hours later he heard movement headed in their direction. Untangling himself from Melissa, he threw on some boxers and left the tent to see who approached.

The Whittaker brothers appeared in the dense foliage and shook their heads.

"No sign of him or anyone else who might look like they're...them," said Luke, the slightly taller of the two brothers.

"I hope we don't have a total no-show on this," Melissa said, coming out of the tent wearing shorts and a T-shirt. She was brushing the hair out of her eyes and looking sexy, like she'd been well loved. "Even if...

You-know-who wasn't sure about the agent wanting to buy us, you'd think he'd come and take a look."

Huntley and the other men just stared at her and then smiled.

"What?" she asked, sounding annoyed.

Huntley had to admit that she looked damn good.

The brothers chuckled. "I should have joined the JAG," Luke said.

"You and me both," Jason said.

Chapter 15

Right at dusk, Melissa, Huntley, and the Whittaker brothers took the same steps as they had the night before. Melissa and Huntley shifted into their jaguar forms, and the Whittaker brothers packed up the gear and hid it in the same tree. Then Luke and Jason followed the jaguars to the beach and remained hidden in the vegetation.

Since this was the second day of attempting the ruse, Huntley was having a devil of a time feeling casual, afraid that at any moment Jackson and his men would come out of the rainforest and shoot them with darts. It was like taking a test but then having it delayed over and over again, when the test taker had been prepared the first time. Also, the effects of being shot at the last time were still fresh in Huntley's mind. Most of all, he worried about Melissa and how she would manage the drug and the ordeals they might have to face after that.

She was watching the ocean, her ears, nose, and whiskers twitching as she listened and smelled for any sign of a boat or men headed their way. Huntley was sure that if Jackson and his men did arrive, they'd attempt to shoot them from the screen of trees lining the beach. Something suddenly made a thunking sound behind them near the tree line, and both his and Melissa's heads whipped around. A coconut rolled to a stop in the sand. They looked up at the coconut tree and saw nothing.

If Huntley hadn't been worried about what would happen to them if Jackson showed his face, he would have loved being here like this with Melissa. He licked her cheek, and she licked him right back, a glint of the devil in her pretty green eyes. Then she nudged at him playfully, and they began frolicking on the beach like they had last night. Sure, they knew why they were there, but for the moment, they enjoyed themselves, tackling each other, playing, licking, and nipping. Besides, this was part of the show, even if Huntley liked to believe they truly were jaguars in love.

He paused to consider the unbidden feelings coursing through his thoughts.

Not only had he never done this with a female agent on a mission, but he realized he'd never done this with a female jaguar ever. When he and Genista were on missions together, they hadn't had the time or need to do this. And back home, their dating activities were strictly of the human kind. He realized then that Genista wasn't a playful sort, and he really liked that in Melissa.

He and Melissa chased each other back and forth along the beach, kicking up the sand, growling playfully, and exploring a bit until they spied a turtle and came to a dead halt. Jaguars ate turtles. Not that he or Melissa intended to bother this one, but she loped over to it as if to pretend an interest, which would be natural for a jaguar. The sound of a motor rumbling as a boat headed to the cove caught their attention. He and Melissa were a long way from the cove. Dense vegetation hid it from their view so they couldn't see the boat and identify it as the same one that had taken off with the Carringtons.

Still, this was it. Or it could be. He was ready to get

this over with—to get to wherever the poachers were holding the Carringtons and free them. Before he could do something to indicate he thought that might be them, and maybe they should head more in that direction, he heard something move in the trees near them. One of the Whittaker brothers?

A shot fired from the rainforest, and Huntley felt the damn solid prick of the dart as it hit his rump. Melissa jumped at the sound of the gunfire. Huntley dropped against the ground, pretending to be completely knocked out before they shot him again. He wished now he'd told Melissa to run if they shot him first, that only he was needed to accomplish this part of the mission. She could have come for him after he was at the compound. Not that she could easily find him. But at least he knew she'd be safer. Though he highly suspected she wouldn't have gone along with the plan.

She poked at him with her nose. He grunted to let her know that he was alive. Another shot sounded, and she fell next to him. He feared she had dropped too quickly, and he listened hard to hear her heart beating. As the seconds ticked on, her heartbeat that had been thumping wildly was drifting to barely anything.

No one moved from the trees. He kept waiting and waiting and waiting. And no one moved. What the hell?

What if the men who shot them weren't Jackson's men, and the Whittaker brothers had taken the new poachers down because of it? That would mean Huntley and Melissa were knocked out for no good reason! Or at least he was nearly knocked out. He couldn't lift his head or open his eyes, but he could listen for the sounds around him.

Nothing was happening. No sound of human movement. Hell, what had gone wrong?

Huntley's brain was filled with fog, and he was having a difficult time hearing anything over his own slowed heartbeat and the rainforest noises and the waves hitting the beach.

Forever, the minutes seemed to tick by. Maybe an hour had passed. The Whittaker brothers were supposed to take down any other poachers, but what if Jackson wasn't with his men this time? What if he'd just sent them to capture the jaguars? On the other hand, Jackson liked the thrill of the hunt too much, and Huntley didn't believe he would stay away and let his men do this. Not to mention that Huntley suspected Jackson got off on doing something illegal. Unless he was indisposed again.

Huntley must have drifted off until he heard footsteps running through the sand. He played dead—or asleep— for whoever approached.

"Hurry," a man said.

Jackson. Huntley wanted to rip him to shreds, yet he was relieved the right man had finally come for them so they could get this show on the road and rescue the Carringtons.

"We don't know how long the cats have been out," Jackson said, "so move it!"

"Why don't we just shoot them again?" one of his cohorts said. "Better safe than sorry."

"We might as well just pump them full of live rounds. Giving them too much of the drug or something different could kill them," Jackson said, sounding irritated with the man.

"Yeah, but where are the other guys who were here before us?" another man said as Huntley felt his limp body being lifted and carried.

He really wanted to see how Melissa was faring, but he couldn't open his eyes to look or he'd worry that the poachers might think he was coming to. Actually, he wasn't certain he could open his eyes anyway.

"Hell if I know what happened to the bastards. They probably heard something and got spooked. Good deal for us all around. After that buyer spouted off that he wanted these two—and for the price he is offering— hell, everyone's going to be out here looking for these cats. We're just damned lucky we got here in time," Jackson said.

"Never seen a black one up close," a fourth man said.

Huntley frowned. *Phil Gorsman*? The man who shot Timothy Jackson's sister and nearly killed her? He had come down here after all. Huntley was certain once those in charge realized they'd released him accidentally on bail bond, they'd have to correct the situation pronto. He must have figured he'd be returned to jail while awaiting trial. He wouldn't have been allowed to leave the country.

Huntley would love to tell Jackson the story if he was unaware of it. Unless Jackson already knew and needed Phil more than he cared about his sister.

The men carried Huntley along the beach because it was easier than trying to walk through the tangle of plants and vines in the rainforest. It was still dark out, so it would be difficult for anyone to see them. The poachers had to be wearing night-vision goggles because Huntley hadn't seen any sign of artificial light.

"The male is a son of a bitch to carry. Just like that other one," Phil said.

Avery Carrington?

"Quit your bellyaching and hurry it up," Jackson said.

Huntley knew the cove was a lot farther away, but all of a sudden they were there, the sound of the ocean breakers no longer nearby but around the bend now. He must have dozed off. He was trying his damnedest to fight the drug slipping through his veins so he could be ready at a moment's notice.

"Hey, Danny, where are you?" Jackson called out, but his voice was hushed.

Everyone had stopped in place. Huntley heard the boat grinding against the sandy shore, gentler waves rocking it.

"Let's get the cats loaded in the cages," Jackson said.

"What about Danny?" Phil asked.

"We can't hang around here waiting for him to take a leak or whatever," Jackson said. "You know what happened to my crew the last time."

"They said jaguars attacked them. But we all know jaguars don't attack people. They're not like other big cats—they'll run away."

"They had to have had cubs nearby, Monty," Jackson said, sounding aggravated.

"What about these two?" Monty asked.

"No. If they had cubs, the male wouldn't be hanging around the female. Don't you know anything?" Jackson turned away from him and said, "Danny!" He paused. "We got to get out of here, damn it. The park rangers nabbed my other men. We don't want that to happen this time."

A cage door opened. Huntley was shoved into the cage and the door slammed shut. The same happened to one close by. All he could think about was Melissa, and he prayed she was all right.

"Danny," Jackson called out again. "You got two minutes to finish what you're doing and get your ass back here."

No response.

Huntley waited to hear a reply, but the boat's engine started and then the ropes were thrown across the deck. The boat was pushed away from shore and took off. So much for waiting two minutes.

If Danny was still alive, which Huntley doubted, he was stranded. If he wasn't alive, good riddance. Then Huntley wondered if Luke and Jason had something to do with it. Had one of the brothers found the boat and taken care of Danny? Hell, could they have had time to put a GPS tracker on the boat?

Hot damn, if they did. They hadn't discussed doing such a thing, but he could see the brothers winging it if the opportunity availed itself. They wouldn't let Melissa and Huntley take all the risks without another backup plan.

Feeling a little easier that Martin might soon learn where they were, Huntley was about ready to drift off to sleep again when Phil said, "So what are you going to do about that other male?"

"If we can't get a buyer by tomorrow, he's dead meat, as much as I hate that it might come to that after all we went through to get him. But we can't risk having him around much longer."

Huntley knew he and Melissa were going to have to

kill the whole lot of them. No turning this bunch over to the police.

~~~

The motor roared on as the boat sliced through the water, and Huntley was certain the men wanted to get to where they were going as soon as they could. It was bound to get light out before long, and if they got caught transporting a couple of cats in cages, they would be arrested.

That made him think again about the cubs and how glad he was that he and Melissa didn't have to worry any longer about getting caught while caring for them. He couldn't wait to tell the Carringtons that their babies were safe and on the way home.

Water splashed up into the boat as they sped along, the boat bouncing and slamming into the rough water. The boat smelled of cats—margay, ocelot, puma, jaguars. Different boat, though. The other must have been confiscated. Jackson had been a busy bastard.

Huntley didn't remember much after that, only that the men were moving around on the deck of the boat and he could hear water lapping at the sides, rubber rubbing the exterior, the sound of ropes hitting the dock, then the dock lines being tied from the boat to the dock cleats.

"Okay, get the cages into the truck pronto, and Phil, you get the boat out of the water. Huey and Monty, you help."

Four men grunted as they hefted Huntley's cage out of the boat, then jarred him as they carried him down the wooden dock. He was shoved into a dark enclosed truck, and then he heard and felt Melissa's cage bang against his.

Then the door was rolled shut. He listened for the sound of anyone in the back of the truck with them, but the men seemed to still be working on getting the boat out of the water. He suspected no one was going to ride in the back. No need to.

He grunted at Melissa, but she didn't stir. He felt dead to the world too, unable to move a damn muscle to lift his head. How the hell was he going to rescue anyone now, let alone himself and Melissa? He sure hoped like hell he could throw off the drug and do what he was supposed to do.

And he prayed again that Luke or his brother had attached a GPS to the boat and that it would lead Martin's men to their location before long.

Then the truck began to pull forward, the engine grinding and clattering, the cages rattling and shaking as the truck rolled over the uneven ground. Huntley closed his eyes. Maybe if he could sleep just a little, he would be ready to wake up when they arrived at their destination.

At least he hoped so.

Truck doors slammed and Huntley didn't know if the truck had driven very far from where the boat had docked or not because he hadn't noticed when the truck had actually pulled to a stop. He must have dozed off again. A latch on the back of the truck was opened, and then the door rolled up. Huntley kept his eyes closed, but he could tell it was getting to be dawn, just a hint of light in the sky. Then he heard a male jaguar roaring and hoped it was Avery Carrington. The cat was agitated, and from the sounds of his roars, he was moving from one side of his cage to another.

The men carried Melissa's cage out first and set it on the ground with a thunk. Then they pulled Huntley's cage out of the truck and carried it to its final resting place.

"Get the truck out of here," Jackson ordered.

An engine started up and then the vehicle drove off.

"Where's Jackson going?" Monty asked.

"To meet with the buyer? Hell if I know," Phil Gorsman said. "He's sure pissed off about the other male cat, though, and how he couldn't sell him and the female off at the same time."

Huntley still wondered how Phil had been able to leave the States without being stopped after nearly murdering Jackson's sister.

Huntley risked opening one eye to see what he could as they carried him over to the angry big cat's cage and set Huntley's next to it. A small adobe home was about a half acre away, high wooden fences surrounding the yard and tall trees towering over them from all sides. Four cages were empty. One held an ocelot, another, a margay.

A larger cage held a pacing male jaguar. Huntley studied his rosettes and recognized the pattern as Avery Carrington's. Unfortunately, the Avenger agent had no clue that Huntley or Melissa were shifters and there to help him. What alarmed Huntley the most was that Avery's wife, Kathy, wasn't there. Phil had claimed that she had been sold off, which had to mean they'd already shipped her off somewhere else. Judging by Avery's pacing and roaring, he would rip every human to shreds that got anywhere near him.

Huntley figured it wouldn't matter now if Jackson and his men knew he was awake. He lifted his head and looked around for Jackson, but he was gone. Maybe he had taken off to meet with Huntley and Melissa's buyer and it was one of their fellow agents. At least Huntley hoped that was the case. The men moved Melissa's cage next to Huntley's.

"Jackson's sure pissed that the buyer didn't want the male because he was way too aggressive," Phil said.

Huntley couldn't blame Avery when he had to be worried to death about his wife. As soon as he could, Huntley had to let Avery know that his babies were fine and headed back to the States. And that he and Melissa would help him get free, then do everything they could to learn where Kathy had been taken. Avery probably wouldn't realize that all the branches were working on this.

Avery glanced in their direction for only a moment, too agitated to be interested in the new jaguars, so Huntley couldn't get his attention.

Melissa was still doped up and sleeping, and Huntley kept worrying about her. She wasn't stirring at all. Concerned they had overmedicated her, he watched her chest rise and fall. She was still breathing, her heart still pumping blood, but at a slower rate.

Wanting her to show him she'd be all right, Huntley growled at her. He poked his nose a short way through the steel bars of his cage, trying to get her attention, to wake her.

Phil said, "As long as the two new ones keep up the courtship and they behave, I believe we've got real money in them."

Huntley stuck his paw through the cage, trying to reach Melissa's cage. They were too far apart.

"Hey, let's move the female's cage closer to the male's. If the male cat is still trying to connect with her when the buyer arrives, it'll help seal the deal," Huey said.

Huntley backed off to avoid getting his leg caught between the cages. As soon as the men finished moving her cage against his and lined the cases up so the steel rods bumped against each other, Huntley poked his paw between the two cages again. Phil and the other two men watched in fascination.

Huntley couldn't reach her. She was lying in the middle of the cage and still fast asleep. But he noticed Avery wasn't roaring any longer.

Huntley glanced back at him. The cat watched Huntley curiously. Huntley raised his brows and grinned. To the humans, he was certain his reaction looked like he showed off his very wicked teeth in a primal way, saying to stay the hell away from his mate.

"Would you look at that," Phil said. "The badass cat isn't so big and bad now that there's another male here."

"Good. Maybe he'll calm down enough that we can sell him and don't have to shoot the bastard."

Huntley padded over to the other side of his cage, nearer to Avery's, and did something so uncharacteristic for a male jaguar under the circumstances that he hoped he could clue Avery in that he was a shifter and not all jaguar.

Huntley truly hated to do it because it was so demeaning. The shifters didn't just wear their jaguar coats from time to time. Being a wild cat was part of the whole of who they were. He lay down on his stomach, then rolled over on his back and exposed his belly and throat.

No grown male would do that with another grown male when the one had claimed the female as his mate, even if they were in cages.

Avery grinned and his sharp teeth looked just as deadly as Huntley's. But at least he thought Avery had gotten the message.

"Well, hell, what's that all about?" one of the men asked.

"Maybe they're brothers."

Yeah, brothers in different branches of the Service and ready to kill a bunch of poachers.

The cat sat down and looked at Melissa. Huntley nodded. Then she growled softly and Huntley was on his feet—and so was Avery. Huntley rushed to her cage and roared. Her ears and whiskers and a paw twitched. Huntley tried to reach her through the cage again.

Phil said, "Jackson's going to love the way these two act toward each other."

"Maybe the buyer will take all three off our hands, since the first male seems to get along with the other," another man said. "The new male has sure calmed him down."

If the buyer was their own man, the situation couldn't be better. Except for the fact that Kathy Carrington was gone.

—◦◦◦—

Huntley hated to have to bide his time to break out of there, wanting to learn where Avery's wife was being kept pronto, but they had to wait until night fell. As soon as it got dark, the rains came. One dim security light fluttered on and off at a corner of the house, and the fence had a locked gate. Phil and the other men had retired inside. All but one of the lights finally went out inside, cloaking the house in darkness. Jackson had never returned, as far as Huntley could tell.

Melissa had been lying on her stomach for about an hour, her head up. She had tried to stand a couple of times, but the effort seemed to take every ounce of her energy. Each time, she collapsed on her belly. And each time she growled softly. He was dying to help her up, but he couldn't. Then on the third try, she finally made it to her feet, but she swayed a bit. Huntley was feeling back to his normal self. And glad of it. But he needed Melissa to be in better shape before they attempted to escape.

He examined the latch on the cage. A snap lock, easy to open as a human but impossible as a cat. Many big-cat rescue facilities used them. He recalled the story of the chimpanzees that had watched their keepers opening the gate to their enclosure. One of the large chimps had learned to open the gate, and several escaped and killed the owner. But the cats couldn't manage such a thing.

The cages were shadowed in darkness and the rain was coming down lighter now. Huntley assumed anyone in the house would be sleeping, and even if someone looked out at the cat enclosures, he wouldn't be able to really see what was going on. Only the cats could with their night vision.

Time to make an ally. He shifted, moved next to Avery's cage, and said, "I'm Huntley Anderson with the JAG, and that's my partner, Melissa Overton, JAG also. Your kids are safe. They're on their way back to the States in the care of a couple of Guardians who are providing for them in the meantime."

Avery shifted and frowned at him. "Thank God the babies are safe. But these bastards said they've sold my wife to some guy named Pierre Beaufort. He wanted us both for a breeding program. Then I lost my cool when he was poking around at Kathy, and he wouldn't buy me. Said I would be too dangerous."

Huntley nodded. "Understandable. We weren't sure what we'd find. So we have to wing it. Our best chance is to storm the house, shift, and take them out—no witnesses, no leaving them for the police like we'd first planned. I'll notify my boss, and then we'll locate your wife. We do have an agent who's supposed to be buying Melissa and me, but we can't risk that he's the one who arrives here first. If he did, he'd buy you too. If someone else shows up instead, we might end up getting separated or in a worse situation."

"I agree. I'm damned glad to see you. Kathy said she left the cubs in a jaguar shifter's tent and had smelled both a man and a woman. It must have been your tent."

"It was."

"She prayed the two of you could handle the girls and alert our people that we had gone missing."

Huntley smiled a little. "It was kind of a shock. I came to your rescue, but they fired a shot at me, and I was knocked unconscious. I sure as hell wish I'd been able to rescue you before you had to go through all of this hell. I think Melissa was a little more shaken since she was a lot clearer headed than me at the time. She just missed taking the bastards down before they took off with the two of you in the boat."

Avery sighed. "Would have saved everyone a lot of grief. But I could see where your partner wouldn't have been able to handle all the men on her own. I'm just grateful you're here now and the kids are safe."

"Two of your Avenger buddies are helping out also—the Whittaker brothers."

Avery smiled a little at that.

"I want to wait a little while longer until Melissa is more herself," Huntley said.

"I want to get the hell out of here and find my wife." Avery glanced in Melissa's direction. She was curled up in her cage sound asleep.

Damn.

"But we'll do it your way. We can't risk it with your partner still so out of it."

Huntley hated to have to wait as much as he knew Avery did, but otherwise one of them would have to carry Melissa. It was much too dangerous.

Both men shifted back into their jaguar forms. Huntley headed to Melissa's cage and grunted at her. She grunted right back at him.

He smiled, knowing she was aggravated that she couldn't shake off the drug. Then he lay near her cage, breathing in her relaxed scent, and waited. After what he suspected was another hour, Melissa stood and yawned, then grunted at him, letting him know she was awake and ready. Well, maybe not completely ready, but enough that she was able to escape. Huntley was immediately on his feet. So was Avery.

Huntley shifted at once and worked on unfastening the latch to his cage. So did Avery with his, then they dropped the latches on the ground and closed the gates to the cages, in case anyone chanced to look out and saw the gates wide open. Though Huntley suspected it was too dark to see.

Still in her jaguar form, Melissa leaned against the bars of her cage, waiting for Huntley to get her out, and he worried then that she still felt a little loopy or she would have freed herself. He unlatched her gate. When she moved out of the cage, he ran his hand over her head in greeting. She nuzzled him in the crotch. He was sure his face turned a little red, and he thought she wasn't quite with it.

He closed her cage and then shifted, and the three of them sprinted in jaguar form for the house. Standing by one of the open windows, Huntley peered through the screen. It was a bedroom, with a man sleeping on a full-size bed, sprawled out on his belly, arm slung over the side, face toward the opposite wall. An empty tequila bottle sat on the bedside table. The room smelled of liquor, sweat, and body odor—which could be a disadvantage for the shifters with their enhanced cat sense of smell.

Huntley went around to each of the windows, avoiding the one nearest the security light, though it shuddered and stayed off more than it stayed on. He finally found an open window to the kitchen, which he hoped was far enough away from anyone who might hear them entering. Still, the window looked to be situated over the sink, and that meant leaping in through the window and trying not to make a big racket. But with all the dishes and dirty food in the sink, Huntley opted for the first bedroom he'd investigated.

With everyone still in their jaguar forms, Avery stuck close to Melissa, guarding her, for which Huntley was grateful. Even though she had a viciously strong bite, he wasn't certain she could attack that well in her current condition.

Huntley inserted his fishhook claws into the screen mesh on the bedroom window and tugged, making a racket, his heart drumming. He yanked the screen out quickly with his powerful claws. The man on the bed was too drunk to wake and didn't stir. Huntley leaped inside and then shifted into his human form.

Melissa and Avery jumped through the window and waited while Huntley woke the man to question him about Pierre Beaufort's whereabouts. Huntley had his hand on the man's throat, threatening to strangle him. "How can I reach Pierre Beaufort?"

"Who…?" the man said, looking up groggily and then beginning to stir. "What the hell." He couldn't see Huntley in the dark, which was to Huntley's advantage because he didn't believe the poacher would think a naked, unarmed man was too dangerous.

The man was still drunk and half asleep. "Huh?"

This wasn't going to work.

Avery quickly moved into the living room in his cat form, and Huntley assumed he would question one of the other poachers. Melissa stayed close at hand, protecting Huntley, he thought. Or she still wasn't able to shake off the effects of the drug and wanted to stick close to him until she could. Either way, he was glad she stayed with him.

"How can I get in touch with Pierre Beaufort?"

The man began to reach under his pillow, as if some of his tequila-soaked brain cells warned him to kill the man towering above him before it was too late. Huntley assumed he was reaching for a weapon.

Huntley took hold of the man's head and twisted with a swift jerk, breaking his neck. Maybe the next guy would be more cooperative.

Melissa jumped onto the bed and checked out the dead man. Huntley smiled at her tenacity, then peered into the living room. A man was sleeping on the couch, a leg hanging off it, lying on his back and wearing only a dirty tank shirt and a pair of boxers. He was snoring, so Huntley figured Avery was in one of the other bedrooms. Maybe he'd have better luck.

Huntley hurried across the bare wooden floor, the darn thing creaking with his footfalls. Melissa moved into the room but remained in her jaguar form, protecting his back.

In the living room, a low-watt bulb lit the room sufficiently for the man to see Huntley once he woke. At Huntley's approach, the man opened his eyes and Huntley quickly clasped his hand over the poacher's mouth. He had to question the man about the buyer who took possession of Kathy, or he would have just killed the poacher where he slept. The man looked up at Huntley with bleary eyes, but then his eyes widened as he saw the naked stranger peering down at him. He tried to get up off the couch, but Huntley's hand was on his shoulder, and he shook his head in warning.

"What…who…?" The man still looked half out of it, unable to shake off the effects of overdosing himself with liquor.

"Speak softly and answer me this—where is Pierre Beaufort?" Huntley asked, his voice hushed.

"Who the hell are you?" The man looked like he didn't believe Huntley could cause him bodily harm, naked and unarmed, as he glanced around the room to ensure no one else was there. Then he saw Melissa standing in her jaguar form, eyeing him. She showed off her teeth for good measure, causing her nose to wrinkle and her whiskers to bristle. "Holy shit!" He scrambled to get off the couch.

Huntley shoved him back onto the couch.

"Stay! Where can we reach Pierre Beaufort?" Huntley asked again, losing patience.

"Hell if I know," the man said, not looking away from what he had to have figured was the greater threat to him—Melissa in her very growly jaguar form. "What the hell's going on?"

"If you don't know anything…" Huntley said, a threat in his voice.

"Phil Gorsman maybe knows. He's sleeping it off in that bedroom down the hall. Maybe just Jackson knows. He usually deals with the buyers." Then the man made a fatal mistake. He dove for something under one of the sofa's cushions. He fell into the cushions, searching frantically for something, and came up with a gun in one hand. Despite trying to be quick about it, he was too drunk to manage and fumbled with the gun, nearly dropping it before Huntley seized the man's head, jerked it hard, and broke his neck. That was the problem with being inebriated. Slow reflexes were no match for a cat's quickness. The man slumped back onto the couch, and Huntley stalked in the direction of one of the other bedrooms.

In there, Huntley found Phil sprawled on the bed. His poison of choice was whiskey, and he had a half-empty bottle sitting on the floor next to the bed. Celebrating the capture of a bunch of jaguars? Huntley flipped on the light switch.

"Hey, Phil, remember me?" Huntley asked.

Phil opened his eyes. They grew saucer-sized and he tried to sit up, but when he saw that Huntley wasn't wearing any clothes and had no weapons on him, he grinned. "New look for FBI agents these days? Government running out of money again? Or maybe you think you'll scare a man into confession like that." Then he slipped his hand under his spare pillow.

Huntley pinned him down, one arm tight against Phil's neck and his other hand gripping Phil's right wrist to keep him from getting hold of a weapon.

"Where's Pierre Beaufort? How can I reach him?"

"Jackson," Phil choked out. "He's the only one who deals with him. If any of us did, he'd think we were trying to sell the cat behind his back. He's got another guy who can deal with the buyers from time to time when Jackson's on another job, but we don't even know the man's name."

"So you don't know where this Pierre is or any way to contact him?"

Behind Phil, Melissa hopped onto the bed and showed off her wicked teeth.

Phil jerked his head around and stared at her, struggling to get free from Huntley. "Holy shit! How did she get loose?"

"She'll bite—hard—as soon as I tell her to."

"What the hell's going on?"

"You captured the wrong cats this time. They bite back. One last time. Where's Pierre?"

"I...I don't know. I'd tell you if I knew."

"Did you tell Jackson you shot and very nearly killed his sister?"

Phil's eyes bugged out again.

"Didn't think so."

In his jaguar form, blood on his mouth, Avery loped into the room.

Phil's mouth gaped. "What the hell…" Then he said, "The bitch led you to me. She deserved what she got. If she'd done that to her own brother, *he* would have killed her!"

"So you're lying to him. How can I believe you're not lying to me?"

"Screw you."

"Wrong answer. But I'll make it easy on you." With killing precision, Huntley did the same to Phil as he'd done to the other two men, ending his miserable life. The whole while, Huntley recalled how Jackson's sister had nearly died because of this man and had been fortunate enough to get a second chance at life. But this sick bastard had been free to go right back to a life of crime. Not any longer.

After that, Huntley and Avery searched for clothing. They both found clean T-shirts and jeans and slipped them on. Then he searched for shoes, but only managed to locate a pair of flip-flops—not his usual style for a mission like this, but the guy's feet were so big that it would have been like wearing clown shoes. Avery managed to find a pair of one of the guys' tennis shoes that fit.

"Did you get anything from anyone?" Huntley asked as he saw Melissa come out of another room wearing a long T-shirt. The edge of a pair of black boxers could be seen at the bottom of the T-shirt.

"Nothing. Two men back there. But they had the same to say as the others. Jackson's the only one who knew. I was searching in a desk to see if I could find anything else," Avery said.

"We'll grab their cell phones, report the stolen cats, seize one of their vehicles, and take off," Huntley said.

"What about my wife?" Avery asked, jerking a cell phone out of a pair of men's trousers.

"Martin will have every available resource looking for her. And your cohorts may have been able to attach a GPS locator to the boat that brought us here. Although the boat might be locked up in a garage some distance from this location. I don't hear any nearby water source. Still, it's probably not too far away because it was beginning to get light when we landed and we arrived here not much later."

Melissa had grabbed a phone and was staring at it.

Huntley searched for keys to one of the three vehicles parked out front and found another phone. "Avery, if you would, call the Whittaker brothers because hopefully they're nearby, depending on where we are."

"Sure thing." Avery tried to get hold of Luke and Jason, while Huntley was about to give up on looking for the car keys and just hot-wire one of the vehicles.

Melissa lifted the phone to her ear and said, "Martin, we're…" She hesitated, as if she didn't remember what she meant to say next.

Feeling bad for Melissa, Huntley located a set of car keys and called Martin on another phone, wrapping his arm around Melissa's shoulders and giving her a heartfelt hug. "Hey, boss, we're at the compound where Jackson was keeping the cats. We've taken care of Jackson's men, including that bastard Phil Gorsman. Jackson's gone, though. We're grabbing a vehicle and getting out of here." He paused and said to Melissa, "If you'll hide the phone you're holding under some papers over there on the table, Martin can have our men locate the house using GPS."

"Okay," she said, and he watched her as she did what he asked.

Then he said to Martin, "We've got Avery, but Kathy was sold to a buyer named Pierre Beaufort. As soon as you get a fix on our location, let us know where to go. We need to find Kathy as soon as we can. Have you heard from our guy who's pretending to be the buyer?"

"Your brother wanted the job. So Everett said he's following the man who wanted the payment to your current location, but he's not Jackson."

"Crap."

"My sentiments. The man was planning to buy the two of you, but now he's waffling about the price. Said it would cost Everett twice as much."

"Good thing my brother doesn't really need to pay for our release. Can you give him the kill order? Unless you think the man can tell us where this Pierre Beaufort is and that will lead us to Avery's wife."

"Yes. I'll give the order."

Huntley clicked the car keypad and the Jeep's lights flickered. "We're taking a Jeep." Then he gave Martin the license number. Huntley noticed as soon as they walked outside the house that the ground was littered with glass and stones, and Melissa wasn't wearing any shoes. He said, "Hold on, Martin."

Huntley pocketed the phone, lifted Melissa into his

arms, and carried her to the Jeep. As soon as he set her in the backseat, she sprawled out to sleep.

Okay, so she really wasn't fully awake. Avery climbed into the front seat.

Huntley pulled the phone out and got behind the wheel, then said to Martin, "Once you find the location of this place, they've got an ocelot and margay caged up that need rescuing."

"Got it. Is Melissa all right?"

"Drugged still. With her smaller size, they over-dosed her."

Martin cursed.

"The Whittaker brothers are ready to meet us and help get us out of here as soon as we learn where my wife is," Avery said to Huntley. "Luke said they found the place where the boat was stored. They *had* tracked it with GPS."

"Martin, did you hear that? We just need the coordinates for where we are now."

"I've got agents on it now. I've got a man talking to Jason Whittaker, and we'll report the location of the boat once they're out of there."

"All right. Road's bad. Gotta go."

"Call you in a few minutes and let you know where you are and where you need to go."

Then they signed off.

The road was muddy and chock-full of holes, with thick vegetation growing up right next to it. Occasional sightings of dark homes back off the road caught Huntley's attention.

As soon as they saw headlights coming in their direction, Avery said, "Turn off down that side road."

Huntley turned off and drove toward a residence until the vehicle passed. "What if it's Jackson? We could take the bastard down. Learn where Pierre is."

"We can ambush him down here if he follows us."

The car turned off onto the same road, and Huntley thought one of two things: the driver *was* Jackson, recognized the Jeep, and wondered why one of his men would be taking a spin in it at this time of night when he was supposed to be watching the cats, or the driver of the vehicle was the owner of the house they were headed for.

If it was Jackson, they'd make their stand here and take him out. Huntley pulled over on the rutted road and stopped the Jeep.

"Want me to shift and take care of him?" Avery said.

Before Huntley could reply, someone shouted out the vehicle's window from behind, "It's me!"

"My brother, Everett," Huntley hurried to say, thrilled to hear it was him and that he was fine. But Huntley had really hoped Jackson was coming for them. He'd hoped they could learn where Pierre Beaufort was and take Jackson out once and for all. He and Avery got out of the vehicle and headed back to the car parked behind them. Everett jumped out of his vehicle and gave Huntley a warm embrace.

"I had to make sure the Jeep was the one you stole and confirm it with the boss first. Where's Melissa?" Everett asked, sounding worried.

"Asleep in the backseat."

"Is she okay?" Everett asked, his brow creased in a deep frown.

"Yeah, she'll be okay."

"Good." Everett shook Avery's hand. "Damn glad to see you."

"Likewise," Avery said.

"Grab Melissa, will you, Huntley? We'll take my car. The boss called me and told me what happened. The guy that was trying to sell the jaguars to me had a fatal heart attack—with my help. He didn't have any clue where Kathy's buyer is, or Jackson either. My mission was to pick the three of you up and haul ass out of here." Everett was still talking while Huntley lifted Melissa out of the Jeep and carried her to Everett's rental car.

As he opened the back door for Huntley, Everett said to Avery, "Your cubs are now back home safe and sound. They arrived a few hours ago."

"Thank God for that. Now we just need to get my wife home," Avery said.

"Totally agree with that," Huntley said.

"As soon as I verified that you were driving the Jeep, Martin notified the police," Everett said, as Huntley got into the backseat with Melissa, and Avery climbed into the front seat. "We want to be as far away from there as possible."

"That's for damn sure," Huntley said. Melissa rested her head in his lap. "Are you all right?" He stroked her arm, wishing this was all over with and they could take a real vacation together.

"Yeah," she said, her voice soft with sleep. "Can't kick the way the drug is making me so drowsy."

"No problem, honey. Just sleep. It'll wear off." Huntley saw his brother glance at the rearview mirror. Yeah, Huntley *was* dating the she-cat. No ifs, ands, or buts about it.

"Thanks so much for all your help," Avery said.

"You would have done it for any of us. Hell, Everett," Huntley said to his brother, "I thought you were working a cold case. Martin didn't tell me you were down here trying to buy Melissa and me from that scum, Jackson."

"I applied for the job as soon as I learned my fool brother was trying to martyr himself along with his new girlfriend."

Huntley shook his head. "I don't see myself as the martyr type." Melissa appeared to be asleep, but when Everett made the comment about her being Huntley's new girlfriend, she slid her hand lightly over Huntley's leg. He hoped that meant she agreed with him. He smiled down at her.

"Not a martyr, but bait then. Dad would have had me drawn and quartered if I hadn't come down here to help free you. Not that I needed the extra push. As soon as Tammy and her mate heard, they wanted to come down here too. Boss said no. They're still training those teens and that's their priority. But yeah, as soon as Martin told everyone in the branch that you and Melissa needed help finding a couple who had been captured and how you were left to cub-sit, everyone who wasn't on an urgent mission dropped everything and started trying to solve this case." Everett paused, then said, "How did cub-sitting work out, by the way?"

Melissa chuckled.

Huntley rubbed her shoulder and smiled. He knew that would come up in the conversation soon enough. In fact, he suspected that once the family was all home together, and he and Melissa were back stateside,

everyone in the JAG would give them a hard time over
it in a lighthearted way.

"They can be a handful when I'm at home and Kathy
leaves them for me to take care of so she can get some
things done. But I have to admit, I wouldn't give them
up for the world," Avery said.

"Which was which?" Melissa asked.

Huntley was also curious to know.

"The smaller, less aggressive one is Jenny. Jaime's
the one in charge."

"Goldie," Melissa said. "We had to give them nicknames. She was more golden. And the other, Jenny, we
called Sweetpea."

Avery chuckled. "She can be quite a scrapper too,
when she wants to be." He let out his breath in aggrava-
tion and folded his arms. "She's not like us. My wife, I
mean. She's wild and used to the jungle, but she's not
trained to fight like we are in our human forms."

"She shifted four times. The cubs followed suit,"
Melissa said softly, still resting her head on Huntley's
lap. "Scared us to death."

"We tried to make an escape on four separate occa-
sions, but it was impossible. Too many armed men at
the place at the time. Each time she shifted and we
thought we'd make a run for it, someone would come
out to feed the cats or do something. Managing by
myself, no problem. But with her safety to think about,
no way. They were poking at her, and I got angry. They
drugged me again. I didn't even know she was gone
until I woke this morning. The buyer was supposed to
take both of us, but the bastard chickened out and only
took her."

"In case you didn't see them, I've got some of your bags back there," Everett said.

"Hell, yeah," Huntley said, then passed one up to Avery. As soon as Melissa was awake enough, he'd try to change into his own clothes in the car.

Avery got a call on the poacher's cell phone, glanced at it, then smiled. "Yeah, Luke? Okay." He ended the call. "Luke and his brother will meet us in an hour at Santa Eduviges in the forest reserve of Los Santos. They've got a lead on Pierre Beaufort. He's living near there. Apparently, the reserve is another place where they're picking up animals and selling them off. Beaufort doesn't catch them. He just lives close to the reserve so that the seller can reach him quickly."

"Good show," Everett said and headed on the road that would take them there.

"Thank God for that," Huntley said.

"Yes," Melissa murmured.

Huntley was glad she was awake enough to be listening in and able to respond. Avery yanked off the poacher's shirt and began pulling on one of his own.

"Trouble up ahead, folks," Everett said. "Police car is approaching. He's motioning us to stop. Everyone clean? No blood splotches anywhere?"

Chapter 16

"NONE OF US HAVE PASSPORTS ON US," HUNTLEY warned, caressing Melissa's arm as they watched the police approach their rental car and were about to be interrogated.

Everett pointed at the console. "Thankfully, Martin and the Whittaker brothers thought of the trouble you would all be in once I came to free you. I picked up your passports, driver's licenses, and badges and some of your bags from the Whittaker brothers while they went to search for the boat that took you to the cat holding area. I've also got Kathy's for as soon as we're able to rescue her."

Melissa tried to sit up, not wanting to look like she was out of it because of using drugs, even if she was. She hated feeling this way, hated that she wasn't able to help question the poachers and was only able to snarl and show off her teeth. Even when she'd jumped on Phil's bed, she nearly fell off it, but she guessed he hadn't noticed with her wicked canines distracting him.

She desperately wanted to go back to sleep. She leaned against Huntley's shoulder as he wrapped his arm around her and they waited for the police to question them.

Two police officers approached the vehicle, one going to the driver's side, the other to the passenger's. Both pointed flashlights into the car to see who all was in it.

"Can we see your passports, *por favor*?" the police officer standing on the driver's side asked.

"Certainly." Everett handed him everyone's passports.

"Holiday?" the other police officer asked, peering into the backseat at Melissa and Huntley and shining his flashlight on them.

"Checking out the rainforests," Everett said. "Beautiful beaches, birds, everything. Hoped we'd catch sight of a jaguar, but they're awfully elusive."

"Recreational drugs?" the police officer asked, looking at Melissa, who felt her whole body chill with concern.

"No, officer. Not into that sort of thing." Everett pulled out his JAG badge. "We're all with a Special Forces agency in the United States. If we ever got caught using drugs, that would be the end of our careers."

"Can we see the rest of your badges?" the officer said, looking at Melissa as if he was certain *she* wouldn't have one.

Everett pulled them out of the console and handed them to the officer, but the officer just shook his head. "Just open them up and show them to me."

"What's wrong with you?" the other officer asked Melissa. "Been drinking?"

"Allergy medicine. It made me drowsy. I thought it was the non-drowsy formula," she said. "Last time I use that brand." She made a face of disgust.

"Fernando, we have all we need here," the first one said after checking the badges and quickly looking at Melissa and Huntley in the backseat.

"We haven't checked the trunk of their car, their car

rental agreement, or—" Fernando said, but the other man was already handing over the passports and bidding them a good night.

"But—" Fernando said, hurrying to join his partner.

"They are the ones!" the police officer hissed.

Fernando glanced back at the car.

"The ones Alvarez and his partner got into trouble over."

Fernando glanced back at the car, though he couldn't see in the dark interior now. The other officer waved for them to move along and Everett did.

And Melissa relaxed again against Huntley. Then she leaned over to pull some clothes out of her bag, wanting to get out of her borrowed stuff. Huntley helped her out of the long men's T-shirt and boxers, and smiled when he was assisting her into a pair of lace-trimmed robin's-egg blue bikini panties and the matching bra. She hoped that everyone sitting up front was watching out the window and not slipping peeks in her direction.

But it was hard to get changed in the backseat of a car. She pulled on a pair of jeans shorts and a royal blue tank top, leaving off her tennis shoes for later. She wanted to help Huntley change, not because he needed her help, but because she wanted to have her fingers on him. She slid the poacher's shirt off him, slipping her hands over his body while he tugged his own T-shirt over his head. He smiled back at her, kissing her forehead, then worked on the hard part of pulling off the jeans in the cramped quarters. His cock stood at attention. She smiled. Shaking his head, he smiled back at her.

"Your fault," he said. He pulled on a pair of briefs

and then his own jeans. After he tied on a pair of boots, he gathered her close again.

She smiled, thinking of Everett's comment about her being Huntley's new girlfriend. She had thought she'd just try it out—staying with him and seeing if they were really cut out for being together. But now she wasn't sure she was ready for it.

She'd believed that she could do this, but maybe not. Working with him was one thing. But worrying about him getting killed on a mission when they were mates? She realized that she really did like that Oliver was safe and sound at home so she didn't have to worry about him when she was on a mission. Sure, she worried about her partner on missions, but it was different, wasn't it? What if they had cubs, like the Carringtons? What if the cubs were home, and both she and Huntley were on jobs, maybe not working together on an assignment, and neither made it back?

At least someone who had a job like Oliver's would be home to take care of the cubs. One parent would be there for them growing up.

Not that she wanted her kids to be tame shifters. Then again, she didn't want to worry about them getting into a situation like Avery and Kathy's cubs had either.

Beyond that, how would it look if she and Huntley were together on jobs like this and no longer strictly partners? She realized they were displaying too much affection toward each other in public, when they should have been strictly equal partners on a mission. She sat up straighter, trying to be more agent-like and less like a wilting, drugged cat.

Huntley sighed and encouraged her to lie down on his

lap again. No matter what, she couldn't fight the urge to go along with his suggestion. As soon as she nestled her head in his lap, she promptly fell asleep.

Melissa felt the car stop and the engine shut off, so she lifted her head and then sat up, feeling a hundred percent now. Huntley had fallen asleep too, so she didn't feel bad that she was the only one who had been so out of it. She glanced at Avery and smiled. He was snoring a little, his head planted against the passenger's window. He probably hadn't had enough sleep either as he worried about how to rescue himself and his wife when they were still together, and then again after he lost her.

"Catnap time's over, folks." Everett gave them all a big grin as Avery and Huntley stirred, and then they climbed out of the car and headed inside the eatery.

The aroma of rice, beans, and chicken filled the air while the chatter of conversation surrounded them. They quickly spied Luke and Jason seated at one of the red vinyl-covered tables, and each man rose from his chair to give Avery a bear hug.

"Hell, man, we thought we might have lost you," Jason said.

"Not me. But I'm more than concerned about my wife. What do you have?" Avery asked.

A pretty waitress took their orders, and then left.

"See that guy over in the corner? The redhead?" Luke asked, his voice hushed as he leaned forward a little to speak privately to them.

The men were far enough away that they couldn't hear Luke, but she knew he was ensuring that others wouldn't overhear him and become suspicious about their interest in Pierre, in the event anyone knew him.

Surrounding each of the tables, vines hung from the ceiling like a screen, simulating the rainforest, to give each of the customers some privacy. The agents all looked in that direction.

"That's the jerk who's buying the animals. Pierre Beaufort," Jason said. "The one who bought Kathy."

Avery tensed so much that Melissa was afraid he'd make a scene. But he was good. He was seething, ready to shift and rip the man to shreds—after he intimidated him enough to locate his wife—but he remained seated, hands clenched, grinding his teeth, eyes narrowed, his posture rigid.

"He's living a half mile from here. Alone. Has a bamboo privacy fence with a locked gate. We couldn't see any cages from our vantage point, but we could smell cat urine. So we know he's had cats there before," Luke said. "We called out Kathy's name, but we didn't get any response. He wasn't home when we checked, so we picked the lock to his gate, slipped in, and found cages and your wife's scent, so we knew we were at the right place, but your wife wasn't there. We checked the house just in case and found a note on his calendar showing he was going to be here at this time. We headed on over here and waited in the car until we saw him park at the café. We couldn't take him in front of all the patrons. We figured we'd meet up with you here if you arrived in time."

"Now that we have a couple of vehicles, some of us could wait for him at his place while some of us followed him if he doesn't head straight home," Melissa said.

"Agreed," Huntley said.

"So who wants to do what?" Jason asked, looking at Avery, given that it was his wife who was at risk.

"I'll go with whoever's following the bastard," Avery said. "If he doesn't return home, he might be picking up more cats or something. I don't want to be sitting at an empty house, waiting to hear word."

"Melissa? Huntley?" Luke asked, still giving them the lead on the case.

"If he doesn't go to the house, he might be meeting up with Jackson. The man would most likely not go to Pierre's house," Melissa said.

"I agree," Huntley said. "We'll stay with Avery and follow Pierre. But we have a problem with rental cars. We don't want to get stopped by the police and have them learn that whoever signed for the rental car isn't driving it."

Everett nodded. "I'll have to go with you while the Whittaker brothers are house-sitting."

"Once we saw the note on Pierre's calendar about coming here, we didn't have a whole lot of time to do a thorough search of his place. We'll do it this time and maybe discover another lead," Jason said. "We did grab our GPS tracker off the boat before Martin let the authorities know it was being used to steal cats from the park. After Pierre went inside the café, Luke attached the GPS tracker to Pierre's car."

Melissa smiled. "You guys really come in handy." She saw Pierre sit up a little taller in his seat, then motion with his head to someone in greeting. "Did he say who he was meeting?" Melissa asked.

All heads turned in Pierre's direction. None of them recognized the swarthy, dark-haired man.

"He only scribbled the words: 'noon,' 'lunch,' and the name of this café," Luke said.

Pierre and his lunch companion huddled over the table discussing some matter.

Then suddenly Pierre straightened his back, lost all the color in his face, and stared at the man for a moment.

Melissa didn't want to voice the concern she had, but Pierre seemed to have received bad news. About Kathy? Or something else?

"Look away," Melissa said, getting a cat's wary sixth sense that the man would glance around the room. Everyone at her table did what she told them as the waitress served up their meals. True, the vines helped to screen them from view, but if Pierre managed to see a glimpse of all the agents watching him, she figured that would spook him.

Melissa continued watching Pierre, but in a more inconspicuous way. He didn't notice her as her lunch companions hurried to scarf down their meals. When Huntley was through with his, he said, "Eat yours, Melissa. I'll keep an eye on the situation."

Pierre and the other man were again huddled together, talking to each other. She wished she could hear what was being said, but she ate her meal while Huntley continued to surreptitiously observe the men. She felt that any second, Pierre would flee.

"I think we need another plan," she said. "Instead of the ones who were planning to house-sit, I believe you should follow his friend. I suspect he knows what Pierre is up to."

"Sounds like a good change of plan to me." Huntley took a sip of his coffee. "Same deal as before?" He was still watching the two men when she finished her meal.

"Yeah," Avery said. "I'm all for still following Pierre."

Luke paid for their meals. "Okay, same setup as before."

"Let's go before they do," Huntley said.

"Got to use the little girls' room," Melissa said. She couldn't imagine that no one else needed use the facilities.

"Actually," Huntley said, "I could use a pit stop too."

Avery got up with them.

"Guess that leaves us holding down the fort," Everett said to the other two agents.

"We'll be quick," Huntley said.

Melissa hated that she had to run to the bathroom at a time like this, but it might be the only opportunity she had. She rushed through her business and headed out of the bathroom, nearly colliding with Pierre.

"Sorry," she said, rattled. She smelled the scent of jaguar on him and wanted to growl, but instead gave him a pretty, faked smile. She hoped that if Avery was still in the restroom, he didn't kill the guy when Pierre walked inside the men's room.

Pierre smiled back at her as if he thought she might really be interested in him, but then Huntley and Avery exited the men's room and an instant of barely controlled tension rolled off the two agents. She hurried back to the table where the others were waiting, while Huntley and Avery followed after her, thank God.

"Ready to go?" Huntley asked everyone.

"Yeah, let's do it," Everett said.

The other agents waited for Melissa and her party to leave the place first.

The man who had been eating with Pierre was just

finishing up his meal when Melissa and her group walked past his table. Everyone was taking in deep breaths, trying to determine if he had been around the jaguars or other big cats. He had.

Melissa was dying to learn if the jaguar cat's scent she had picked up on Pierre and at the compound was Kathy's. As soon as they got into Everett's rental, Pierre exited the café, moving fast. He wasn't looking anywhere but at his pickup truck.

Luke and Jason stalked outside, then got into another vehicle.

Before their "game" made his appearance in the parking lot, Pierre started his rumbly engine and drove off down the road.

Everett followed him at a distance.

"As soon as we learn where Kathy is, he's a dead man," Avery said.

No one said a word. She understood just how he felt. Huntley wrapped his arm around her shoulders as a nonverbal way of saying he'd feel the same about her if something like this happened to her.

Well, ditto if it happened to Huntley. Which had her thinking about how dangerous being lovers while on a mission could be. They could get careless, too concerned about each other, and not pay enough attention to the tasks they had to perform to get the job done right.

They watched Pierre as he drove down one street, then another. Everett turned off on another road so the guy wouldn't realize they were following him. They continued to monitor his signal with the GPS tracker.

"He's stopped, next road over," Avery said, sounding a tad anxious.

Everett drove onto another road and then turned onto the one that Pierre had taken.

"There," Avery said.

Pierre had parked at a house where a man greeted him outside, dogs bouncing around them. The man shook his head, then Pierre said something. The man shook his head again.

Then Pierre was back in his truck and headed down the road.

"Something's up," Avery said.

"What if he got word that a bunch of Jackson's men died and he's checking his sources?" Melissa ventured.

Everyone was quiet for a moment. Then Huntley said, "Possibly. I'm certain the word would have gotten out to all these lowlifes."

Melissa speculated that the guy was trying to hide his tracks in case anyone discovered he was involved.

"He appears to be heading to his house, from the address Luke gave us," Avery said.

"Good. Once he goes inside, we can question him in private," Melissa said.

Everett drove into the driveway and blocked the man's truck in case he decided to make a run for it. The place was isolated, most likely because Pierre was dealing in the illegal transportation of exotic wildlife.

They all hurried out of the car to intercept him as he headed for his house.

"We'll go with you." Avery took hold of Pierre's arm. And the way Avery gripped it, Melissa knew that if the guy lived very long, his arm would be wearing Avery's handprint in the form of a very large bruise.

"What do you want?" Pierre sounded like he was

about ready to expire on the spot. His face was as red as his hair. He was middle management, not one of the men running around in the rainforest risking his neck. Nope, he was living quietly here, just handing the cats— or anything else he managed to get his hands on—over to someone else, maybe another middle man?

That was what they were eager to learn.

Chapter 17

HUNTLEY WAS AFRAID AVERY WOULD KILL PIERRE before they got anything useful out of him, so he was the good cop in this scenario, giving Avery a warning look to release the man and back off. Melissa and Everett let Huntley handle it.

Avery gave Huntley the darkest, most dangerous smile he had ever seen on a man who was on *his* side.

"You had a female jaguar here. Where is she now?" Huntley asked, forcing Pierre to sit on a chair, then towering over him.

The man looked at Melissa and said, "You! You were at the café. You followed me here." His gaze focused again on Huntley. "What do you want with me? I don't know anything about a stolen Jaguar. Look around here." He waved his hand at the rundown place. "Would... would I have a car like that and be able to sell it?"

Huntley almost smiled. But he didn't and instead said, "Let me try this one more time. You bought a female jaguar from Timothy Jackson. She was here. DNA evidence proves it." He lied, but Pierre would never know that. "Now, we can do this the easy way and you tell us where she's gone, or we can do it the hard way. Believe me, you don't want to do this the hard way."

The man swallowed visibly. "How...how did you get my name? Phil Gorsman...that's who told you? He's... he's dead. You guys... Oh God."

"Easy or hard," Huntley said.

"You're not going to let me live, are you? If I tell you anything, that's it."

Avery yanked off his shirt. "The hard way it is."

"You had your chance," Huntley said.

The man's eyes couldn't have gotten any rounder. "Wait, okay. I...I sold her to Carlos Ranchero."

"Where is he?" Huntley asked.

"I don't know where he lives or—"

"How do you get in touch with him?"

"His phone number. I...I have it on my cell phone."

"Get it."

Pierre fumbled in his pocket, then finally pulled the phone out and nearly dropped it because his hands were shaking so badly.

Huntley scowled at him. "Call him."

"What?"

"Tell him you want to see him right away. You've got a deal for him. A cat or something that you might sell him that would be so incredible he can't resist," Huntley said. "Your life hangs in the balance here, Pierre. You either get him to come here pronto, or well, let's just say you won't like the alternative."

"What if he gets suspicious? What if he thinks something's wrong? I just met him for lunch and didn't say a thing about this."

"You make him believe that nothing is wrong. That you just got a sweet deal that you hadn't expected. Make it real, something the man can't resist. A couple of mating jaguars."

"All right, all right." Pierre licked his lips, then took a deep breath and called Carlos. "Hey, man, I got to unload a couple of cats real quick. They're a mating pair of jaguars. Yeah, no shit. Why didn't I mention it earlier? The guys just dropped them off. Said they were in a rush to get some quick cash. But you know that trouble I got into with Merco, the loan shark, a month ago? Yeah, yeah, I know, but I need some quick cash again. The cats are really healthy. Can you drop by my place? You want a picture of them?" He glanced up at Huntley, looking panicked.

Huntley nodded.

"Okay, I'll get back to you in a couple of minutes and send it to you." Pierre ended the call. "How the hell am I going to get a picture that doesn't look like I took it off a website?"

"You watch him," Avery said, "and I'll do this."

"No, wait. You watch him," Huntley said. "Everett?"

"Got your back," Everett said.

Then Huntley and Melissa headed for one of the bedrooms.

"What…what are they doing?" Pierre asked Avery.

In the privacy of the guy's bedroom, Melissa and Huntley stripped out of their clothes.

"Getting a couple of jaguars so you can take your damned picture," Avery said.

As jaguars, Melissa loped into the living room and Huntley followed right afterward. All the color blanched out of Pierre's face. "What…what's going on?"

"Take the picture," Avery said.

"In…in the house?"

"Will he recognize your backyard?"

"Yeah. I have a tiled bird fountain he's often remarked he likes. It has a tile mosaic of a jaguar eyeing the birds."

"Okay, let's do this. And don't pull anything stupid because they're friends of mine," Avery said, motioning with his thumb to Melissa and Huntley. "And if I say so, they'll rip you to shreds."

The man was so shaky that Everett finally grabbed hold of his arm and helped him out of the house, while Huntley and Melissa followed them outside.

"He won't believe it if the cats aren't in a cage," Pierre said, eyeing Huntley and Melissa with trepidation.

"Skip the cages," Everett said. "Take the picture and call him back."

Huntley nuzzled Melissa as she stared at the camera in front of the bird fountain. He thought it was a nice salable shot. He was glad his brother said no more cages because he really didn't want either Melissa or himself to have to get into another one anytime soon.

Pierre called Carlos back. "Hey, Carlos, I took a couple shots of them. Here they are." Pierre paused, then said, "Yeah, um, the black one is even rarer." He looked up at Avery and Everett eyeing him, both wearing scowls. "The jaguars are really…agreeable. The tranquilizer hasn't worn off yet. I'll have them back in the cages before you get here. Okay, see you in half an hour."

Pierre ended the call and looked like he was about to fall down. "Where the hell did they come from?"

"Believe me, you don't want to know." Everett guided him back into the house and Melissa and Huntley followed behind Avery, joining the others inside.

Pierre glanced again at the cats and then back at Everett. "You were already at the house, weren't you? I thought things were out of order in the living room. So you left the cats in my bedroom before? What if they'd killed me?"

"Sit," Everett told him, directing him to the same wooden chair.

"So what do we do now? I did all that you asked," Pierre said, starting to whine.

"We wait nice and quiet-like. When Carlos gets here, we'll see what he has to say about the female jaguar. If he tells us he doesn't know anything about it…we start over from the beginning. Only we're doing it *my* way this time," Avery said.

They waited for well past the half hour. Huntley worried that Avery would lose his cool. Melissa began to pace. Huntley lay down on the floor next to Pierre and rested his head on Pierre's boot. The man didn't dare move. Everett was observing Pierre, his arms folded across his chest.

Avery watched out the window. "Forty-five minutes and he's a no-show."

"Maybe he's…he's spooked. You know, we got the word that some of Jackson's men were taken down," Pierre said, grasping at any reason the buyer might not show up.

Avery sliced him a glower.

"I don't know! Maybe he was suspicious that the cats were out of the cages. I would be. Or maybe he had to get some men to help him load the cats into his truck. Just the two of us couldn't do it."

Avery tensed. "A truck is pulling up. What do you usually do? Greet him? Wait for him to knock?"

"He'll call to let me know he's arrived. You got your car blocking my truck. It might make him wary."

Pierre's phone rang. He glanced at it, then uneasily at Avery. "It's him."

"Answer it and watch what you say."

Pierre nodded. Then he said, "Yeah, Carlos. I'm here. The car? It belongs to the two guys that had the cats delivered. They're still here. I couldn't pay them off until you paid me. The cats are too valuable to just... I know, I know. We don't usually do it this way. But I told you I'm in a financial bind. I can't pay them. So they're hanging around until they get paid. Okay. I'm coming out." Pierre ended the call. "He wants me to come out. *Alone*. He sounds like he suspects something."

Avery smiled, but the look wasn't at all pleasant. "Do you think I was born yesterday?"

"No...no, man. I promise," Pierre said, spreading his hands out wide. "No tricks."

Avery's phone rang, and he lifted it to his ear and smiled a genuine smile this time. "Good to hear from you. Perfect timing. The truck parked in front of you belongs to the next middleman. Make sure Carlos and whoever else is with him join us inside." Avery turned to Pierre. "No problem. Carlos and his cohorts are being escorted inside as we speak."

Huntley could just imagine what Luke and Jason, as that's who they had to be, thought of the situation when they walked into the house with Carlos and two other men and saw him and Melissa in their jaguar coats.

Carlos tried to back out of the house as soon as he saw the uncaged cats. Luke knocked one of the men out cold as soon as he fought to leave. The other wet his pants.

"Not so tough when the cats are out of their cages, eh?" Avery asked, his voice hard.

Luke and Jason smiled.

Everett said to Carlos and his henchman, "Take a seat, Carlos, and you too."

"Where is the female jaguar this piece of shit sold to you?" Avery asked as soon as the two men were seated.

Carlos looked at Pierre as if he wanted to kill him. Probably would if he lived through this.

Melissa grew closer to Carlos and snarled, baring her teeth.

"She hasn't eaten lately," Everett said. "Give us the answers we want and we'll be on our way."

"If we tell you—" Carlos said, his voice shaking.

This time Huntley roared and displayed his very sharp, very long teeth.

"Yasmine Baker," Carlos spit out.

"A woman?" Everett asked, sounding as though he couldn't believe it.

"I don't ask. Some woman, or anyone for that matter, asks for something, I check with Pierre and he gets with his source and gets it for me, and I give it to the buyer."

"How do we get in touch with her?" Avery asked.

"You think you're going straight to the buyer with a couple of…" Carlos looked at the jaguars as if he couldn't believe what he was seeing. "She already bought a female. She wanted a male, but the one we had was acting so vicious that she wouldn't have wanted him. So I sold her the female. But if you think I'm going to tell her where…"

Patience gone, Huntley bit into his thigh.

Carlos cried out in pain and agony, and the other man tried to scramble off the couch, but Everett grabbed his shoulder and made him stay put. Pierre's face drained of color.

"Where can I get hold of this Yasmine Baker?" Avery asked again.

Huntley had only given Carlos a minor taste of what he could give him if he didn't cooperate, but the way the man's face was sweating and his heart was racing, Huntley didn't want to give him a premature heart attack. Carlos was clutching his leg, applying pressure to the wound.

Carlos struggled to get his cell phone off his belt, then found Yasmine Baker's contact information and gave it to Avery. Then clasped his hand over his bloody wound again.

"You come with us," Avery said. "Who's staying with Pierre?"

Huntley nudged at Melissa and she grunted at him, then they returned to the bedroom, shifted, and dressed. "We go with Avery," Melissa said, rejoining the men.

Carlos and the other man just stared at them.

"We'll leave the jaguars here in case you have any trouble with Pierre," Huntley said to Luke and Jason. "If we track down the woman and the jaguar, we'll give you a call. Do you want to stay with the three of these men?" he asked his brother.

"Sure."

"Good luck," Luke said.

Jason nodded at them.

"Let's go." Avery grabbed Carlos's arm, but the man had nearly passed out from the pain. "He didn't bite you that hard. Hell, if he'd wanted to, he would have crushed the bone. All he did was sink his teeth in a little. Enough to let you know we mean business."

He hauled Carlos out to Luke's rented car, and then they were off. Huntley hoped they wouldn't get stopped and have the police want to see the car rental papers.

"Had the woman wanted a mating pair of jaguars?" Huntley asked, sitting in the backseat with Carlos while Avery drove and Melissa was the passenger up front.

"Yes. She said she wanted…cubs. Once she had them, she wanted to know if I'd buy the pair of adult jaguars back from her. I told her if they were in good shape and the deal was right, I would consider it. As long as I made the money off the sale to her and then got to sell them again, I'd do so. I wouldn't have to pay the poacher any money this time. But then she didn't want the male because he was too aggressive, and she wanted me to get her another male."

"But she lives here in Costa Rica?" Melissa asked, sounding like she couldn't believe it.

"Yeah. Well, for a few months of the year. She's American. So she returns after she gets what she wants. She'll be hanging around for a couple more months. Then I heard some poachers were killed and…" His eyes widened.

"Call her and tell her you have a male jaguar for her," Melissa said.

"I always send her a picture first."

"Okay, then tell her you have a mated pair, but they're inseparable. Show her the picture that Pierre sent you," Melissa said.

"Then what? If she wants them, I deliver them. She's

not going to believe I'm delivering them in the trunk of your car. And, hell, I'm injured!" Carlos said.

"He's got a point." Avery turned the car around.

"What are you doing?" Melissa asked, upset.

"Getting his truck. The buyer will believe Carlos has the cats in the back of the truck," Avery said.

They were only a short way away when Avery had turned around and drove back to Pierre's house. They switched vehicles, Huntley waving at Luke who was watching out the window, and then they piled into Carlos's truck and took off again.

"So what are you going to do? Threaten the woman to give up the cat? Did the man who sold it to Pierre steal it from you? Or promise to sell her to someone else?" Carlos asked. "What's so special about this cat?"

"You know what you're doing is illegal, right?" Melissa asked, as if the bastard didn't have a clue.

"So what? You're some animal activists and you intend to release her back to the wild? How the hell did you ever train those cats to act the way they did? When I saw the picture Pierre sent to me, I thought for sure that he had Photoshopped them. If he even knew how to do such a thing. But when I examined it closely, I knew it hadn't been. When those other guys strong-armed us into Pierre's house, I was certain that the cats weren't really there. But then there they were. Are they…highly trained guard cats or something? Wait, the one I sold wasn't a guard cat, too, was she? Ah hell, sure. Somehow Pierre bought a cat that you guys already owned and…you probably paid a fortune to train her."

Huntley wanted to tell the guy to shut up, but instead

he said, "Call her. Tell her you've picked up a mating pair, but you have to deliver them quickly or you'll have to sell them to another interested buyer."

Carlos nodded and made the call. "Ms. Baker, I've got just the cats you want for your collection. They're a mated pair." He frowned. "Good natured." He glanced down at his bloody leg. "Yeah, the female might be carrying cubs already. I'll send you some pictures." He put his hand over the phone. "She said I can come over tomorrow."

"Now," Avery growled, "or the deal is off."

"I've got another buyer I'm supposed to take them to this evening to let him look at them. If you want to wait until tomorrow, that's fine by me. But if you want to see them now, you can get a jump on the other buyer." Carlos took a deep breath. "I understand. I'll let you know if the other deal falls through, and then I'll see you tomorrow morning at eight." He ended the call. "I can't force her to see me," he said to Avery, who jerked the truck into the ditch.

"Okay," Huntley said. "We scope out the place, Avery. And we'll take it from there."

"She has a nice place," Carlos warned.

"Drug money?" Huntley asked, getting suspicious.

Carlos shrugged. "Hell if I know where she's getting her money from. It's near the beaches and rainforest, and has a walled-in backyard and a swimming pool."

"And a cat run?" Avery growled.

"Large, partly landscaped. Trees inside, but the fencing stretches across the top. She spared no expense on it. Even a small pool for the cat. So it's a nice deal, really."

Melissa sighed. Huntley felt some relief too.

"Just the woman lives there? Any man around?" Huntley asked.

"A couple of men. I think they are her bodyguards or security. The place is safe, but you know how it is."

"Yeah, lots of characters like you doing illegal stuff," Melissa said.

"So what do you think *you're* doing?" Carlos asked. "Keeping exotic cats as guard animals? Hell, that's worse than anything *I've* ever done."

"Did she have plans to be out tonight or something?" Huntley asked. "And that's why she can't meet with you? Or is she really not interested?"

"She said she had a prior social engagement that she couldn't break."

"Calling this in," Melissa said, and Huntley thought she sounded frustrated.

He didn't blame her. He hoped that they would find Avery's wife there and then fly her back home as soon as they could.

They drove through the small town of Quepos, past six blocks of restaurants and bars, hotels, gift shops, and bakeries. The town was situated along the main beach, and a sports fishing fleet was harbored there.

"Used to be a big market for bananas here," Carlos said as if he couldn't shut up—probably nervous. "Then there was a big market for palm oil. Now all the tourists hit the area in the dry season for eco stuff."

"Like seeing the beautiful animals that you and your buddies threaten to eliminate from their natural habitats?" Melissa said.

Carlos shut up after that. Thankfully.

They noted the streets were wet and there wasn't a lot of traffic. Which Huntley was glad for. And it seemed to be getting ready to rain again, the sky darkening.

"Hey, boss, we hope we're getting closer to picking up the female cat. We have one of the middlemen with us and he's helping us to reach her. Let me ask him." She turned and said, "Do you know a Timothy Jackson?"

"Hell, yeah. I heard a bunch of his men were taken out some time recently."

"Do you know where he got off to?" Melissa asked.

Carlos shook his head. "I don't deal with the poachers. It's safer for me that way. You'll have to ask Pierre. He's the one who deals directly with them."

"That's a negative, boss. We'll keep you posted. We should be there momentarily. Out here."

The housing development was nice. Huntley had looked it up on his borrowed phone and discovered that a home selling in this area was worth $350,000. For there, that was a lot.

But Carlos was right. The area was a little pricey for the old truck they were driving. Though Huntley imagined some of the places had gardening crews. As rainy as it was, they didn't see anything like that.

"Here it is," Melissa and Carlos said together.

The two-car garage door was going up and the backup lights on a yellow Maserati were shining as someone began to pull out of the garage.

"That's her," Carlos warned.

Avery hightailed it out of there until he reached the next street in the development and turned off there so she wouldn't see Carlos's truck and become suspicious.

Using a map on the phone, Huntley guided Avery around the development so he could return to the house. It wouldn't be dark for another hour, though.

"What do you want to do?" Avery asked. "If she's in there and safe, I'm good with waiting until it's dark."

"Good. That's what I'd opt for," Huntley said.

"I'm all for it. What are we going to do about him?" Melissa asked.

"It may take all three of us to go after her," Huntley said.

"I'm wounded. I'll just wait for you in the truck. I'm not even sure I can walk any distance," Carlos said.

No one said anything, but Melissa figured knocking him out was their best bet.

Avery drove back to the town and parked at one of the restaurants so that no one would notice them much. Not like driving around the ritzy development.

When the rains began pouring down and the sky darkened sufficiently, they figured it was time to chance it.

They still hadn't decided what to do with Carlos. Then Melissa said, "We can lock him in the back of the truck. Like he would do with one of the cats. Got any cages back there?"

Huntley held out his hand. "Give me your cell phone."

Carlos gave it to him. Huntley had to help him into the back of the truck, then climbed in with him and shut him up in a cage. "Stay there. When we get the cat, she's going to be in the back with you. Except she'll be on the outside of the cage guarding you. So if you don't want a jaguar to finish you off, do as I tell you."

"*Sí, sí,*" Carlos said, sitting on his butt and looking anxious, his hand clutching his thigh.

Not that Kathy would be joining Carlos back there, but the threat appeared to make the man compliant.

Then Huntley closed the cage door, left the truck, closed its door, and locked it.

When they reached the house, they knew they didn't have any choice but to pull into the driveway and deal with this. If the guards were watching, they'd come check them out. There wasn't anywhere for them to park inconspicuously nearby.

"Let's go," Huntley said, and the three of them were out of the truck in a flash. He hoped the hell that Carlos was right, that Kathy was here and safe—and none of the three agents or Avery's wife would be injured while freeing her.

Chapter 18

MELISSA WAS READY TO KILL THE GUARDS OR ANYONE else who tried to stop them from freeing Kathy. And she knew by the way that Avery was giving off an angry scent that he was also ready to kill. A guard, at least they thought he might be, came out to speak with them. They assumed at least another was waiting in the house for them, watching to see what would happen.

"Where's Carlos?" the man asked, his skin a light brown, his English heavily accented with Spanish. He was wearing a suit coat and black trousers that looked completely out of place there in the tropics.

"He wanted us to bring the jaguars here so Ms. Baker could see them," Melissa said. "He said that she didn't want to miss out on them."

"She had a social engagement and told him she would see him tomorrow."

"Do you want to see the cats? The male is a black. Rare. Beautiful," Melissa said.

"I don't care anything about the cats," the man said. "Now leave before I have to call the police."

"She buys exotic cats stolen from a reserve. That's illegal," Melissa said, arching a brow.

The man reached his hand into his suit coat, but Huntley grabbed his arm and said, "Don't move or I'll break it."

"Who the hell are you people? What do you want?"

"A stolen jaguar," Melissa said. "We don't care about Ms. Baker or you and your bodyguard friend. But we do care about the cat."

"Where's Carlos?" the man asked again, and she got the impression the guard knew him.

"Safe. So shall we go into the house and pretend to be friends? Or do we get…rough?" Melissa asked.

He smiled down at her a little like he didn't believe she could best him.

"Don't test me," she said.

Huntley removed the man's weapon, and then they headed for the house. "Ms. Baker's not going to like this," the guard said.

"She doesn't have to like it. And the cat doesn't belong to her," Melissa said.

She was certain they would have trouble as soon as they entered the house. If they could enter it. But the other guy inside wouldn't unlock the door.

Avery headed around to the back gate. Melissa was torn between getting into the house and taking out the other guard, or going with Avery in case the other guard intercepted him back there. Then she said, "Come on, let's go."

Huntley followed her lead, thankfully, and they rushed the guard to the back gate. "Got a key?" she asked.

Avery was still trying to break the lock with a rock.

"No," the guard said.

"Screw this." Avery jumped over the wall.

They heard running footsteps and Melissa climbed over the wall after him, leaving Huntley to deal with the guard.

Two men were coming for Avery. Two guards. Damn

it. Melissa went for the second guard. Being a woman, she found that men didn't take her seriously. She was too cute and petite to be dangerous. Avery and Huntley, on the other hand, looked like they could dish out some injuries, as well built as they were.

The men both went for Avery. That gave her the advantage she needed since they were armed with knives and they ignored her.

She proved the one wrong, jumping with a sidekick to the guy's leg just as he sliced at Avery with a knife. The men probably didn't want to fire off guns in the high-priced neighborhood and risk having one of the neighbors, or several, call the police.

The man went down, crying out in pain. She immediately kicked him in the head and knocked him out. Then she raced for the cage the jaguar was in.

Avery was still fighting the last man, who was trying to stick him with a knife.

Melissa had just reached the locked cage when she heard Huntley rush to help Avery. Between the two of them, they knocked the last guard out.

"Locked!" Melissa called out.

The cat was pacing in front of the gate, roaring to get out. And then Melissa saw a smaller "exhibit" that contained two margays. As soon as Melissa and the others were out of here, they could notify the authorities, and when Ms. Baker got home from her social engagement, she could deal with the fallout.

Huntley found a rock, and he and Avery ran to the cat enclosure. Huntley struck the lock several times before breaking it. Avery jerked the lock off the cage door and let Kathy out. She was all over him, licking and hugging him with her forelegs while she remained in her jaguar form. He was hugging her back, and Melissa swore he had tears of relief in his eyes.

"Why don't you guys... Where's the other guard?" Melissa asked.

"He's in the truck. Knocked out. We'll leave Carlos and the guard in there and drive back to Pierre's place," Huntley said.

"Okay, good." Melissa turned to Kathy. "I'm Melissa Overton, JAG branch, and this is my partner, Huntley Anderson. Your babies are home safe. Why don't you and I go inside and find some of Ms. Baker's clothes to wear? You should have seen Huntley and I take care of your babies. He wore more of the bottled milk on his shirt than he was feeding to them at times."

Kathy gave her a jaguar-sized grin and the two of them headed for the house.

"I won't feel good about this until she's on a plane headed for home," Avery said.

"I don't blame you," Huntley said.

Avery let out his breath. "I don't know how you do it."

"What's that?" Huntley asked.

"Work on assignment with Melissa and not worry every second about her."

"She's got great instincts and is a hell of an agent," Huntley said, and when Melissa turned to give a smile for the compliment, he winked back at her and then got on the phone to call the boss.

The house wasn't quite as posh as Melissa had expected, but it was nice. All tropical decor: green and purple floral fabrics, tiled floors, ceiling fans, and a huge entertainment center. Melissa and Kathy quickly located the woman's bedroom, and while Kathy found some undergarments, Melissa looked in the closet. "Something fancy, or simple?"

"Anything will do. After what the woman put me through, I should borrow her most expensive clothes, though I have to say this cage was a lot nicer than where I had been. But I couldn't believe a woman would buy exotic animals from the park so she could raise cubs. She didn't want Avery. She planned to buy another male. I could just imagine being stuck in here with a full-time jaguar. Then she was on the phone to someone earlier and told her guard that the seller had another pair of cats for her to look at.

"She said they were a mated pair. Scared me because I was afraid she'd figure I was of no use to her now. And she'd sell me off to someone else where the conditions were lots worse. I was so worried about Avery and what they would do to him. And if anyone could find me before something really awful happened. Then too, I couldn't quit worrying about Jaime and Jenny. I smelled your scents in the tent, and you were my only hope. I went to rescue Avery, but that was a big mistake."

"We'll get you home as quickly as possible." Melissa gave Kathy a hug. The poor woman had to have been terrified. At least Melissa had training in escape and evasion. "What about this T-shirt?"

"That will do." Kathy pulled the aqua T-shirt over her head, then found some jeans with sequins on the pockets, and a pair of hiking shoes. "Good fit." She turned and gave Melissa a hug this time before she broke into tears.

Melissa's eyes misted. "We've got to get you and Avery back home to your kids." She hugged Kathy back. "We were so worried about you." She told Kathy all that had happened while they took care of her cubs, hoping to cheer her. The poor woman wasn't a fighter, not trained for ordeals like this. She was simply a mother wishing to be back with her babies.

When they went outside, the bodyguards were missing. "Where are the two other bodyguards?" Melissa asked.

Huntley jerked his thumb at the cage. "In there." The guys were still unconscious, naked now, and Avery and Huntley had managed to find another lock and locked them in. "See how they like being in there."

"Maybe we should put the other one that's in the truck in the cage too," Melissa said.

"Already done."

Melissa glanced back at the cat cage and then realized three men's naked backsides were flashing her instead of two. "Good." She got on the phone and called "their" local policeman to alert him about Ms. Yasmine Baker and her illegal possession of the margays and the location of her property.

Sounding surprised that she'd call him with a heads-up, Alvarez asked, "Will you be there when we get there?"

"No. We've secured Ms. Baker's bodyguards in another pen where we found evidence indicating she also had a jaguar here, but it's gone now. Got to go. We'll alert you if we find any other cases."

He thanked her and she thought he now believed that she and her partner really were here to help them out. Then she and the others left and headed to Pierre's house. Kathy sat on Avery's lap on the drive back as if they couldn't get enough of each other. He told her all that had happened to him after the poachers had sold her, and she thanked Melissa and Huntley for taking care of the babies and all they'd done.

Huntley rested his hand on Melissa's leg as if he wanted what Avery had with Kathy.

Time would tell, she figured. She scooted closer to him anyway and called Luke. "We've got her. We'll be there in a couple of hours to drop off the truck and pick up the car and leave." Then she called Martin.

"We'll make arrangements to fly the Carringtons home at the earliest possible time. Let me know when you meet up with Luke and Jason," Martin said, still tense. They wouldn't feel good about this until the Carringtons were on their way home.

Two hours later, they were back at Pierre's house. And then they left Carlos in his truck for Pierre to deal with, giving a stern warning to all four men that if they ever sold anything from one of the reserves again, they were dead men.

Pierre was wringing his hands, glancing at the bedroom where Huntley and Melissa had shifted into jaguars and then back again. When they headed outside, he hurried after them. "Wait! You left the jaguars in my bedroom. Aren't you going to take them with you?"

"It's illegal to take jaguars anywhere. Didn't we just tell you that?" Huntley said. "We certainly don't want to be caught red-handed hauling them around. You deal with it." Then he stopped and turned and gave Pierre a steely glower. "And that means return them to the park where they were taken from. Not selling them to someone else."

"But…"

"Do it. But watch that female's bite. It can be worse than the male's."

The shifters were all fighting smiles. Then Everett, Melissa, and Huntley climbed into Everett's rental car and the Carringtons headed out with Luke and Jason. Their mission was to get the couple home. Melissa's, Huntley's, and Everett's task was to go after Jackson.

Everett was driving, Huntley riding up front, while Melissa called Martin back and put the call on speaker. "Any leads on Jackson?"

"First, I just wanted to say you all did a damn good job on rescuing the Carringtons. As to Jackson, we suspect he got word that his men are dead and that the police are crawling all over the place. Why don't you find lodging for the night, get some rest, and tomorrow I'll update you," Martin said.

"Okay, will do." Melissa said to Everett, "Find some place near the forest reserve. Until we have to leave here for our next assignment, I want to enjoy the rainforest atmosphere right next door."

"You got it," Everett said. He glanced at Huntley. "I wonder how long it will take for Pierre to check out his bedroom and find that the man-eating cats aren't in there."

Melissa chuckled, then sighed. "Do you really think the two men will quit selling poached exotic animals?"

"Hell, yeah. Not that either of them will get legitimate jobs if they give up dealing in exotic animals. Now, Carlos? Unless he can get medical care without arousing the suspicion of the police, or he pays them off, who knows what might happen to him? My bite left punctures in his leg, and if he doesn't get some antibiotics and get it taken care of, he might end up losing the leg, or more. As to Pierre, I think he knows we'll be back if we have any hint that he's selling again. In fact, it wouldn't hurt for one of our guys to pose as a buyer in the near future and test him. If he offers to deal, no more chances."

"Did you at least open the bedroom window so that Pierre doesn't wonder what happened to the cats?" Everett asked.

"Yeah. I was damned tempted not to, though. Let him figure out what was going on," Huntley said.

Melissa chuckled. "I closed it."

The brothers laughed.

"How about this place?" Everett asked, driving into the parking lot of a two-story hotel.

"Looks good to me. It's situated right next to the rainforest reserve so I can still enjoy all the jungle sounds," Melissa said.

"Perfect." Everett added, "So, Huntley, are we sharing a room like usual?" He smiled like he had made a joke, but it forced Melissa into considering the situation, when she hadn't given it any thought before this.

She and Huntley weren't a couple dating each other on a vacation. All three of them were agents on a mission. As soon as Everett made the comment, she felt obligated to remind everyone that she was just another agent working with them on an assignment.

"Yes. The two of you can share a room. If we can get another one next door, that would be great. If not, no problem," she said, shrugging and perfectly straight-faced because she meant it.

But the two men were staring at her as though she'd shifted into a jaguar right there in front of God and everyone, their mouths gaping a bit, their eyes widened. Then Everett looked like he wanted to bow out of this one fast and quickly said, "I'll get us a couple of rooms."

Before Melissa could follow Everett and avoid talking with Huntley about this, he stopped her, hand on her arm in a gentle, worried way. She looked up at him, saw the concern in his expression, and worried that he felt they were breaking up when they hadn't even officially dated yet.

Even more now, she didn't believe going home and setting up housekeeping with Huntley was a good idea. She needed to move her stuff into her own space so she could have time to consider what she was doing. Maybe they could date on and off between missions. She'd like that. But moving in with him right away—no.

"We're teamed up on this mission," Huntley said, as if hoping that would remind her of their assignment to work together and would make all the difference in the world.

She had to admit, it did to an extent. When the boss sent a team together, they stayed together until they solved their case or were ordered home. But now that three of them were there, working together, it felt awkward to her to stay with Huntley when Everett normally did. As if Huntley was truly her boyfriend. Which he wasn't. They were...teammates.

"Right," she said. "And we'll continue to work on the case until the boss says otherwise. We will all stick together. But concerning the rooms tonight, since we're agents on a case, this will work out best. Like you said, you do well talking with your brother about a case. Maybe he can come up with some ideas we haven't thought of."

"You and I can do that tonight," Huntley said. "You come up with plans that are just as well thought out."

"I…I think we both need a little time to know what's right." She sighed. "When I return home, I'll find a place and get moved in. Then whenever you and I are home from our own missions, we can find time to see each other."

He let out his breath and released her arm. "All right."

She was a little surprised when he didn't fight her on it, but then again, he was probably feeling the same needs as she'd been experiencing, and knew this was all too soon and too fast for both of them.

"Come on. Let's join Everett." Huntley kept his distance from her, treating her strictly like his partner, which was a good thing.

So why did she want his arm around her shoulders, feeling him close? Because she was damned needy. That alone proved she needed to keep her distance.

They entered the lobby, where a couple of blue parrots in a golden cage chattered and tropical fish swam around in a saltwater tank nearby. Everett sat in one of the floral-covered chairs, room keys in hand, waiting for them.

"Do you want to get dinner together before we go up to our rooms, or did you just want to get room service?" she asked.

"We can eat dinner down here," Everett quickly said, as if he'd already said the wrong thing regarding the rooms and didn't want to further upset his brother.

Everett would probably get hell for teasing about it in the first place. But even if he hadn't said anything about staying with Huntley, she would have opted for her own room while the brothers roomed together. She was just glad Huntley hadn't made some crack about having to stay with her to protect her.

"We'll eat together," Huntley said and walked toward the hotel restaurant without a backward glance.

Now Everett's face was flushed. "Sorry about the rooms. I was just…"

Melissa smiled brightly. "No problem. This works out perfectly." Then she headed for the restaurant, while Everett took a couple of long strides to catch up.

"I just thought…" Everett said.

"We're on a mission together, just like usual," Melissa said, not wanting to hear what Everett thought. She was certain everyone who had witnessed their affectionate behavior during the mission thought the same.

When they sat down at the table, Huntley was looking at a menu, ignoring them. Melissa took a deep settling breath and let it out. She didn't want to upset him, but couldn't he see this was best for both of them? If Everett hadn't been here, it would have been fine with her to sleep with Huntley.

They soon ordered, ate their meals in silence, and then retired to their separate rooms. Everett didn't say anything, but he had damned well looked like he either wanted Huntley to escort her to her room, or for the both of them to. But when she said good night and headed for her room, one that ended up being three floors above theirs and in another wing of the hotel, they didn't follow her and she reminded herself that this was the way it should be.

Yet leaving them made her feel isolated and alone, and she truly missed the two of them. Especially Huntley, and that was not good.

Chapter 19

HUNTLEY WAS HAVING A DEVIL OF A TIME LETTING Melissa have her space. As soon as she said she wanted her own room, he knew that he had to let her have it. He didn't like it. Not that he didn't feel she was safe enough. If he'd had any inkling she wouldn't be, he would have stayed with her. Not just because he wanted to be with her, sleeping with her, and making love to her. He wanted to talk to her about the mission, about her goals, about anything.

He couldn't shake loose of his growly nature, as much as he tried at dinner. Everyone knew he was upset — mainly with himself — because he couldn't act like it didn't bother him. That was because it damn well did.

He knew that Melissa pulling back had to do in part with Everett's comment, like it brought her back to her senses that they were on a mission. But he worried that it went deeper. Maybe it had something to do with speaking with Kathy in Ms. Baker's home. Or maybe something to do with the babies. He could second-guess Melissa's concerns all night, but it wouldn't do him any good.

Knowing Huntley was in a blue funk, and without a word to him, Everett tossed his bag on the bed, then went into the bathroom and closed the door. The water in the shower whooshed on.

Huntley sat on the bed and couldn't think of anything

but Melissa in her jaguar form, lying in the cage so drugged she couldn't wake from it. And then later cheering Kathy up, sharing stories of Huntley and her taking care of the Carringtons' babies, and trying to ensure Kathy wouldn't be upset that she'd lost those precious days while she was separated from her youngsters.

He ran his hands through his hair. Damn it. He wanted to be with Melissa tonight. And the next, and every day after until they finished this mission. And then when they got home, he wanted her to live with him. In a condo he'd buy. Or maybe she'd prefer a house. Hell, he hadn't even asked her what kind of a place she'd like to live in.

He called her up on the hotel room phone. "You said you'd cook the meals."

"What?" Melissa said, sounding confused.

He lay back down on the bed and stared up at the ceiling. "I said I'd buy a condo and you offered to cook the meals, though anytime you want to go out to eat is fine with me. But I was thinking about it. Maybe a house would be better. With a big yard full of trees. Living out in the country."

"I think…we need to hold up a bit on that. I mean, I could come over sometimes and fix us a meal, and we could go out at other times, but I need to get a place of my own."

Huntley didn't want her to get a place of her own, and he was worried this might have something to do with Oliver's call. "You're not considering going back to Oliver, are you?"

"What? No."

"He won't talk you into it when you return home to pick up your clothes, will he? Saying that things aren't working out with Chad like he thought they would? And it was just an experiment or something?"

She didn't say anything for a moment.

"He's not right for you," Huntley said and was proud of himself for sounding caring and not growling with annoyance.

The shower shut off in the bathroom.

"Call me if you get lonely," he said.

"Night, Huntley. See you in the morning for breakfast." And then the phone clicked dead in his ear.

Everett left the bathroom wearing a pair of boxers. He glanced at Huntley as he hung up the phone. "Sorry about smarting off earlier. I didn't mean to upset you and Melissa."

Huntley got up off the bed. "It wasn't your fault. She's just feeling the need to have a little space. I think she felt kind of awkward about the sleeping arrangements with you joining us."

"I could ask for another assignment, but I think you need me on this one." Everett sounded like he had no intention of leaving them after all that Huntley and Melissa had been through.

Besides, Huntley knew his brother well. He was certain that the cold case wasn't half as exciting as what was going on down here.

Huntley slapped him on the back. "We can use you. She and I will work things out."

"For what it's worth, I think the two of you make the perfect couple."

Huntley smirked at him. "You and I both, but it looks like I'll have to work harder at it to get her to agree."

"You're not really going to let her sleep alone, are

you?" Everett slipped into his bed. "I love the company, but, man, if I were you…"

"If you were me and you cared anything about her, you'd give her some space."

Everett shrugged, then smiled. "I might. But I sure didn't think you'd go for it. There's an extra key on the dresser if you decide to take a walk tonight."

Huntley chuckled, shook his head, walked into the bathroom, and shut the door. In the shower, he soaped himself up and thought about Melissa lying in a bed all by herself. Was she already asleep? Or was she thinking about him, like he was thinking about her? He just *bet* she was thinking about him.

He heard the phone ring, and he was out of the shower in a flash, grabbing a towel and rushing out of the bathroom.

Everett said, "She's all right, Brother. Just wanted to tell you thanks for watching over her when she was so out of it earlier."

Huntley threw a fresh pair of clothes on. "I'll be right back."

Everett smiled. "Remember to grab your key…just in case."

Huntley seized it and shoved it in his pocket, just in case. Though if he had any say about it, he wasn't staying with Everett tonight. "Night."

"Good luck," Everett said.

And Huntley was out the door feeling much more lighthearted, a man with a mission, and just a little apprehensive.

Wearing a tank top and mini boxers, Melissa had finished blow-drying her hair and was ready for bed when a knock sounded at her door.

She stared at it for a moment, not believing anyone would have the wrong room, and surely, Huntley would not be at her door. From what Everett had said, Huntley was in the middle of taking a shower.

She got up and strode to it, then peeked out. Huntley stood there, waiting patiently.

She let her breath out and smiled. She knew just what he wanted and well, hell, just what she wanted. She opened the door. "You could have called if you wanted to talk."

He stood in the entryway, looking at her like he wasn't sure what to say. Then he said, "You wanted to thank me for watching your back earlier today?"

She smiled. Hell, she couldn't help it. "Come in." She let go of the door and he shut it.

Then he secured the safety latch and the second lock.

"You're not planning on staying a while, are you?" she asked, knowing damn well he was. Not that she was going to object.

"Didn't bring a room key. And when Everett goes to sleep, there's no waking him. Besides, you wanted to thank me?" He moved toward her and she backed up toward the bed.

"On the phone. Yes."

He prowled toward her, and she bumped the back of her legs against the bed. She was smiling. He was too.

She liked his playfulness. Oliver didn't play. If she'd told him she wanted space, he'd have given it to her. No trying to change her mind.

"It wouldn't be the same if you thanked me over the phone," Huntley practically purred—big cat like.

Then he tackled her. She was expecting his moves to be more human and less jaguar-like, but she should have known better, and squealed out a startled response. He pinned her firmly to the bed, his body nestled between her legs. He felt hard and hot and eager. For a long moment, he just held his body against hers, pressing his growing cock against her mound and letting her know for herself how much she turned him on, which she had to admit she enjoyed. She loved his impulsivity, recognizing he was like her in so many ways.

He looked into her eyes with such longing that she knew he wanted her—here, now, and for longer.

"We agreed to a condo, but I'm open to buying a home if you prefer." He moved a little against her, making her ache between her legs for him, making her wet and eager. She couldn't believe how just his touch could turn her on, even when they were both fully clothed.

He kissed her chin. "And you agreed to cook. I'll do everything else. We had an oral contract. We agreed."

She laughed. "I'll have to be really careful about what I agree to with you in the future."

He smiled, the warmest, most loving smile, and then it turned wicked. She loved it.

He began kissing her. She still wasn't certain they were meant to be together forever if missions got to be bad news, but she couldn't send him back to the room to stay with Everett for anything. She began tugging off Huntley's shirt, and he quickly yanked it off the rest of the way, flinging it across the room where it landed on the TV. Fascinated with his bronzed skin and ripped abs, she slid her fingers up his tightly corded muscles, felt them tense, and loved the way they were so firm and strong, knowing just how strong they were when he flexed them as a cat or a man.

His eyes darkened with desire as if he was a jaguar caught in the spell of the moment, enjoying the way she touched him and stroked him, the tactile exploration of his body serving even more as a total turn-on.

It amused her to see the control she had over him. When she dipped her hands underneath his belt to reach his buttocks, he shook his head and murmured, "Too many clothes…for both of us."

He moved off her then and began pulling off his boots while she watched the muscles in his back tense. Unable to keep herself from touching him, she got onto her knees behind him, spreading her legs so they rested at his hips, and she rubbed his shoulders and back, kissing his neck, licking, and nipping at the skin.

His pheromones were firing up and doing a number on hers as he groaned. "Woman…" he said, half pleading with her, half growly with warning, definitely ragged with craving. Instead of getting up and taking off his pants, he struggled to remove them while still sitting down on the bed.

She assumed it was because he didn't want to separate from her for even a second while she kneaded his muscles and he melted to her touch. She'd never thought the hunky jaguar would melt under her strokes. Sex with him wasn't just sex. It was way too much fun.

While he worked his jeans down his thighs, she yanked off her tank top. Then she rubbed her breasts against his smooth back and wrapped her arms around his chest, toying with his nipples and loving how they were just as rigid as hers were.

"Hell...no fair," he growled and jerked off his boxers, then turned and pinned her to the bed again. "Vixen." His hand cupping a breast right before his mouth clamped down and feasted on the other.

He made her hot and wet and ready for him, and feeling his erection press between her legs stoked her fire even more. She arched a little to rub against him. His mouth suckled on her rigid nipple, his thumb stroking the other. She ran her nails through his hair, making him growl.

She wrapped her legs around him to give herself better leverage.

He slid his fingers beneath her waistband and down between her legs. Forget the slow buildup. He was going for the gold.

His fingers stroked her slowly at first. "Faster," she whispered, closing her eyes as she centered herself on the sensation, arching toward his fingers and wanting more, harder. She didn't say anything, didn't need to as he pressed harder all of a sudden, then slipped two fingers inside her and began to penetrate her as deeply as he could go.

She was racing to the top—not slowly climbing to the peak, but ready to make a jaguar's leap—and went flying. "Ohmigod, yes!" she cried out.

And damn if she didn't love that about him. He was one hot, sexy, turned-on cat as he claimed her mouth, licking and tonguing her, his fingers magically wringing her out as she writhed at his touch.

Her pulse and his were beating fast when he pulled

her boxers down and centered himself on her. She was so ready, opening her legs up to him, her knees bent, wanting his cock inside her now, filling her to the max.

Huntley loved the way Melissa was eager to play, wanted to make love, and hadn't been totally serious about them staying in separate rooms tonight. He was certain she'd been feeling awkward with Everett joining them, or none of this would have been an issue. As soon as she called back and wanted to thank him, Huntley knew that was her way of reaching out and letting him know she didn't want to be alone.

This felt damn right. Well, better than right as he pushed the head of his cock into her wet sheath and her inner muscles grabbed him, holding him. She was tight, stretching and stroking him as he drove home. Sliding against her silky skin, he was hot and she was hot—a jungle heat that made their pheromones mix and mingle, primal, natural, and wild.

"You're beautiful," he said and watched the way she opened her green eyes, sultry with warmth and desire. For him. For his touches. For what he made her feel.

She smiled at him and moved her hands from his sides and slid them down his legs, her every caress unhinging him. "You…oh…"

He watched as she seemed to lose all conscious thought of what she was going to say while she groaned out his name in a wild and satiated way. He loved the way he could bring her to orgasm. His body rigid with the need to let loose, he followed, surging into her to the hilt, exploding deep inside her and continuing to drive into her until the end.

Not wanting to separate from her, he slipped his arms

around her and held on tight. This was what he had envisioned they would do after dinner. This was the way it was meant to be. Their hearts were still racing, their breathing fast, and he knew he had to move off her and let go, yet he didn't want to. She seemed fine with his body planted against hers, between her legs, his cock still pulsing inside her.

"You are beautiful," she finally said, reaching up to caress his cheek.

He leaned down and kissed her mouth again, slowly, thoroughly, tongue to tongue, lips brushing and caressing. Then he smiled. "Better than talking on the phone now, wasn't it?"

She chuckled, and he rolled off her, then pulled her to lie against his chest. He could really get used to this— missions with Melissa, off-time with her, a home. He knew she wasn't ready to make any commitments yet. But he was fine with it. He aimed to show her just how much she needed him in her life, and how she couldn't live without him.

In the aftermath of their lovemaking, Melissa cuddled with Huntley, glad he'd come to see her and that he was staying the night.

He let out his breath in a satisfied sigh.

"What?" she finally said, feeling well loved and totally satiated.

"If you ever want to talk about anything… What I mean to say is that Genista and I never talked about anything important."

"You said she wouldn't discuss missions." Melissa yawned.

Huntley ran his hand over her shoulder in a light

caress. "About anything important. Not just about missions, but about how she was feeling concerning us or life in general. Nothing. She never would open up. I don't want that to happen between you and me."

"You mean if I think that we should live apart for a while, I should tell you that, and then—"

"Move in with me anyway," Huntley said, and she heard the smile in his voice.

She chuckled. "Okay, so whose idea was it for her to move in with you in the first place?" That had Melissa more than a little bit concerned. Had Genista not been able to resist Huntley's persuasiveness, and in the end it didn't work out either?

"*She* did."

Surprised, Melissa looked up at him to see if he was smiling or serious.

Appearing completely serious, he raised his brows and shrugged a little. "She had been living with her grandmother, and when her grandmother died, Genista sold off her grandmother's house. Since we were dating at the time—"

"You offered for her to move in with you."

"No, she asked if she could stay with me until she could find a place. I said sure, thinking she would find her own place if she needed to, but then she didn't seem to want to. She never looked for one. In retrospect, I don't think she wanted to be alone after her grandmother died. But she really didn't aspire to be with me for the long term either. I think in the end she was ready to move on with her life and let me get back to mine."

"Then here I come, looking for a place to perch for a short while," Melissa said with a sigh.

"Yeah, but you're not moving on."

She chuckled. "Why does that sound so much like you telling me what I'm going to do and not giving me a choice?" Even though staying with him was just what she chose to do. How could she not after everything he'd done for her during and after the mission? How he made her feel sexy and well loved, and she wanted to show him the same consideration? He was gorgeous, so virile, funny, and loving, and she had no intention of giving him up.

"Ahh, honey, I would never force a decision on you. I just need to know if you'd prefer a real home, maybe out in the countryside, or if a condo would work."

She didn't say anything at first, just thought about a house on a lake with woods all around and how much fun that would be to take runs in the middle of the night in their spotted coats when no one was about.

"Or something else. Or just staying where we are now?" He sounded like she had already moved into his apartment, and he desperately wanted to do whatever was needed to make it work for the two of them.

She couldn't help but love him for caring so much. "A house in the woods on a lake. But that's my ideal place, not anything I would suggest for us to get— because you never know when I might decide I need to move on."

He didn't say anything for a long time, then kissed the top of her head. "A house in the woods on a lake it is. And if you move on, the next wild she-cat I hook up with will surely like it better than my studio apartment."

She smiled up at him. "Already planning for the next live-in girlfriend?"

He smiled down at her. "Trying to make sure *this* live-in girlfriend doesn't decide to up and move out on me."

"I enjoy being with you, you know."

"The feeling's one hundred percent mutual."

She thought about what he had said when he first arrived at the room—that he didn't have a key to his room and wouldn't be able to wake his brother. For one, she'd felt the key in his jeans pocket when he had pressed his hot, clothed body against her. She hadn't said anything then because she was too wrapped up in the moment. And truly, his saying so had tickled her. But she wanted him to know she knew.

"By the way, in case you didn't realize it, you did too have your room key with you," she said, her head pressed comfortably against his chest. They seemed to fit so nicely together this way. And she could really see this being forever.

He stroked her shoulder for some time, then finally said, "Well, I'll be damned."

She chuckled. "Don't worry. I like it that you didn't assume I'd let you stay the night."

He laughed and then they settled down to sleep like two big cats curled up together in perfect bliss, and she knew being with him was just so right. She was glad he hadn't slept in the same room with his brother.

Before dawn the next morning, the hotel phone rang next to Huntley's ear, and he needed a minute to register what was making all the racket. Four in the morning?

He lifted the receiver and grumbled, "Hello?"

"Hey, got a call from Jackson," Everett said.

"What?" Huntley and Melissa, looking sleepy and well loved, scrambled to sit up. "Our Jackson, as in Timothy Jackson the poacher?"

"Yep, one and the same. Get dressed. He's really upset he missed meeting with me the other day to sell me the two cats. He knew I wanted them for a special project. He said the man who was to sell them to me disappeared and he feared he'd met with foul play. And then Jackson said his cats were stolen. But he's getting me another cat. This one has cubs. It won't be a mated pair, but he's going to give me a real deal."

"Jaguars?" Huntley growled.

"No. A puma female and two cubs."

"Hell. Okay, where are you meeting him?"

"At the park where you and Melissa were taken. He wants to meet me at that same beach."

"Wait, why there? You're just a buyer. Why would he want you there?" Huntley was getting a really bad feeling about this.

"It's a good place for him to transport them. He said he had trouble with the transfer of the jaguars due to unforeseen circumstances, so he couldn't meet up with me at his usual location."

"The compound where we got rid of his henchmen and freed Avery," Huntley said.

"Has to be."

"So why the beach?"

"I know the location since I have been there 'watching' the courting jaguars. I know my way around the jungle. I'm sticking to the story that I have no way to capture the animals or to transport them out of the rainforest without getting caught. He wants assurance that I had nothing to do with the raid on his place.

"He said it was important to keep good connections with buyers, and he didn't want to lose my goodwill. So he wants to take me from the beach to the location of the cats, and then from there, we'll ride in the boat to another location where I can arrange to have the cats picked up if I'm agreeable."

"It sounds like a setup to me," Huntley said, watching Melissa as she hurried into the bathroom, naked and beautiful.

"Right. But I suspect he's hedging his bets in case I'm legitimate. He's a greedy bastard. I told him it would work for me, and once we were at the new location, I would make arrangements to have someone pick up the cats and me. He would be long gone by then. At least, that's his plan."

"When are we supposed to be there?"

"At dusk. It'll take us that long to drive back to the park and then hike through the rainforest to reach the beach. He'll take me to where they have the cats after that."

"You're not going alone."

"Hell, no. I'd better have my two favorite guard cats with me. Hidden in the foliage, of course. When we spy him, they're going to take him out."

Huntley shook his head. "Still sounds like a trap to me. Like he knew you killed his man and then had something to do with the dead men at his compound and the theft of the jaguars. He's getting you into the rainforest alone, so he can learn from you just what went down."

"That's what I figure. But he's greedy too. If there's

any chance I could be a legitimate buyer, he doesn't want to screw it up. On the other hand, if he suspects I'm on the side of the law, he'll plan to eliminate me. I already called Martin and the Whittaker brothers. They got Avery and Kathy Carrington on a plane going home, but aren't returning until tomorrow themselves. So they canceled their return flights and will join us for the show."

"As cats?"

"Yeah," Everett said. "Everyone else gets to have all the fun. I let Martin know what's going on. So we meet up with the Whittaker brothers, take a tent and field packs, you all change in the rainforest, and I go for a long hike as a regular old human."

"Did Jackson ask if you were coming with anyone?"

Everett said, "Yeah. He warned me to be careful. Did I have some men with me, just in case I have any trouble due to the high water in some areas? That kind of thing. I told him I always go to the rainforest alone. Having others with me kills my being in tune with nature. He didn't say anything after that, just said he'd see me then."

"Either he believes you're lying, or he assumes you're a nutty biologist. After what happened to his men and the cats, I'd guess that he believes you're in on it somehow. I'm surprised he would even contact you or believe you'd meet him then."

"If he suspects I had anything to do with it, he probably figures I'll meet with him because I'm after him next."

"Right. Okay, let me get dressed. We'll see you, grab a bite to eat, check out, and hit the road."

Melissa came out of the bathroom wearing just a towel, looking damned sexy, and he was ready to eat her all up. Huntley growled low. "On second thought, we'll meet you downstairs in half an hour."

She gave him a small, very wicked smile, and slipped the towel off her sweet, naked, slightly damp body.

Chapter 20

AFTER BREAKFAST, EVERETT DROVE THEM BACK TO Corcovado National Park. Luke and Jason Whittaker met up with them at the resort that they'd stayed at before. It was good that it was the rainy season, because the place was still half empty. But Melissa worried about the logistics of the situation, and she couldn't help feeling anxious about being shot again. However, a thick fog coated the whole area in a blanket of gray. Visibility in the rainforest proved difficult enough, but with fog, it was even worse.

Which could be good for the cats.

"What if Jackson has men watching for any sign of you and he sees you with three men and a woman?" Melissa asked, as they unpacked what they didn't need for the rainforest at the cabana.

"He might have men at the park entrances," Everett admitted, tying on a pair of hiking boots.

"He didn't ask you which one you would be coming in at?" Huntley asked.

"I figure he'll expect me to come in through the one closest to the beach. Since that's *not* the one we'll be entering, we should be fine. I doubt he'll have enough men to watch all the entrances," Everett said. "He doesn't even know what I look like."

"He could have paid a park ranger to call him when you showed up and gave your ID."

"True."

"And asked if you had any men with you," Melissa warned.

"Okay, so I go in alone. Some of you go in before-hand, and some of you follow me in afterward," Everett said. "How will that work?"

"Sounds like a better plan. Melissa and I'll lead the way. I doubt he or his men would suspect us of being with you because of Melissa. Then Luke and Jason can follow behind you."

They all agreed that the backup teams would come in about fifteen minutes apart.

So that no one would think that she and Huntley had anything to do with poachers and stealing big cats, they would play up the couple in love as they made the long hike through the muddy jungle. He liked the way she kept hugging him and kissing him, and he stopped to give her a thorough kiss like he really meant it and wasn't playacting in the least. Despite all his muscle and hard agent training, he was cute.

All the vegetation dripped from the recent rains, which had subsided for now. The team had opted for leaving the tent behind because they couldn't give it to Everett to carry once they all had shifted into their jaguar forms. Besides, the fog created enough of a gray screen to make them practically invisible when they changed.

After moving off any human-created trails, Melissa and Huntley found a nicely isolated spot in the middle of the rainforest and stripped in the thick mist.

"Don't take any unnecessary risks," Huntley said, pulling Melissa into a tight embrace.

She held on to his naked body, pressing herself as

close as she could. "Ditto, you know." She frowned up at him. "When we get back—"

He smiled down at her. "We're getting a place together."

She tried to smile, but she was just too worried about him, his brother, the other men, and the cats.

Huntley leaned down and kissed her. "This is a hell of a mission."

Then she smiled up at him. She'd never dropped her clothes before shifting, then hugged a fellow agent before they went into danger. "Be careful."

"Always."

She kissed him back, wishing they'd already taken down Jackson, freed the cats if he really did have them, and were back home having hot sex in Huntley's studio apartment.

Reluctantly, she pulled away from him, the first time ever that mission wasn't the only thing on her mind.

After shoving their clothes into a field pack, she and Huntley shifted. He grabbed the pack with his teeth and jumped onto a high tree branch. There he shifted and secured the pack, before shifting back into his jaguar form and jumping down to the muddy earth.

Then they headed toward the main entrance to locate Everett so they could watch his back while listening and looking for signs of anyone who might be coming for him.

Before, Melissa and Huntley were fairly secure with the knowledge that nobody would bother the two love-birds. Not when they were humans. No one would know them. Not unless the two buyers, Carlos and Pierre—or Carlos's henchmen—ended up coming to the rainforest.

Everyone else who might know they had anything to do with the case was dead.

But now? They were two courting jaguars—looking suspiciously like the two that Jackson had caught earlier. Another pair like that would be extremely unlikely. So what would Jackson think if he came across them? That whoever had killed his men had returned the cats to the rainforest.

They hadn't gotten very far when all hell broke loose. Four shots rang out in the vicinity of where she guessed Everett had to be. Before they could move in that direction to help protect him, someone fired at Melissa and Huntley. A tranquilizer dart smacked a tree inches from Huntley. Both of them leaped away from the direction of the man who'd fired and had run some distance into the thick foliage when another tranquilizer clipped ferns only half a foot from Melissa.

Her heart skipped beats as she and Huntley made their way back around to where the one shooter had to be. One advantage they had, a really *big* advantage, was that the hunters would never expect the jaguars to hunt *them*. It just wasn't in the big cats' nature to do so. Though if it had been Avery and Kathy, they would have fled the area just so he could keep her safe. But not Melissa and Huntley. They lived for missions like this.

They moved cautiously, listening for any hint of men in the area, anyone moving through the brush like men normally would. The birds and monkeys and bugs were making a ruckus, but even so, Melissa could hear if a man moved through the brush. All was quiet now. No weapons being discharged. No sound of anyone crying out in pain from having been wounded. No roaring from any jaguars letting them know they were all right. Or men calling out to do the same. Or anyone on cell phones nearby, signaling what was going on.

Everyone was in hunting mode.

As much as Melissa wanted to stick close to Huntley—to ensure that she knew he stayed safe—she had to move away from him, keep her distance, and travel silently through the rainforest, hidden from his view so that the two of them couldn't be ambushed at the same time. Someone began talking some distance from her, trying to be quiet, but she heard the man's low, gruff voice and headed in his direction.

She couldn't see Huntley, but someone else moved through the tangled vines, sloshing in the water and mud, fast—away from her location. The farther she went, the wetter it got. The rains had created a perfect swampy habitat for caimans and crocs, the soupy water rising several inches up her legs now. She headed for the person speaking, watching for signs of anyone else hidden nearby and for any movement in the water. A howler monkey swung from one tree to another, catching her eye. He'd seen her stalking and hunting, which shook him up. He screamed a warning to his own kind that danger was on the prowl nearby.

But then a cat screamed—a cougar's blood-curdling human-like scream, as if in a horror flick—and Melissa's skin tingled with unease. The cougar was about a hundred yards away, if she could guess the distance despite the thick vegetation. Whoever had been talking on the phone had grown quiet.

Between the fog and the vegetation, only a couple of feet were visible as she continued to move in the direction she'd heard the man talking. She heard splashing, and she turned and listened. Then she saw a crocodile floating nearby, only its eyes above water, watching her. She moved away from the crocodile, not believing he'd go after her, but she could never tell.

After wading another twenty or so feet, not seeing or hearing anything but insects buzzing, birds twittering, and butterflies, she heard something else…cat snarls? She lifted her head and listened. *Cubs*.

Jackson had told Everett he'd caught a cougar and her cubs to sell. But he would have tried to draw Everett into the swamp and then questioned him about his involvement with the jaguars stolen from Jackson's compound.

Everett hadn't gotten hold of Jackson and asked him where the cats were that he wanted to buy, or what had happened to the man that was supposed to meet him. Had Jackson's man called Jackson and told him he was going to speak with Everett? If so, did Jackson know that Everett was probably the last one to see his man alive?

Well, the JAG agents had pretty much figured out Jackson had set up a trap for Everett.

When she heard the cubs crying, even though she knew better, Melissa couldn't help herself. Their woeful cries drew her toward them. But where was the mother?

Then she saw a burlap sack hanging from a tree branch and two little cubs squirming inside, crying. Had to be cougar cubs, which made her think of the ones they had rescued earlier. She couldn't free the cubs out there in the swampy area—something might prey on them. She had to locate the mother and free her.

She was fairly certain someone was watching the sack of cubs, waiting for someone to go after them. That observer wouldn't expect a golden jaguar to come for them. Though the observer might believe the jaguar was a female that had responded to the sound of cubs crying due to maternal instinct. A she-cat's need to foster the abandoned cougar cubs. She'd heard of a big cat killing a baboon, then discovering an infant crying nearby. The cat had actually nursed the infant. So anything was possible.

A footstep in the squishy mud alerted her that someone was to her right. She dashed into the large leafy understory and came around to attack the man, but he'd taken off into the swamp. She could sort of run in the water by leaping through it until it got too deep, and then she had to dog-paddle.

Whoever it was splashed away, trying to swim through the mucky swamp.

When she saw him, he turned, and the horror on his face meant he knew she wouldn't let him live. He brought up his rifle and fired as she leaped at him. As close as she was to him, she thought he would have hit her. Probably would have, if the rifle hadn't misfired.

Thank God for small miracles. She landed on him, shoving him into the swamp. He struggled with her, trying to move her forelegs off him, but then he quit trying and she was certain from the way he moved about that he was going for a knife. If she could just hold him down long enough, he'd drown before he could cut her. She felt a slice of pain in her right foreleg, but didn't give up, didn't move off him, and waited until he quit struggling. She got off him and he floated to the surface of the water, and then she saw movement in the water. Another crocodile. But where was the mother cougar?

Leaving the man to the crocodile, she swam away from him and headed back to the tree where the cubs were suspended from the branch. Then she made circles around the area, looking for the mother cat until she found her in a sack tied to another tree. She was quiet, and Melissa assumed she'd been tranquilized, but the cubs hadn't been this time.

Now what was she to do? She couldn't move the mother cougar, and she couldn't move the cubs. She returned to the cubs and jumped into the tree, hoping Huntley was all right. That his brother and the Whittaker brothers were all right as well.

She licked at her bloodied wound. Not too deep, but she'd need to clean it up once she was out of there. She wanted to roar for Huntley, to let him know where she was, but she couldn't without also letting the poachers know she was there. So she lay down on the branch and guarded the cubs like she'd done with them before. Only that time they'd been on dry land and not hanging in sacks over swampy land. And this time she was alone, praying that everyone else was okay.

———

Huntley heard the cougar scream and the cubs snarling, and he knew beyond a doubt Melissa would head their way. He was chasing his own prey—the man who had shot at him and missed. Huntley heard something moving in a tree nearby. The fog clung to the trees and earth, making the visibility nonexistent for anything any distance away, but the man couldn't see him either. The poacher couldn't hear the jaguar like the cat could hear him, though.

Huntley moved around the tree to come in from the back in case the shooter was ready to hit him with another dart.

And then Huntley saw him, his rifle ready, waiting for the jaguar to move into his sights.

Huntley jumped into the tree, let the man see an up-close and really snarly view of an angry jaguar, and then killed him with one swing of his paw, breaking the man's neck and sending him flying into the muddy swamp below.

Now Huntley had to locate Melissa, and then he was going back for his brother. He roared for Melissa, and way off in the distance, he heard her roar back for him. Thank God. He ran through the shallower areas of the swamp-covered land, had to paddle some, and saw a damn fer-de-lance swimming toward him. They were so aggressive that it wouldn't hesitate to attack, but neither would Huntley. Then it veered off and went on its way as if it suddenly realized the jaguar wasn't one to mess with.

Huntley continued to swim as fast as he could. Though jaguars were powerful swimmers, able to go against strong currents and long distances, they couldn't paddle very fast. Then he saw a dead man floating in the swamp and a rifle next to him. Melissa's handiwork, he was sure. A crocodile had already taken a bite out of the man's leg. Huntley continued on his way when he saw a sack hanging from a tree, no movement in it, and as he looked higher, perched on a branch was Melissa, his beautiful golden jaguar.

He leaped into the tree and nuzzled her as she practically purred to him. Then he shifted and saw her bloodied leg. It wasn't cut badly, but she still was bleeding a little and he wanted in the worse way to carry her out of here and take care of her wound. "If you're all right here, I'm going back to make sure my brother and the others are okay. Can you hold out without us for a little while longer?"

She nodded and he gave her a hug, then she shifted and he gave her a kiss. "Stay safe. Stay here. Do you know where the mother is?"

"In another tree about hundred feet from here. She's been drugged and tied up in a burlap sack to a tree branch like her babies."

"Okay, we'll move them to dry ground and watch over them like we did before. I'll be back."

"Be careful." She gave him another hug and kiss.

"We're house hunting when we get home," he said, as if to tell her she was staying with him for the long run.

She lifted a brow and smiled a little.

"I'll be back."

Then he shifted and so did she. He licked her cheek, then jumped to the swampy ground and took off through the fog to locate his brother. He couldn't help the anxious gnawing at his gut. Everything had become too quiet after the shots had been fired. He even thought that when Melissa and he had roared, one of the Whittaker brothers would have followed suit.

He tracked his scent trail to reach the place where he'd heard the shots fired, about three hundred yards from there, and headed in that direction.

He saw Luke in his tan jaguar form looking dead to the world, only he was sleeping, not dead. Thank God. Huntley whipped around, looking for signs of the shooter, and then found him lying on the ground hidden by vegetation. He *was* dead.

Huntley continued to look for Everett and Luke's brother, then heard talking—a man's low voice. "You were involved with the stealing of the jaguars. Tell me the truth. You wanted me and my men to risk coming out here to catch the cats, and then when they were in the compound, you stole them from me so you wouldn't have to pay for them. Where are the rest of your men? You can't tell me you took out all of my men on your own." Jackson held a rifle on Everett, looking anxious to use it.

So Jackson hadn't realized Everett was one of the good guys. Just thought he was a double-crosser.

"Listen, Jackson, I don't know what the hell you're talking about. I met with you in good faith. Your man said I should follow him to the compound, but the next thing I knew, someone stopped his truck and killed him. I didn't know what the hell was going on, so I turned around and left. I didn't even know where your compound was."

"You lie."

Everett folded his arms. "I take it that you don't really have a cougar and cubs for me to buy."

"I'll sell them to someone a little more reliable. You and I are going to take a walk in the swamps. You'll make a damn good meal for some hungry crocodile."

Everett turned to look behind Jackson as Huntley got ready to ambush the bastard.

"Oldest trick in the book," Jackson said, not about to turn his head and look until Huntley roared.

That got Jackson's attention in a heartbeat. Before he

could turn around and center his rifle, Huntley leaped and knocked him down. Then took a swipe with his forepaw and killed the bastard. Huntley shifted and said, "Where's Jason?"

"Shot, tranquilized."

"Crap."

"Where's Melissa?"

Huntley shook his head. "Cougar cub-sitting. We've got a hell of a lot of work to do. We need to move these bodies into the swamp. On second thought, one of us has to stay with the brothers and protect them. You do that. I'll take care of the bodies. Hell, what a mess."

"Take care, Brother."

"You too." Huntley shifted as Everett went to move Luke to where Jason had fallen. Huntley grabbed Jackson's belt and tugged him toward the area where the swampy area started. He thought of doing this as a human, but in truth, he could carry large animals into trees as a jaguar, and he could move a couple of measly humans just as easily with his jaguar muscles. As a human, he'd be at more of a disadvantage.

When he reached the swamp, he dumped Jackson into the water, then headed back for the last man. It was still so foggy that he didn't see the body or Everett trying to wake up the two agents until he was practically on top of them. Then he hauled off the last man until he reached the water and dumped him in.

After that, it was time to take care of Melissa's charges. He dove through the vegetation to reach her, swam out to her, then jumped into the tree and she brushed her muzzle against his. He shifted. "The Whittaker brothers are asleep. Everett's good. Jackson and his other man are dead. I'm going to untie the bag with the cubs and give them to you to take care of. I'll get the mother, and we'll take them to dry ground, open the sacks, and watch over them until the mother revives like we did before. Okay?"

She nodded.

After another hour, they were sitting together high in a tree, watching the mother stir and the cubs drinking milk from her. They hoped it wouldn't make the cubs sleepy, but they'd guard them until the mother could. They were still a long way from where Everett and the other agents were, but they wanted it that way. After what had happened to the mother, they didn't want her tearing into the agents.

When the mother woke sufficiently, she led her cubs away. As soon as they were gone, Huntley and Melissa leaped onto the muddy ground and ran through the rainforest to locate Everett. He paced back and forth in front of two drowsy jaguars, both sitting up now but unable to shake off the effects of the drug.

Huntley smiled a little at the brothers, then nudged for Melissa to go with him. They found their field pack and shifted and dressed. Then they rejoined Everett. "We need to get them dressed and walk them out of here before anyone runs across us with a couple of doped-up jaguars and thinks we're trying to capture them," Huntley said.

"This I've got to see," Melissa said.

The men all smiled at her.

"This is one part of the mission you don't need to watch," Huntley said, then found where the men had stashed their gear and brought it back.

"What? You think one of the other guys has something that you don't have?"

Huntley cast her a look that meant payback time. She smiled at him, then turned around to watch the birds in the trees or something while the two brothers shifted.

After having a horrendous time trying to dress the brothers, as loopy as they were, Everett and Huntley each took one of the men in hand and helped them walk. It would be dark before they reached the park ranger's station, and hopefully by then, the Whittakers wouldn't look like a couple of drunks.

Melissa slipped underneath Luke's other arm and helped out. He gave her a sloppy grin. She smiled up at him.

"She's mine," Huntley growled.

She and Everett laughed.

By the time they reached the ranger's station, the men were still dead tired, but they managed to walk on their own and appeared to be beat by the heat, humidity, and all-day hike they'd taken. Recognizing Melissa and Huntley from before, the ranger said, "You didn't find any poachers?"

"Didn't see anything worth mentioning." Huntley wrapped his arm around Melissa's shoulder and kissed her on the cheek.

He couldn't wait to get to the cabana, get cleaned up, and get some sleep before they flew out tomorrow. He decided as much as he loved being a jaguar in the wild, he wanted some human time to spend with his new live-in partner. Who he hoped would become much more than that in short order.

The next day at the airport, they both picked up new phones at a kiosk, and the first thing Melissa did was call the Carringtons to get an update on them and the kids. And then she made a play date with them, arching a brow to see if Huntley wished to be included.

"Hell yeah," Huntley said, enfolding Melissa in his arms. All of this felt so right. Better than right.

But as soon as they arrived in Dallas, he felt antsy about Melissa having to deal with Oliver. When they saw him at the airport, Huntley felt her sag a little, like she didn't want to deal with this right now.

Huntley was all for having a showdown with the man—telling Oliver he managed to drive away the most alluring she-cat ever, and now he had no claim on her.

So that's just what he said. And Melissa looked at Huntley as if he was crazy!

Chapter 21

MELISSA WAS TIRED. AFTER MAKING LOVE AS QUIETLY as she and Huntley could in the cabana half the night, and with the energy it had taken to heal up from the cut she'd received, and then the long drive to the airport and the long flight, she couldn't deal with Oliver. Actually, she was shocked to see him standing there, hands shoved in his pockets, giving Huntley a nod as if he was still just her partner on a mission, and then acting as though she was supposed to get a ride with Oliver home. When he was supposed to be seeing Chad. Unless that was already over before it had started. She hoped not.

She had to admit this was a new one on her—Oliver coming to pick her up from the airport and not allowing Huntley to drop her off. Then again, Huntley wasn't planning to drop her anywhere but take her to his studio apartment.

And then Huntley had opened his big mouth. As if *Huntley* had any claim to her! Though she did like that he said she was precious. And alluring. But she hadn't expected Huntley to say anything about her to the ex-boyfriend.

Oliver nodded, but he didn't budge either.

She sighed. "Thanks so much for discovering the Carringtons' identities. That was a real big help to us. About packing up my stuff and moving out—"

"Can we talk, alone?"

She felt Huntley tense beside her.

"Tomorrow. When I come to pack up my stuff. But I'm tired. Certainly not tonight."

Oliver opened his mouth to speak, as if to object or try to change her mind.

"She said no," Huntley growled.

Melissa glanced up at him, telling him in no uncertain terms that this was *not* his business.

"Just saying," Huntley said, still looking all growly.

"I'll see you tomorrow, Oliver. Again, thanks for everything." Then she walked past him and Huntley hurried to catch up to her.

"You might want to ask Genista why she really left Huntley Anderson," Oliver called out to her.

Melissa glanced over her shoulder at Oliver. He still stood there, arms folded across his chest now, his expression concerned. Did he think to protect her from Huntley?

She didn't need any protection from him. He was perfectly suited to her.

Huntley wrapped his arm around her shoulders as if he was afraid she might just stop and talk further with Oliver, and he wanted to ensure she didn't. She snuggled against him, loving the way he was ferocious, charming, sexy, and protective.

She wasn't going to buy into Oliver's words. Yet, was there more to Genista's moving out suddenly without doing it face to face with Huntley? Not that it would have anything to do with Melissa's relationship with Huntley, but she was curious.

She shook her head at Oliver and walked with Huntley to his car.

"He doesn't know what he's talking about," Huntley said as they climbed into his vehicle.

"Are you sure there's not something more to her leaving? Something she wouldn't discuss with you? You said yourself she didn't like to talk about anything important."

"Well, hell, maybe. Then again, why would Oliver know about it when I wouldn't?"

"Maybe he told her he was worried about me, and she felt sorry for me and told him the truth of why she left."

Huntley grunted. Then he glanced at her. "You're not really going back to him, are you?"

"Are you kidding? When I can't get enough of you?"

Huntley smiled a little.

"He's never called me precious or alluring. And as far as I know, he's still seeing Chad. So no."

"Why don't *you* call Genista? Maybe she'll open up to you when she wouldn't with me."

"I really don't need to."

"I'd like to know what it was all about if there's something more to it."

"Are you sure?"

"Yeah, I am."

"All right, but only because you want to know what's up with her." Melissa didn't want him to think she believed that anything that was an issue for Genista would be one for her. They were just too different from one another, and from the sound of it, Genista hadn't shared the heat with Huntley that Melissa felt for him. The whole way back on the plane, they'd cuddled and were close, and she loved it—realizing she truly did love him.

—◦◦◦—

"Better watch out. His dad has a lot of influence over the JAG," Genista warned Melissa over the phone as Huntley drove Melissa to his place.

"What do you mean?"

"Everett and Huntley served exclusively as a team on missions for a few years because Martin knew they were good at it. Never got injured. Always got their man…or woman. They were totally in sync with one another. Good at their job. Why break up a great agent team?"

Melissa had an idea but didn't think it was true, so she ventured, "The brothers weren't getting along? They asked for others on assignment?"

She glanced at Huntley. He was frowning at her.

"No. They were perfectly happy to work together. All of a sudden they were split up, and I was given the mission to work with Huntley. I almost felt bad for him. He was happy to work with me, and we hit it off great. But at first, I could tell he was having a difficult time getting used to me and the way I work. That soon changed, and well, you know where that led."

"You were dating him and moved in with him. I thought you were getting married." Melissa didn't want to hear anything bad about Huntley from the ex-girlfriend, because from the sound of it, she and Huntley just weren't that compatible.

"It has nothing to do with Huntley, truly. He's a likable guy. Well, a real sweetheart. Busy, dedicated to the job, focused on mission—which I loved about him. It also drove me crazy. When I'd come home from a mission, I'd want to forget all about it. He'd want to talk about it. Help me work through mine. I couldn't.

"He said he always did that with his brother. I didn't want to. Maybe some part of me resented that he wanted to treat me like I was his brother." Then Genista laughed. "Not in any way other than the need to discuss missions. Anyway, then he'd want to talk about his job. I didn't want to hear about it. Maybe that's why he and his brother were so good on their assignments. They worked through things and were ready for the next mission. I don't know. It just isn't the way I like to handle it."

Melissa could see Genista's point if she wasn't geared the same way as Huntley. "He really wants the best for you, you know." She wanted Genista to know that he hadn't said anything bad about her. She knew Huntley had to have been upset by the way Genista left him without telling him she was moving out. But even so, he hadn't said anything about how he'd felt to Melissa.

He glanced over at her as he parked in his parking slot.

"Yeah, I know. I told you, he's a sweetheart. That's why I moved out like I did. I was afraid he'd get all woeful looking, and I wouldn't be able to leave because I didn't want to hurt his feelings."

Melissa could envision him like that. He was a nice guy. More than nice. She leaned over the console and kissed his cheek. He gave her a hug back. He was just perfect for her on and off a mission.

"I was being a total coward, I know. But if I hadn't moved out, the next time he asked about my last mission and he wanted to talk about his, I knew we'd been in the same boat all over again. It was for the best that I cleared out, and well, then there you were," Genista said.

"I got an ultimatum from my ex-boyfriend—leave my job and work at his, or move out. But then I learned he was seeing someone else." She didn't want Genista to think she'd been making the moves on Huntley while on assignment when both he and she were seeing someone else.

Genista didn't say anything for a moment. "Oliver told me he was concerned that you'd hooked up with Huntley after I left him and Oliver left you. He wanted to know the real reason I left Huntley. Oliver was worried you'd get hurt since he felt he'd already hurt you. I always knew the guy wasn't meant for you, but he still seems protective of you. I've never seen a wallflower like him at the Christmas party. Not everyone is a wild cat or works for the JAG, and yet there he was, holding up a corner of the wall."

Melissa smiled. She'd tried so hard to introduce him to everyone, but had finally given up to enjoy herself a bit. "Okay, so you alluded to a reason that Huntley and Everett began to go on missions with other agents. And that was?"

"Huntley wasn't paired with anyone else but me. Did you know his dad has a lot of influence with the JAG branch?"

"Wait, you're saying his dad had something to do with it? Like he wanted the two of you paired on an assignment in a matchmaking attempt?"

"Yeah, that's exactly what I'm saying. After two missions, I made the mistake of moving in with Huntley. My grandmother had died, and well, it just seemed to be the solution for me at the time. He's a great guy, really. Don't get me wrong. Only he's looking to settle down.

I'm not. Especially if his dad is pulling the strings. Huntley just wants more than I'm willing to give right now. Oh, and by the way, if you're being paired with him on missions, it probably isn't Martin's idea either."

"Why would that happen when you were dating Huntley? I've been on three missions with him already." Melissa really didn't believe this, though she knew Roy Anderson was involved heavily in the politics of the organization, and he certainly had the money to invest in projects that the JAG wanted to support. Like funding more rangers for the Corcovado National Park.

"His father probably got word somehow that Huntley and I weren't going to last. Betcha anything that if you and Huntley look like you're not getting along, he'll suddenly be paired up with another female agent for the next assignment."

"Do you have any proof?"

"You know Roy investigated the Patterson brothers, ensuring they were acceptable to him for Maya and his daughter, Tammy, right?"

"Yeah, but that doesn't mean he's getting into the matchmaking business with field agents."

"I wouldn't be surprised if he hadn't already checked into your background before you were assigned to work with Huntley. You know Roy was at the Christmas party and watching his sons and his daughter, Tammy, right? Did you speak to Huntley at all at the party?"

"Yeah, I did. Someone bumped into me when I was getting some eggnog, and I spilled it on Huntley's shoes." Melissa smiled a little at the memory and realized that was the first time she had really interacted with him.

Genista laughed. "He doesn't care for the stuff, and I wondered why he smelled of it when we went home that night."

"We got to laughing, and I was helping him mop up his shoes, and I don't know, maybe his father saw us talking and laughing and thought there was more to it."

"We'd had a bit of a row, so we weren't exactly speaking to one another. Then there you were, being nice to Roy's son, and well, I bet you were paired with him on a mission not long after that."

"Yeah. The next week, actually. Thanks, Genista." Melissa didn't know what to think, but she didn't like being manipulated. She'd believed that Genista was way off base on this, but the more she thought about the way Roy was, the more she wondered if there was some truth to it. Not that it changed her mind about how she felt concerning Huntley.

"Huntley's a great guy. But I didn't want his father getting into our business, and the other issues were just unresolvable as far as I was concerned."

"Did you ask Huntley about it?"

"No."

"The boss?"

"Nope."

"Why not?"

"I figured it didn't really matter. I wasn't ready to settle down with him or anyone else. I hope it works out for the two of you. I just thought you should know. Talk later."

"Yeah, thanks." Melissa ended the call and realized Huntley had already parked the car at his complex. She climbed out of the car, shocked about this whole situation. If it was true, did Huntley know anything about it? She suspected he didn't.

Huntley watched her, curious and a little worried looking as he grabbed their bags and hauled them to his front door.

She called her boss while Huntley unlocked the door. "Martin, I've got something to ask you." She looped her finger around one of Huntley's belt loops as he carried the bags inside and shut the door.

Then he pulled her into his arms and kissed her cheek, waiting to hear what was up. She ran her fingers down his buttons, ready to start unfastening them as soon as she had both hands free. This was how she wanted to unwind from missions from now on—in this hot, *wild* jaguar's loving embrace. No more tame cats for her.

"Did Roy Anderson have anything to do with my working with Huntley on a mission?" she asked her boss.

Huntley immediately stiffened.

Silence. She smiled up at Huntley, letting him know she wasn't upset if it was true.

"Martin? Did he?" she prompted when there was too long of a delay, and she knew then Huntley's dad had been involved.

"He might have said he thought you'd make a good team," Martin said carefully. "He doesn't decide who goes with whom on assignment. That's my call."

"So he suggested we'd work well together."

"You do, don't you?"

"Yeah, we do. But I want to know the truth."

"I wouldn't have paired the two of you if I hadn't thought you could be good as a team."

"All right. As of now, Huntley and I are on vacation. Take us off the work roster, if you will."

"Will do. Glad you're back. I'll be in touch in a week."

Melissa took hold of Huntley's arm, led him to the couch, and began yanking couch cushions off. "Make it two. We need a *really* long vacation." Starting…now.

Martin chuckled. Huntley grinned at her, pulled away, and began to make up the sofa bed for them.

She ended the call with Martin and said to Huntley, "What's your dad's number?"

Huntley joined her again and took the phone from her. "I'll take care of this one."

She folded her arms and watched him as he called his father. Huntley's gaze was on her, already darkened, already interested. She loved him for it. So different from the way she'd been treated when she returned home to Oliver. Nothing would change the way she felt about him, about this, about them.

"Dad, it's me. Did you have anything to do with me teaming up with Melissa on an assignment? You did. How's it going for me?" He grinned. "She's just perfect for me in every way that counts. Thanks, Dad. Love you. Talk to you later."

He ended the call right before Melissa swung one of the couch cushions at him.

"I love you, Melissa," Huntley said just as he tackled her and pinned her to the sofa bed. And she realized how much she loved how he did that to her. But then again, next time, she was tackling him first.

She looked into his heated gaze, felt his hard body that was getting even harder by the moment as he rubbed up against her, and knew beyond a doubt that after all they'd been through, he really was the one for her.

"I love you, you big, ol' sexy cat." And she meant it—glad that Genista hadn't been the one for him and that she and Oliver could remain friends but that they'd gone their separate ways in the romance department.

"We make a great team, don't we?" Huntley asked, kissing her cheek.

"Yeah, we sure do. On and off missions."

Thinking about the time she'd spilled eggnog on Huntley's shoes at the Christmas party, and how she'd admired him on assignments for the way he handled missions and worked with her as a team, and how she'd wished she was with someone like him after hours, she realized this was really meant to be. The fun, the loving, and the serious side of the business.

The next thing she knew, they were kissing and his hands slid up her top and cupped her breasts, his body nestled between her legs, his cock fully aroused, and she was ready for everything—maybe even a couple of cubs—later.

Tomorrow, they would look for their dream house, and she was moving in for good. No other she-cat would *ever* have the opportunity. She couldn't help but be tickled by the way Huntley had handled his dad. But she agreed that she was glad it had all worked out that way.

Huntley loved Melissa. He knew as soon as he called his dad about the arrangement he must have had with Martin that he could humor her into submission if she was bothered about it. He loved that about her—how she could melt at his touches and how she did the same with him. How they could go on a mission and come down off it like this.

And then over dinner, they could discuss that same mission or the next assignment they had coming up or… do more of this.

The home on the lake, setting the marriage date—that was all in the works, starting tomorrow, but for now he wanted to show Melissa just how right they were for each other. What two wild cats in love truly meant. Never again would she come home to a cold relationship. And neither would he.

"About cubs…" she murmured against his mouth.

He grinned against her lips. "We're getting married."

She smiled up at him and said, "That was my line."

"I love it when we think the same thoughts."

"When we have cubs, we're leaving them home during missions."

He smiled at her. "But we'll have to take them on trips to the jungle—to teach them to be wild like us."

"Hmm." She began to kiss him all over again.

"I love you, you know," he said, then kissed her mouth.

She sucked on his tongue and looked up into his eyes with longing and need. "I love you, Huntley Anderson, and I'm ready for whatever tomorrow brings."

And then the time for discussion was over. Melissa had taken hold of his heart. He still remembered that first time he'd really met her—at the Christmas party— her all dressed in a sparkly red dress crouching to wipe up the eggnog spilled on his black dress shoes, and him crouching down to join her. Her cheeks had flushed beautifully as he'd laughed about the mess, and

she'd laughed and said she was making it worse. And
then he'd been delighted to work with her on missions,
as dedicated to solving them as she always was. He
couldn't have been happier.

Melissa loved Huntley like this, loving her or running
through the jungle as cats or humans. Sleeping in a
hot tent and making it hotter, or in an air-conditioned
cabana. She wasn't sure if watching movies or dinners
out were exactly for them, but they could give them a
try. But this—

Yeah, they couldn't be more perfect for each other
like this, on dangerous missions, or just on vacations in
the wild.

Read on for a sneak peek from

SEAL Wolf Hunting

TERRY SPEAR

Coming soon from
Sourcebooks Casablanca

"DAMN IT, PAUL. YOU COULDN'T HELP WHAT HAPpened," Allan Rappaport said as they unloaded their bags from the SUV. The two men had taken a red-eye and arrived at Allan's family's mountain cabin in Northern Montana in the predawn darkness.

Paul Cunningham and Allan, his U.S. Navy SEAL buddy, had just returned from one hell of a mission in the Ecuadorian Amazon, tracking down four college students on a field trip who had been taken hostage for ransom. Paul and Allan had managed to rescue the three young men. But not the woman.

Paul couldn't quit envisioning the woman pleading with him to hold on to her as she dangled off the cliff the rest of them had just climbed—the humidity and stress made her hand sweaty, but he wouldn't let go of her for anything. Then the gunfire had erupted. Paul knew before it happened that he was going to lose her.

From across the stream that Paul and the others had so recently forded, the kidnappers had shot her three times in the back, and a fourth round had slammed into Paul's arm. Yet he still hadn't let her go. Not even after he felt her hand release his.

"Thanks for helping with the woman," Paul said to Allan, looking around the cabin's familiar, rustic living room, trying to shake loose the images that haunted him. He'd been so wrapped up in chastising himself with regret, he had never even thanked Allan for taking out the men who had been shooting at them.

"Hell, I owe you for all the times you've saved my ass. I was only too glad to shoot the two bastards who killed the girl. Besides, you think I could have gotten the others to safety without you?"

Yeah, Paul knew Allan would have. He was good at his job. All of their SEAL wolf team were. But he knew, too, that Allan would never have left him behind.

Because of their high success rate on extractions and other jobs like this—though only the wolves on Hunter Greymere's team knew it was their wolf senses that gave them the edge—they were often hired to do special contract work. They were no longer serving with the U.S. Navy—due to their longevity and not aging the way humans did, they didn't want to raise suspicions. Even so, they still considered themselves a SEAL team; they had met and operated that way for years, usually under Hunter's leadership. In this case, no one else had been free to conduct the mission. When an undercover operative called Hunter with the job of extracting the students, he relayed the information to Paul and Allan. They had been the students' only real hope at being rescued without suffering for months in the hostage-takers' care—or dying at their hands.

With his added wolf's strength, Allan had carried the dead woman at a grueling run in the steamy jungle, insisting that Paul lead the way. It was true that Paul always took the lead when they were on a mission when Hunter wasn't with them. But Paul suspected Allan also knew he would have had a rougher time carrying the woman, wounded as he was. The burning pain in his arm had been so great that combined with the heat of the jungle, it made him woozy and he'd had a hell of a time keeping a clear head for some of the trek. His driving concern had been to save the rest of the students in all haste and ensure he didn't lose his partner, who was like a brother to him. And to take the woman's body home to her family.

"You did everything you could to save her life. We got the others out. We saved their lives. Sometimes we have losses. You know that."

Paul knew how hard it had been on Allan also. The two men just dealt in different ways with losing a hostage.

At least with their wolf's fast healing genetics, a short stay with Hunter and his pack had been sufficient for Paul to recover from his injury. He was glad he hadn't returned here first. Allan's mother would have fawned over him and his injury ten times worse than Hunter's pack mates had. That was also why he wasn't about to tell Catherine Rappaport what had gone down.

"Better call your mother. You know she'll have a fit if she learns we didn't contact her as soon as we got here. I swear she has spies in the area watching for our arrival," Paul said, trying to get off the subject of the mission.

"Old Man Stokes at the gas station. I bet you anything he's the one who calls her. We always stop there and fill up the tank before we come out here for our vacations.

And he knows we're usually here for the last two weeks in July, unless we're held up for some reason."

Northern Montana was the perfect place for hiking, fishing in the streams, and running through the woods as wolves. But as Paul sorted out his gear, he still couldn't sort out his feelings about this last mission. *He* was on vacation. And the third-year botany student, Mary Ellen Wister, was *dead*.

Paul let out his breath in exasperation, recalling the way the woman's parents had dissolved into tears when they gave them the news. He'd tried to give up the ghost and quit rethinking the Ecuador mission. But he couldn't hide his feelings from Allan, who had been like a brother to him since Allan's mother had raised the pair of them.

"I'm fine. I'm not thinking about it."

Allan grunted and headed into the kitchen. "If you're not thinking about it, why are you mentioning it again?" He opened the refrigerator door. "No food in the fridge. We need to go into town and get some things."

"I'm not thinking about it. Okay?" And yet Paul was. He had nightmares every time he drifted off to sleep—envisioning staring down into the woman's frantic gray-green eyes, hearing the barrage of gunfire popping, feeling her jerk with the bullets' impact against her back, seeing her mouth open and her eyes widen. Her last words gritted out, "Thank you," not for saving her, because she knew in that instant he couldn't, but for trying. Then she had closed her eyes and released his hand. He'd shouted for her to grab his hand, not wanting to believe she had died as he continued to pull her up. He'd held on for dear life, not about to let go. He wouldn't leave her in the jungle. He'd had to get her home—to her family.

"We did the best we could," Allan said, returning to the living room, his dark hair tousled, his green eyes stern. "Her family was grateful we brought her home. Can you imagine what a nightmare that would have been for them? Envisioning her left behind in the jungle? You have to accept it and move on."

"Right." Paul still wondered if they shouldn't have taken a different path. One that would have ensured they all had made it out alive. Which was the problem with being the leader. Any mistake and it was his responsibility. He couldn't be like some men, who considered casualties a part of doing a mission. No one was ever expendable as far as he was concerned, and he had a hard time letting go of the tragedy. She hadn't been just a casualty. She had been a flesh-and-blood woman with a boyfriend back home, parents and a sister, and tons of friends. He would have done anything to change the outcome and bring her home alive too.

"I know what you're thinking. And no. They were coming at us from all directions. The only way out of there was to climb the cliffs. If she'd been stronger, like the men, she would have made it. But we had no other choice. You made the right decision. For all of us. Listen, feel free to talk about this anytime, but we've also just got to take the time to let it go and enjoy our time off, to decompress. All right?"

"Yeah. Right."

"Did you get hold of Emma and ask about her cabin?" Allan asked, stowing his scuba gear.

"Yeah, she said we can use it any time we want. I told her we'd stay there near the end of our two weeks here. I don't know why we've never done it before."

The Greypaws' lakeside cabin was on the opposite side of Flathead Lake from the Rappaports' property. The Cunningham family originally bought the cabin for the Greypaws to live in, since the Greypaws were Native Americans and not permitted to purchase the land at the time. Later, when the Cunninghams could gift it to them, they did. Allan's family's place was on the mountain and didn't have ready access to Flathead Lake, so they were really looking forward to the change of pace. Being right on the water would be great for fishing, boating and diving.

Paul started to haul the bags down the hall to the bedroom he always used. "I agree that we need the time to move forward and not constantly rehash what went down in the Amazon jungle."

"Good. Let me call Mom and—" Allan's phone rang.

Paul paused in the hallway. There was only a short list of people who might be calling this early. If Hunter, their SEAL team leader, had a job for them…

Allan put the phone on speaker, and Paul figured that meant business, until he heard Allan's mother's worried voice. "I didn't know you were arriving this early. I just heard that you're at the cabin. *Don't* come by the house yet. Later. I'll call you and let you know when you can drop by."

Allan wore a worried frown as big as the Grand Canyon.

A chill crawled up Paul's spine.

He'd never known Catherine to be that flustered when they arrived home. Usually she gushed over her son and Paul's visit—and wanted to see them the minute they arrived. He thought of her fondly as a second mother.

His own mother had died along with his father, when Paul was eleven.

Allan said casually, "We'll have to run into town to get some groceries. I thought we'd drop by and say hi. Just for a minute."

"No, we're busy. I've got to go. Talk to you later."

She would never turn down the opportunity to see them right away, no matter how early it was. They'd been on missions for the last five months and hadn't had any time to return and visit with her. And every mission could have been the death of them. Right before she hung up on him, they heard a woman shriek and then another woman yelled out, sounding just as frightened.

It only took a second before Paul and Allan had grabbed their emergency mission gear and headed out the door, hauling ass.

For a few minutes, they didn't speak as they jumped into Paul's SUV and roared down the dirt road.

"Probably nothing," Paul finally reasoned, hoping it was so, but he couldn't help worrying the women were in real trouble.

"Right." Allan was wired so tight, clenching his hands and grinding his teeth. He was ready to spring into action as a wolf. They both were.

"Hostage situation?"

The vision of the half-starved college men and woman crouching near a swamp in the jungle—grungy, and so grateful to be rescued—flashed through Paul's mind right before he imagined Catherine and Allan's sister, Rose, and her best friend, Lori Greypaw, at gunpoint in Catherine's home.

"Could be. Mom must know we would realize

something was wrong and was trying to warn us not to
come, which meant she wanted us to come."

Paul wondered why anyone in their right mind would
want to take Catherine Rappaport hostage in vintage
Cottage Grove. All that existed there was a small com-
munity of humans and the remnants of the Cunningham
wolf pack. Those left in the pack—Lori, her grandma,
Allan, his mother and sister, and Paul—still referred to
the pack that way. Though he'd often said they should
rename it the Rappaport pack, because there were more
of that family left. Still, his mother and father had been
the leaders until their untimely demise, and in memory
of their leadership, those left behind still faithfully called
it the Cunningham wolf pack.

Thankfully, it was early enough in the morning that
they had the cover of darkness on their side. He couldn't
believe they'd risked their necks in the jungle and then
returned to their hometown—where everything was
usually so quiet—and run into real trouble. He'd never
known Cottage Grove to have problems more serious
than the usual small-town drama—a drunk standing in
the road, not sure where he was; minor thefts, usually
from out-of-towners; and once, a newly married woman
who claimed her husband had fallen off the mountain
cliffs "accidentally." But now, he and Allan sensed a
new kind of danger in their hometown?

In any rescue operation, a huge risk was involved—
for *everyone*. But this time, it was personal and hit way
too close to home.

"Rose." Paul thought that one of the screams had
come from Allan's twin sister, Rose, who had been
like a sister to Paul as well: a pain-in-the-butt tagalong

when he and Allan had wanted to do guy things or spend time with girlfriends. And yet they were close and Paul would do anything for her, or take care of anyone who had any intention of hurting her.

"Yeah." Allan's expression was hard, worried, but he looked ready to kick ass.

"And the other? Lori Greypaw?" It was hard to tell. Paul had recognized Rose's shriek, because he'd heard it often enough—like when Allan had had the notion to dump a cooler filled with crushed ice in the lake where she had been swimming. Or the time they caught her kissing a guy in the woods when she was fifteen. Allan swore he was going to kill the human male and took off after him. But Paul didn't recall ever having heard Lori scream or shriek.

Allan glanced at Paul. "I'm sure of it."

They reached the area where Catherine lived, with sparsely scattered homes surrounded by harvested alfalfa crops, rolled bales of hay scattered about, grazing cows in some fields, and horses in others. Most of the houses had lights on inside. Bordering the edge of Catherine's lawn, balsam fir trees reached a hundred and fifty feet into the sky and provided perfect cover for Paul and Allan. Paul pulled onto a dirt parking spot where farm equipment was offloaded to sow and harvest the fields.

He and Allan quickly stripped out of their blue jeans and shirts and yanked on black pants and T-shirts to blend in with the darkness. They quickly applied some face paint, armed themselves with guns and knives, and headed through the dry fields to reach the fir trees, then crossed the grassy lawn to the part of Catherine's house that was dark.

They had done this kind of mission so many times—and though every assignment was unique in the problems that could arise, for them it was like driving a car—they didn't have to think twice about what they would do.

Lights were on in the living room and kitchen only. Lori's bright red Pinto was sitting in the gravel driveway, Rose's pickup truck was parked next to that, and a black sedan neither Paul nor Allan recognized behind that.

Shrubs hugged the foundation and Paul moved in behind the hedge to reach Allan's sister's bedroom, but the window was locked. They headed around to the back patio. Allan pulled out his spare key and unlocked the door as carefully and quietly as he could, then gently opened the door.

It made only a slight squeaking sound, and Paul hoped that whoever was there hadn't heard them enter. Only wolves—like their family—would be able to hear it.

"No!" Lori said from the kitchen. "I won't do it!"

Adrenaline surging, Paul and Allan raced across the family room and down the carpeted floor of the hallway between two of the bedrooms, and from there crept toward the kitchen, where they'd heard Lori speaking.

The living room was all clear. Paul and Allan silently passed the guest bathroom and neared the entrance to the kitchen and breakfast nook, where they heard the clinking of silverware and dishes.

In place, Paul was about to peek around the doorjamb

to determine the extent of the threat when Catherine shouted, "No, watch out!"

The crashing of porcelain against the tile floor spurred the men on. Paul's heart was pounding triple time when he appeared in the doorway to the kitchen, materializing out of the darkness in black clothes and black face paint, gun in hand.

Rose saw Paul first. She screamed and dropped the coffee mug she was holding. It crashed on the floor, splattering coffee everywhere.

Lori swung the broom she was holding and whacked Paul in the head with it as Catherine yelled out in fright. Confused, Paul assessed the situation in the kitchen and found only the four women there. One broken plate. One broken coffee mug and coffee splashed everywhere. No armed hostage takers anywhere.

Overwhelmed with relief, he quickly holstered his gun and tried to wrench the broom away from Lori before she could hit him again. It looked like this time she was dying to, just on principle for scaring her. When he couldn't wrest it from her, he grabbed her shoulders instead, pressed her hard against the wall, and kissed her.

He'd been wanting to do that forever—since the last time they'd resolved an issue in this manner.

His chest pressed against her breasts. She wasn't wearing a bra under the slinky tank top—and his internal thermostat turned even hotter. Her shorts were…short, showing off her shapely tanned legs, and her feet were bare. One scorching, sexy she-wolf package.

Unexpectedly, Lori twisted her body and swept her leg behind him, tripping him up and effectively knocking him off balance. He pulled her down with him as he fell on his backside and she landed on top, dropping the broom. He grinned at the way she'd out-maneuvered him.

"It's me," he said, just in case she hadn't realized it.

"Jeez, Paul, you look like a bank robber!"

Lori was lying on top of him, not making a move to get up. His body immediately responded with raven-ous hunger. He took advantage of the moment, flipped her onto her back, and kissed her again. She smelled of lilacs, woman, and she-wolf, and tasted of honey as he licked the sticky sweetness off her lips.

She finally smiled a little against his mouth about the same time as Catherine cleared her throat. As much as Paul didn't want to move from their stimulating pose—and hoping he could quickly get his body under control—he eased off Lori and pulled her to her feet.

This was how he wanted to see her when he came home from missions.

Brows raised, Allan put his weapons away. "I was going to ask if the two of you needed my help…"

"This is why I didn't want you and Paul to run with those boys any longer," Catherine scolded, picking the broom up off the floor so she could sweep up the broken dishes, while Rose cleaned up the coffee splattered on the floor.

"The boys" Catherine was referring to were the rest of their wolf Navy SEAL teammates, none of whom had been boys for a very long time.

"I told you I was busy and would see you later," Catherine said reproachfully.

Lori's gray-haired grandma, Emma, was sitting at the

kitchen table, sipping tea and smiling. "Now, Catherine, don't scold. Allan and Paul are such good boys."

Catherine snorted. "Running around in the jungle like that…" She turned to eye them, then frowned. "Still practicing your stealth moves? You're *supposed* to be on vacation."

Paul had almost forgotten how he and Allan had taken a few years off Catherine's life when they were young, practicing sneaking up on her, either as wolves or as future SEALs. The whole point was for her never to see them. Only she always did see them—because of her wolf senses—and they'd gotten scolded back then, too.

Paul glanced around the kitchen, trying to figure out what the women were up to. They'd had buttermilk biscuits and honey… Paul licked his lips, still tasting the sweetness on his mouth after kissing Lori. A stack of paper was sitting on the table. It looked to be some project Catherine was in charge of, as usual.

Movement behind them in the dim hallway made Paul and Allan whip around to see Michael Anderson, wearing only jeans as he strolled into the kitchen, his red hair mussed, hazel-green eyes wide at seeing Paul and Allan. "When did you two get in?"

Michael was the brother-in-law of their SEAL team leader, Hunter Greymere. Neither Michael nor his sister, Tessa, had been born as *lupus garous*. Yet they both had been drawn to seek out wolves—Michael painting them, Tessa photographing them. Then Hunter had gotten involved with Tessa, and everything changed.

"We got in just a little bit ago. Hell, we didn't know you were going to be here. Didn't you hear all the racket in here?" Paul stepped forward and shook his hand.

"Heavy sleeper," Michael said, looking a little sheepish.

Paul remembered the Bigfork Festival of the Arts had to have been last weekend on the shore of Flathead Lake. "Was your work at the art festival?"

"Yeah. Catherine and Rose had a booth showcasing their homemade salsas and jellies. I stayed the week and painted a new picture for the…" Michael glanced at the women, then cleared his throat. "For a special auction for a charitable cause. One of the galleries put some of my paintings on display at the festival. I also brought some new paintings for Rose's gift shop. I've got a flight out to Portland this afternoon. I'm going to drop by and see Tessa and Hunter first, then I'm leaving for Brazil for another showing."

"Brazil." Paul was a little surprised that Michael would be leaving the States, but figured he would have someone from Hunter's pack watching over him. Newly turned wolves always had a shadow from the pack. "Are you doing well with your paintings?"

"Can't complain. Still winning awards, selling well," Michael said. "Get lots of dates." He grinned.

Same old Michael. Charming. Talented.

"Doing all right controlling your wolf half?" Paul asked. This was the first time he'd seen Michael on his own, without a wolf chaperoning him—one who had either been born a wolf or who had been turned years earlier. For newer wolves, the call of the full moon could still wreak havoc with their control.

"Been doing great. Thanks for asking," Michael said, sounding proud of the fact.

Still, Paul thought it was way too soon to let Michael

out on his own. Paul was just glad everyone in his wolf pack had been born that way. New wolves could be real trouble.

"If we don't see you before you leave, give Tessa a hug for us, will you?" Paul asked.

Allan said, "Yeah, and good luck with your exhibits."

"Thanks. Who would ever have thought I'd have the opportunity to paint wolves that weren't exactly all wolf? Hey, would you be up to shifting so that I can catch you on canvas?"

Paul smiled and shook his head. "Not this time around." The thought of lying around for hours while Michael painted him didn't appeal.

Michael looked inquiringly at Allan.

"Not me," Allan quickly said.

Diversion over, Paul thought Allan would have to explain to his mother why they'd donned face paint, armed themselves to the max, and silently slipped into her home, ready for a fight. Instead, Allan said, "Come on, Paul. We'll come back later when the situation is less…hostile." He glanced at Lori. "Or…something."

Lori was wearing a small smirk, her dark hair curling about her shoulders, her dark brown eyes smiling at Paul, and he sure got the impression that she was hanging around this time. He hoped he'd helped to change her mind if she had any notion of leaving again.

As soon as he and Allan headed outside and closed the front door behind them, they made their way along the road to Paul's SUV.

"So what was *that* all about?" Paul asked.

"I could ask you the same question. I…didn't know you had a thing for Lori. I mean, I used to think you were interested in her, but then the two of you never went anywhere with it." Allan waited for an explanation, but Paul didn't offer one. "Did it seem to you that the ladies were hiding something?" Allan asked.

"Yeah, it did." They climbed into the SUV and drove off.

"They were being secretive," Allan said.

"Yeah, I agree." Paul recalled the guilty look Catherine had worn. Rose's mischievous expression indicated she knew what it was all about. He suspected it had something to do with Allan and him. Lori had worn a similar expression, once they were done kissing. Even Michael had seemed a little apprehensive—he had glanced at the women as if to get his cues.

"The last time they looked that guilty, they were contemplating marrying me off to Tara Baxter," Allan said. "Mom thought if she could entice me to settle down with a mate, I wouldn't want to tear off on these high-risk jobs any longer." Allan glanced at Paul. "Maybe Mom is working on a mate prospect for *you* this time."

That would be the day. Not only were there no other she-wolves in town besides Lori and Rose—well, and Tara—but Paul loved the job he and Allan did. Every assignment was completely different from the last, exhilarating, fulfilling, heart-thumping excitement. And it meant saving people who might not have a prayer otherwise.

"This place isn't known to have a big wolf population—as in our *lupus garou* kind—female or otherwise. So who would she try to set me up with?" Paul asked, figuring Catherine *wouldn't* attempt that with him.

"I was thinking of Lori, and then you went and kissed

her." Allan grinned at him. "Hell, I thought she would have used one of her more lethal martial arts maneuvers on you, not taken you down and kissed you back. Have you been keeping in touch with her on the sly?"

"Me? Hell, no."

Since she taught martial arts to the local kids and had a fourth-degree black belt in jujitsu, Paul wondered how she would fare if he and she were to do a little workout—when he was better prepared for her take-down maneuvers. Paul had to admit that even if he loved his job, he had wanted to see Lori again. Especially since for the last two years, she had been conspicuously absent whenever he'd been around. He told himself it was just because she was part of his pack and he wanted to know what was going on, but it wasn't true. He had wanted to see *her*.

"So why *did* you kiss her?" Allan asked.

"To keep her from smacking me in the head with the broom for a second time. I couldn't get it away from her without too much of a struggle. Figured a more subtle and different approach might work."

Allan chuckled. "Subtle?"

Paul smiled.

**And in case you missed it,
read on for an excerpt from
USA Today bestselling
*A SEAL in Wolf's Clothing***

OF ALL THE DAMN TIMES FOR HIS SEAL TEAM LEADER,
Hunter Greymere, to take a mate and fly off on a honey-
moon to Hawaii, why did he have to do so now?

The problem wasn't only with the assassin, should
he arrive here and target Hunter's sister, Meara, since
Hunter was gone, but also with the fact that Meara was
on the prowl for a mate. Finn Emerson had discovered
that when he read the advertisement for cabin rentals
that was lying on the white marble breakfast bar in
Meara's cabin.

He would have been wryly amused if the situation
wasn't creating even more difficulties for him. Glancing
down at the counter, he reread the advertisement.

*Cabin rentals with single occupancy located
on Oregon coast. Great for rugged adventurers
looking for a wilderness escape. No nearby
shopping, theaters, or restaurants. Strictly a
roughing-it getaway. For a special fee, management will provide a select menu. Cabin
availability limited, so sign up now.*

Meara Greymere, Owner and Manager

As he considered each point in the advertisement, Finn shook his head and slipped a bug into Meara's phone.

Single occupancy? After searching the five unoccupied cabins, Finn had found that each had two bedrooms and a living area furnished with a fold-down couch for additional guests.

Rugged adventurers? From what Hunter had told Finn, Meara had been searching for a mate for some years now, and he assumed she wanted only alpha males to rent the cabins.

Cabin availability limited? Yep, limited to five alpha males, if she could ensure she only rented to alphas.

Meara Greymere, Owner and Manager? What had happened to Hunter in the equation? Finn knew Hunter wouldn't have given Meara total control over the rentals.

As to the special fee for a select menu, he just wondered what—or more appropriately, who—she would be offering.

Finn spied a notebook sitting next to the phone and flipped it open. A woman's handwriting listed guests due to arrive this week—with abbreviated notes beside their names.

Joe Matheson, investment broker—sounded sexy, first arrival.

Hugh Sutherland, thrill seeker—rugged voice.

Ted Greystalk, bank president—promising.

Caesar Silverman, dive-shop owner—sounded wet and wild.

Finn snorted. He didn't think she liked Navy SEAL types much because he and Hunter were SEALs. So why would the owner of a dive shop be appealing? Maybe she covertly *was* impressed with SEALs but refused to admit it, and the diver reminded her of a SEAL.

Rocky Montana, independently wealthy—mysterious.

The guy sounded like he was a wrestler or something. But the "mysterious" bothered Finn most. A man with something to hide?

Five other names had been crossed out and had merited comments like "not rugged enough," "sounded way too controlling," "by own admission, strictly loner wolf," "too old sounding," "strictly human," and "mated!"

She had another list of eligible and ineligible wolves for the following week.

Finn slapped the notebook closed and set up a hidden camera in the living room, wedging it between books in the bookcase. He would have a couple of his buddies run background checks on each of the men to see if they could turn up anything. Because *lupus garous* lived so long, they had to change their occupations and locations after a time to avoid suspicion, so the background checks might not turn up much.

That was fine. Finn would interrogate the men thoroughly in person anyway. He smiled a little. He'd prove to them that none had what it took to turn Meara's head.

Still, Finn couldn't believe Hunter had left a couple of sub-leaders in control of the pack and Meara in charge of the cabins. So who the hell was in charge of Meara?

The worst-case scenario was that Meara would get stuck with a wolf she wasn't interested in mating due to a poor choice on her part. From what Hunter had told him, she'd always been headstrong and hard to heel, and

Finn figured the years hadn't changed her. Besides, she was always picking up the wrong kind of men.

Finn stalked down the plush ivory-carpeted hall to her bedroom—a nicely appointed room with a queen-sized bed covered in an olive-colored silk comforter and pillows, all trimmed in gold. The walls were a marble-ized olive color, and all the wood was rosewood, making him feel as if he were in a cozy woodland den. On the walls hung pictures of redwoods from the California forests Meara and Hunter had called home for more than a century. Finn wondered if Meara ever got homesick, or if she'd adjusted to living on the Oregon coast. He still couldn't believe they'd been forced to move because of some damned arsonist.

Used to living out of a duffel bag, Finn was surprised to feel an uncharacteristic pang of longing for an ocean-view cabin, comfortable, homey, and appealing for every season. He had a place of his own with an ocean view a couple hours south, having thought he might live there if he ever wanted to set down more perma-nent roots, but he rarely stayed there, renting it out to others for most of the year. Or using it as a safe house on occasion.

His home didn't feel like his own place, having been decorated by an interior decorator. Nothing there was his personally. It was just a spot to drop in when it was vacant, once in a blue moon, and he wasn't on a mission.

Meara's cabin had a different ocean view, and it was warmer somehow, filled with her enticing scent and smaller, homier than his place. A rosewood-framed col-lection of pictures of her family—Hunter, her parents, and her uncle, who had owned the cabin resort before giving it to Hunter and Meara—sat on the dresser. A silver-plated hairbrush engraved with her grandmother's name rested beside the pictures. A tube of lip gloss next to that made Finn think of Meara's moistened lips— succulent, full and petulant, and damned ripe for kissing. He scowled at himself for even going there and glanced out the window.

He could imagine a summer day like today with a refreshing, cool ocean breeze blowing through the open windows, or a wintry landscape where the pines were dusted with snowflakes while he ran through them in his wolf coat, or spring wildflowers filling the woods, or the leaves turning crimson, burnt orange, and brilliant yellow on a fall day.

He shook his head at himself. When had he become an old man?

He stripped out of his clothes and dumped them next to his duffel bag. If any of these vacationing wolves thought they had half a chance of making a play for Meara without Hunter around, they'd soon learn that they'd have to deal with another alpha male.

The situation could be a lot more serious than that— not that selecting the wrong mate wasn't serious enough, since *lupus garous* mated for life and lived long lives. Finn didn't know if, in an effort to get to Hunter, the assassin would attempt to grab Meara.

Finn snatched his cell phone from his belt and tried to call Hunter one last time. According to one of Hunter's sub-leaders, Chris Tarleton, Hunter would be flying out with his mate to Hawaii any minute now and he'd probably already turned off his cell phone. Hell, Finn had to warn Hunter to watch his back. If he'd only known sooner that Hunter had moved his *lupus garou* pack from Northern California to the Oregon coast, Finn might have caught Hunter before he left. A few months had passed since their last contracted mission, and Finn had just assumed that Hunter and his pack were still living in the same place they had for years.

The phone rang and rang. *No answer*. Finn would have to keep trying to reach him. For now, Finn needed to stake the territory as his own until Hunter returned. Finn extended his arms and summoned the quick and painless transformation into his wolf form, welcoming the stretching of muscles and tissue. The softer fur covered his skin close to his body, while the coarser outer coat added a protective layer. He dropped to stand on all four paws before loping down the hall to the kitchen where a wolf door was his ticket to the outside.

Once outside, he raced across the slate-gray patio, then dove into the woods surrounding the oceanfront cottage and ran along a trail already marked by Hunter and a female, probably his mate. By the time the two of them returned from Hawaii, their scent markings would be two weeks old, and another werewolf coming into the area might think it was unoccupied, allowing him to stake a claim to the territory.

Finn loped through the northern pine and Douglas fir forests, scent-marking the area surrounding each of the five rental cabins. Waves crashed below the cliffs, and the Pacific Ocean breeze shook the pine branches as the clean air filled his lungs. He paused briefly at the cliffside to take another heady breath and watch the foaming waves crest and fall against the beach. He could never get enough of the sea.

But instead of striking from the direction of the sea and returning there after accomplishing his clandestine mission, as he would have done while serving as one of the elite U.S. Navy SEALs, Finn was sticking to the land this time. Nothing about *this* operation would be clandestine. Finn wanted the assassin to know he was here protecting his own, if whoever it was decided to make a hit on anyone else who had been with the team.

Hunter had been like a brother to Finn while they'd served as SEALs, and Finn owed it to Hunter to keep him safe—and Hunter's sister also, knowing that she could be a target and Hunter wasn't here to protect her. Not that Meara would see it that way once she learned why Finn was here, he suspected.

Finn leaped over a fallen tree on a pine-needle path farther away from the ocean, breathing in the scents of pine and fresh water trickling by in an ice-cold stream. Neither could mask the distinct smell of another predator. A cougar. And farther in the distance, its potential prey, an elk.

Finn paused, twisting his ears this way and that, listening to the sounds of the ocean, the water in the stream, and the birds twittering and singing to one another, but he could detect no other sound of animals, human or otherwise, traversing the land.

Despite this not being *Finn's* territory, he was leaving fresh markings and *making* it his territory until Hunter returned home. Finn scratched the ground again with his paws to help ensure that any newcomer would know Meara had not been left alone without protection.

Finn loped back toward the house, satisfied he'd left enough of his scent to warn anyone who intended to get close to the territory to back off. He glanced at the drive in front of the wood-frame cabin. No vehicle there yet. From what Chris Tarleton had reluctantly told him, Meara should be returning from the airport in about an hour.

Chris definitely didn't sound happy to hear that Finn was back, nor that he was looking out for Meara's welfare. Finn wondered what interest Chris had in Meara. A pack sub-leader's interest—as in she was the leader's sister, and if she was in trouble and Chris didn't watch out for her, he would be in trouble? Or something of a more personal nature?

Baby-sitting Meara wasn't what Finn had in mind, either. But the assassin had already attempted to kill one of their SEAL team members and was suspected of going after another. Finn had the sneaking suspicion that the assassin intended to go after each of them. Fortunately for them, the assassin was batting zero, and with the SEALs aware of the menace, whoever this was would have a devil of a time succeeding now.

Finn ran around the pine trees surrounding the house to the back patio of Meara's cabin. He'd checked out the cabin farther down the coast and found it was Hunter's and Tessa's. Meara's sweet scent permeated this cabin. And here's where he'd stay until he could reach Hunter and apprise him of the situation.

Butting through the wolf door with his nose, Finn entered the kitchen and headed for the master bedroom to dress. If he had judged the time right, Meara would be arriving soon. He'd have a fight on his hands from the outset. *Guaranteed.*

Acknowledgments

Thanks to my beta readers—Loretta Melvin, Donna Fournier, Dottie Jones, and Bonnie Gill—for helping make the story the best it can be! Also thanks to my Australian Facebook friends who helped me with my Australian campers: Emma Lyons, Stacey Clifford, Karen Roma, Lisa Catherine, Vanessa Carlson, Kathryn Royce Martin, Susan Carrato, and Sarah Le Moignan. And to Deb Werksman, my editor, and the cover artists who once again created a cover that wows, astounds, and is well loved! And thanks to Morgan Doremus, Sourcebooks publicist, for stepping in to help me with promotions and doing a great job of it!

About the Author

Bestselling and award-winning author Terry Spear has written over fifty paranormal romance novels and four medieval Highland historical romances. Her first werewolf romance, *Heart of the Wolf*, was named a 2008 *Publishers Weekly* Best Book of the Year, and her subsequent titles have garnered high praise and hit the *USA Today* bestseller list. A retired officer of the U.S. Army Reserves, Terry lives in Crawford, Texas, where she is working on her next werewolf romance, continuing her new series about shape-shifting jaguars, and having fun with her young adult novels. For more information, please visit www.terryspear.com, or follow her on Twitter @TerrySpear. She is also on Facebook at www.facebook.com/TerrySpearParanormalRomantics. And on Wordpress at Terry Spear's Shifters, www.terryspear.wordpress.com.

Jaguar Hunt

by Terry Spear

USA Today Bestselling Author

Two deadly predators...

As a feline Enforcer, Tammy Anderson has one objective: locate the missing jaguar and return it to the States. She doesn't have time for distractions, and she definitely doesn't have time for sexy shifters with more muscles than sense.

One hot mission...

Everyone and their brother has warned JAG agent David Patterson that Tammy is Ms. Hands-Off...which only makes him more determined to get very hands-on. But things heat up in the steamy jungles of Belize and their simple mission gets a whole lot more complicated. Now it's going to take everything David's got to protect the gorgeous she-cat who somehow managed to claw her way past his defenses...and into his heart.

Praise for *Jaguar Fever*:

"Readers will enjoy this thrilling tale as love and danger collide."—*Midwest Book Review*

"Spear's writing style, as usual, is very detailed and descriptive. A must-read for lovers of paranormal romance."—*Romancing the Book*

For more Terry Spear, visit:

www.sourcebooks.com